PASS THE SALT

The steady airflow from below brought the odor of the creatures, a nightmare stench that was almost human, mixed with the decay of human flesh. The smell was overpowering as the scrabble of their feet came just outside the grotto, and then creatures emerged.

The band came to a nervous halt, making rasping noises that might have been speech.

Remo turned on the flashlight and wedged it in a crack in the wall, filling the grotto with a dismal yellow light. Chiun did not object. They both had ascertained that these creatures were blind.

So the glowstick Remo had tossed up the hall as a lure would be unseen, but if the creatures had an enhanced sense of smell, which was almost a necessity, then they would return to the grotto soon enough.

They did, dropping their jabbering to snake-like whispers. One of them ventured through the entrance into the grotto, sniffing with his head hung low, then following the scent, turning his head up at Remo and Chiun...

CREATED BY MURPHY & SAPIR

THE

DESTROYER

INDUSTRIAL EVOLUTION

REPRISE
OF THE
MACHINES
· B O O K II ·

A GOLD EAGLE BOOK FROM

WORLDWIDE®

TORONTO • NEW YORK • LONDON
AMSTERDAM • PARIS • SYDNEY • HAMBURG
STOCKHOLM • ATHENS • TOKYO • MILAN
MADRID • WARSAW • BUDAPEST • AUCKLAND

First edition October 2004

ISBN 0-373-63252-5

Special thanks and acknowledgment to Tim Somheil
for his contribution to this work.

INDUSTRIAL EVOLUTION

Printed in U.S.A.

And for the Glorious House of Sinanju,
sinanjucentral@hotmail.com

1

To make matters worse, the phone kept ringing. The man with the craggy face and the salt-and-pepper hair ignored it, but the ringing became unendurable. With a curse he tried to lift himself, felt his arm muscles turn to wet noodles, and his cheekbone smacked hard on the iron floor. As he lay helpless, the throbbing pain and the chirping of the phone melded into a song of agony.

He was dying, no doubt about that, but couldn't he at least die in peace? He just had to find a way to get to that telephone and yank it out of the wall—only then could he settle down to suffocate in peace and quiet.

It took all his strength, but somehow he made his cold, trembling arms drag him to the control console and grab at the telephone.

"Who is it?"

"Thank God I found you!"

"How did you reach me? Zee phone has not worked from zee beginning."

"How? Calling a hundred times a day for a week, that's how! Five times I actually got a ring, and then the signal went out. Anyway, how's it going?"

The gray-haired man collapsed, gasping, in the padded chair. "I am dying, that is how I am doing."

"I'm sorry to hear that. Cancer?"

"Asphyxiation."

"Never heard of it. Is it, you know, painful?"

"It is not pleasant."

"Well, how much time did they give you? I mean, do you think you'll have time to finish helping me, you know…"

"Senator Herbie, my son was correct. You are a dweeb. Zee dweebiest. Right at this moment I am buried alive, maybe twenty meters under zee desert. If I could help anybody—"

"What do you mean, buried? How did this happen? What's being done about it?"

"I don't know what is being done about it. I haven't heard a word from the world above until you called. I pray to zee heavens that your voice is not the last one I hear—"

"What about Jack? Isn't he digging you out? I should go help him! Well, I would, except I have these burned feet, you understand. I'll hire people, though. Lotsa Mexicans down there, right? Shouldn't cost too much. What do you pay them, like two dollars a day? We'll get eight of them. Five, maybe. How long would it take?"

Mercifully, the signal faded. The phone display said the batteries were depleted. Thank the heavens for small favors, he thought, and flopped onto the floor to expire in blessed silence.

But his peace didn't last for long. Wouldn't you

know, if it wasn't the phone it was the front door. Somebody was knocking insistently.

"Go away!" he shouted. No, he didn't shout, because he couldn't. Couldn't even speak anymore. Had to have imagined shouting. Did that mean the knocking was his imagination, too? Now it was a grinding sound. Now it was a crackling hiss. A cutting torch? He passed out not caring.

The smell of canned air woke him, and there was a rubber mask attached to his face. He was breathing again, real oxygen, and he realized that the sound of a cutting torch had been an actual cutting torch.

He was still inside the Mighty Iron Mole, but now his son was with him. Just as improbable were the floating stars in primary colors, about the size of basketballs, that faded and flared with every flicker of his eyeballs.

Next time he regained consciousness the red, blue and purple stars were gone, and the green star had stabilized into a typical plastic glow stick around the neck of the phantom of his son.

"Hiya, Pops!" Jack Fast was grinning.

Jacob Fastbinder III tried to make his eyes work better. The details of the mole's interior were crisp. He lifted one heavy arm and poked the teenager in the shoulder. Jack Fast felt real, too.

"Yep, it's really me. I got here just in time, too. The atmospheric toxins were at lethal levels. You were almost a goner."

"How?"

"I made an earth drill."

Of course. The teenage boy simply built his own mechanical mole and used it to drill down into the earth and rescue his father. Why not? the old man thought. He was surely mad, and he poked at the figment of his imagination again.

"Ow!" The kid grabbed his abused nostril.

"Not real."

"Am too."

"Hallucination."

"Take that!" Jack poked his father in the stomach hard, and Fastbinder bent double, hacking. When he stopped coughing he realized the oxygen mask was gone. Jack was holding it. The air in the Iron Mole smelled stale but breathable, and Fastbinder was standing on his own two feet.

"I don't understand. How could you do it?"

"Come on and look."

They stepped out of Fastbinder's Iron Mole and into a tunnel. When Jack turned on his battery lantern, the tunnel sparkled as if it were a room of diamonds.

"Neat, huh?"

"Magnificent!" Fastbinder's eyes fell on the device that created the tunnel, and he was astounded again.

The vehicle had three pairs of treads. It rode on two heavy-duty treads, while two steel supports each lifted another pair of smaller treads to the roof of the tunnel, not quite touching the fragile-looking crystalline walls. The treads were all welded against a gleaming stainless-steel compartment shaped like a stubby rocket. A tapered point extended toward Fastbinder, and when he peered through the treads at the other end he saw another tapered end.

"Cool, huh?" Jack asked. "No back, just two fronts, so if you get stuck you just reverse it. The extra treads extend automatically to grip the ceiling if the descent gets too steep, for one hundred percent traction. The thing can even ride on the extra treads if it gets flipped on its side."

"But, Jack, how does it do zee drilling? And what is all this?" Fastbinder looked at the roof of spun crystal.

"That's the coolest thing, Pops! The whole exterior surface is imbedded with proton discharge devices making really big honkin' wads of static electricity. You should see this thing at work. Lightning everywhere! It makes, like, this air hammer that breaks it all down to particulate, dirt or sand or rock or whatever, and sends it flying around, and the particles at the perimeter of the proton discharge get melted in place, and the swirling crumbles stick to 'em and it builds a crystallized support structure. The crystal makes it strong enough, and the computer guides the protons to make tempered, noncrystalline filaments for more support—like rebar inside of concrete. See?"

Fastbinder was still woozy. He understood the concepts his son was throwing at him, and yet…

"You built this thing from nothing? How long have I been down here?"

Jack's grin faded. "Six days, about. You should have taken more oxygen. You shouldn't have even tried this in that old junker of yours."

Fastbinder glanced at the hole where they had emerged from the Mighty Iron Mole. It was a classic, a one-of-a-kind marvel of engineering, built in 1938 by a demented inventor in Oregon. The inventor used it once, boring just eighteen feet into the rich black soil before the engine seized up. The inventor exited through the rear hatchway and was pulled out of his tunnel by rope. The tunnel collapsed as he and his assistants were discussing engine improvements.

The Mighty Iron Mole remained buried, and over the years its very existence came into doubt. Fastbinder, who was an avid collector of antique engineering oddities, heard the rumors, saw the sixty-year-old photos and paid the son of the inventor ten thousand dollars for excavation rights on the property, then paid another hundred thousand to purchase the MIM after he located it.

Fastbinder told the inventor's son that the mole would be restored and put on display at the Fastbinder Museum of Mechanical Marvels.

"Not restored so's it will *work?*" asked the son, now a retired plumber in Portland.

"Not quite," Fastbinder said.

The inventor's son considered the machine a death trap, but Fastbinder was in love with the Mighty Iron Mole long before he ever laid eyes on it. He'd intended to restore it fully—and he did. He even improved it. Still, it took blind desperation to convince him to actually use it.

The Iron Mole hadn't exactly proven itself to be mighty. Now it looked almost as dead as when he'd first dug down to it in Oregon—a metal hulk, smothered in the earth. The entrance made by Jack was an ugly, burned gash in the aluminum-plated steel shell.

"I would like to put this old junker in zee museum, even if she did almost kill me," Fastbinder lamented. "She is a special machine. Nothing was like her, ever."

Jack looked gloomier. "Pops, the museum was trashed, and I mean totally. They took it to pieces. There wasn't so much as a screw and a bolt still put together. Everything's gone from the house, too."

Fastbinder nodded. "I see."

"These are some bad guys, Pops. Herbie was right. They're freaks or something."

"I know this. I met them, remember? I watched them on zee video when I was trying to make an escape. They used no weapons or tools. They did all the destruction with their hands."

Jack nodded seriously. "That's what Margo told the police."

"Margo? She is okay?"

"She's fine," Jack assured him.

"I would like to see the devastation for myself." Fastbinder sighed. "Is it safe to return?"

"No. Uh-uh. The cops must've got word I was back in town. They started nosing around. We gotta surface somewhere else. Don't worry, this baby's nuclear. She'll go for a thousand miles if you wanna. I've got oxygen for a week, and she'll extract and replenish her air supply from any and all water we run into."

"I am starving."

"I have lunch meat inside JED. We'll stop for supplies a few miles down the road."

"JED?"

Jack looked sheepish. "Well, I been working all

hours and didn't have time to think of a better name, so I just called it Jack's Earth Drill. JED for short. You think it's a dorky name?"

Fastbinder shook his head. "Jack, I think JED is magnificent."

Jack beamed.

Fastbinder crawled through the hatch into his son's gleaming vehicle, never looking back at the old diesel earth drill that had been built by a lunatic in 1938.

FOR EIGHTEEN YEARS Frank Socol operated the This Little Piggy Market and Gift Shop on America's Historic Route 66. He bought the place because he loved the mother road and he wanted to be a part of it.

"But, Frank, it's a convenience store," his wife protested way back in the 1980s.

"It's a market, a grocery, a community meeting place. This Little Piggy is a part of the history of Route 66."

"I know you like Route 66 and all, but Frank, you are an ophthalmologist—you can't give up your practice to run a 7-Eleven, even an antique 7-Eleven."

"Lorraine, somebody has to save the This Little Piggy. We can't allow another piece of Americana to just fade away."

"Why not?" Lorraine asked.

In the end, Dr. Frank Socol had to choose between Lorraine and This Little Piggy. Lorraine now lived in Sioux City with an endocrinologist.

Frank kept This Little Piggy Market and Gift Shop on America's Historic Route 66 in pristine and pseudo-vintage condition, including a screen door that slammed. He did add air-conditioning, and the valuable cool air buffeted out that screen door every time a tourist opened it, but every three-dollar bottle of pop they bought helped offset the A/C bill.

The tourists just kept on coming. The Japanese kept the cash flowing during lulls in American interest. There were also big influxes of Route 66 aficionados from Finland, of all places. Hell, the Finns would pay *four* dollars for a bottle of pop and never even complain—especially the stuff in brown glass bottles that claimed to be handcrafted, even though it came from a big plant in Albuquerque that produced the big soda brands.

Frank's real profits came from water. "The rare water of the desert, hand-bottled at the hidden springs of the American Southwest." That's what the label said. Frank Socol composed it himself and had the labels printed in town, and bought the glass bottles—glass for the authentic look—by the truckload. He filled them in the back room between tour buses and motorcycle gangs.

That's what he was doing—filling Mother Road Agua bottles—when he heard a rumbling noise like a really big truck thundering down the ancient, crumbling asphalt of Route 66. He turned off the faucet and noticed that the droplets in the sink were shivering.

Frank Socol walked out of his living quarters in back. From the narrow aisles of the ancient grocery store he could see the heat-shimmering mother road with nary a vehicle on it.

The rumbling became violent and Frank jogged

onto the old plank porch, his body instantly engulfed in the desert heat.

It felt like the vibration came from behind This Little Piggy. That couldn't be. There was nothing but empty desert for miles. In fact, there was nothing to the left or right of the market, either.

But when Frank went around the back, he did indeed find the source of the vibration.

The earth was bulging, growing, only a stone's throw from the garbage bins. For a heart-stopping second Frank thought there was some sort of freak desert volcano coming to the surface. But who ever heard of a desert volcano?

Then he saw flashing blue electricity and the shape of a metal vehicle of some kind, and the air filled with whipping clouds of dust and sand. The sand engulfed him so fast he didn't have time to close his mouth, and sand pushed into his lungs. Opposing gales of air squeezed him front and back, spinning him.

He retreated, but in the maelstrom he had to have staggered in the wrong direction. He found himself right up close to the machine that clawed out of the earth, and the crackling blue energy reached out for Frank Socol.

The vehicle crawled onto the level surface of the desert. The lightning vanished, allowing the clouds of sediment to settle like sifted flour. A light breeze carried the lingering dust away from Jack's Earth Drill.

The hatch opened.

"Holy smokes! It's hotter out here than at two thousand feet!"

Jack Fast slid out of the hatch feetfirst and stood blinking in the powdery sand, then saw he was not alone. "Hey, cool!"

Fastbinder emerged, merely happy to be alive and back on the surface of the earth again. He found his son examining the blackened, burned remains of a human being perched alongside JED.

Frank Socol was kneeling, his arms stretched out to either side, as if frozen in a state of worship. The static discharge of the earth drill had burned and blackened his flesh and bones halfway through his body.

The false idol to which he was praying was the gleaming, spotless earth drill.

"You like yours extracrispy, Pops?"

"No, thank you." Fastbinder, to be honest, was nauseated by the remains—and now he was worried about who else might be around.

"Don't worry, it's still early. Nobody for miles," Jack explained. "Let's go shopping!"

Fastbinder saw they had surfaced alongside Route 66. Miles to the east along this road were the abandoned remains of his own precious museum.

This place was also on a similar deserted stretch of Route 66, with the quiet mountains rising out of the dry earth a few miles behind it. It was old, but not a bad-looking retail establishment.

They emptied the antique, hand-built wooden shelves of This Little Piggy Market. They took overpriced foam coolers and filled them with everything from the refrigerated display cases.

"Told you, Pops," Jack said as they each navigated

a shopping cart through the desert weeds. "It's too early for tourists."

Fastbinder held up a small box of his favorite sugar-glazed popcorn snack. "Zees Screamink Yellow Zonkers would be a dollar and ninety-nine cents at zee zupermarket, but he was zelling it for six bucks U.S."

"You talk like a real kraut when you get worked up, Pops," Jack observed.

"I like zis place very much," Fastbinder admitted. He typically restored antique machinery, but he could see that a lot of love and elbow grease had gone into restoring the market. The expensive furnishings in the living quarters, and the spotless new Land Rover parked in back, proved that This Little Piggy was quite profitable.

As Jack was tossing groceries in JED's hatch, Fastbinder used the boy's mobile phone to reach his lawyer in Cologne, Germany.

"Herr Fastbinder, I am so glad—"

"Shut up and listen. There is a property I want you to buy for me as soon as possible." Fastbinder described the market.

"A grocery store?" his lawyer asked. "Eet duss goot bizeeness?"

"A tourist grocery store," Fastbinder said. "And soon it will be zee top tourist destination on zee famous American Route 66."

Jack Fast was grinning. "Pretty savvy, Pops. Americans love this kinda bizarro unsolved-mystery stuff."

"And zee Finns," Fastbinder reminded as he ducked back into the earth drill. "Never underestimate zee buying power of zee Finnish tourists."

Jack's Earth Drill rolled into the tunnel and the flashing of lights didn't appear again until it was a hundred feet down.

Nobody was there to witness its departure. Frank Socol, late owner of This Little Piggy Market and Gift Shop on America's Historic Route 66, was too extracrispy to notice.

2

His name was Remo and he was tossing people out of an airplane.

"Three, two, one, go!" He hoisted the skydiver through the open floor hatch with one hand.

"Ten, nine, eight!" Remo said loudly over the wind and aircraft racket, staring at his watch.

"I will exit under my own power," declared the next skydiver, words muffled by the helmet enclosing his entire face.

Remo, who took his job as jump coordinator very seriously, shook his head. "Six! No room for error five! Four!" At zero the skydiver jumped, but not before Remo gave him a quick shove that sent him spiraling away from the plane at an unplanned trajectory.

The next skydiver curled his lip as Remo counted down the next jump.

"You touch me, I kill you," the squat, powerful-looking man called.

"Four! Eat shit 'n' die three!"

The skydiver stepped through the hatchway on three, only to find himself dangling in the thin subzero wind just outside the belly of the aircraft. The jump coordinator was gripping him by the harness in one hand as if he were holding an alley cat by the scruff of the neck.

"One! Wait for it, zero!" Remo released the jumper with a twist. The skydiver with the bad attitude went flopping end-over-end toward Earth.

Only one skydiver left, and he decided it was in his best interest to cooperate. This no-nonsense jump coordinator was clearly not a man to cross. Remo wasn't bothered by the frigid wind. He sucked on a spare oxygen bottle occasionally, but it was almost as if he were doing it just for show. He was thin, but his wrists were so muscular he had to use a six-inch aircraft screw, bent like a twist tie, to extend the bands of his watch. The guy was either inhuman or a lunatic.

But he was a reasonable lunatic, anyway. The last skydiver behaved himself and in return Remo jettisoned him powerfully from the aircraft at exactly the right instant. The launch was smooth and straight—no out-of-control free fall to fight his way out of. The skydiver happily considered that his smooth exit was going to gain him a few vital seconds.

Outside the aircraft, fifty thousand feet above the earth, the skydiver deliberately forgot all about the strange jump coordinator and concentrated on what he was doing. He was a professional extreme athlete. Distractions were lethal to peak extreme performance. Taking control of his fall, he drew in his limbs to cut wind resistance.

The goal was to get to the surface faster than all the

other divers. The winner of this competition was the jumper who used the least total time to get from fifty thousand feet to solid ground—without dying.

"This is a stupid sport," Remo observed.

Free fall was the last place on Earth you would ever think to find yourself with unexpected company. The skydiver jerked and twisted until he found who had spoken.

It was the jump coordinator from the aircraft, the fool in the T-shirt, hovering just above him.

"What are you doing?"

"Skydiving, duh, what's it look like?" Remo didn't shout, but the extreme athlete heard him clearly through the wind noise and his face mask.

"You got no chute! No oxygen! No thermal suit!"

"The chute I'll pick up later. It's not like we don't have time. We're practically in orbit."

"Come here, I'll harness you in with me."

"No, thanks."

The skydiver sputtered and tried to give chase, but Remo turned his body into an arrowhead that slipped through the thin air faster than the skydiver in his bulky gear.

Remo was slightly peeved. He had thought the last man in the line would be the guilty one. It made sense, right? If you're going to kill a bunch of your fellow sky-divers, wouldn't it be optimal to shoot down instead of up?

Remo's boss had agreed with this theory, but the last skydiver had proven to be genuine in his fear for Remo's safety. The guy didn't have the heartbeat or the respiration of a man about to commit murder. You could tell those things, if you just know what signals to look for.

At least, Remo Williams could tell such things. He could read a man's heartbeat, pupil dilation, breathing and other signs of nervous activity that were hidden even to a state-of-the-art polygraph—and Remo did it all without using any equipment at all.

Remo knew the martial art of Sinanju. Remo *lived* the art of Sinanju. In fact, he was the Reigning Master of Sinanju, which was roughly equivalent to having a thousand black belts in karate.

Karate, after all, was derived from crumbs of knowledge fallen from the table of the Masters of Sinanju, who had practiced their art for thousands of years. Kung fu, ninja, judo, all were but flickers of light pilfered from the Sun Source of martial arts, Sinanju.

Sinanju was far more than the other arts. Sinanju worked because it enhanced the senses. Whereas most humans tapped into ten percent of their bodies' capabilities, the Masters of Sinanju used fifty percent. Sometimes seventy percent. In a few rare cases, even more.

Nothing on the planet could match the ancient practice that came from a dismal little fishing village on the shores of what was now North Korea. The Sinanju Masters worked as assassins, traveling the globe centuries before the great European explorers. They were employed by the most powerful rulers of their times, emperors and kings and warlords, and the Masters practiced their art, usually, without weapons or tools.

Remo would resort to using a parachute when jumping out of an airplane, when given the option. There were lots of parachutes around for the taking right now, but he wasn't in much of a rush. These dingbats had jumped from way, way up and it was a long, long way down.

"Hey, got a minute?"

The next skydiver did somersaults trying to find out who was talking to him. "Who the hell are you?" he shouted when he finally found Remo closing in on him.

These knuckleheads weren't so bright. "Jump coordinator, from the airplane." Remo pointed up just in case the guy couldn't remember where the airplane had been.

"You're gonna die!"

Same story with the same result. The guy's bad attitude was now frantic fear for Remo's life. A brief chat convinced Remo that the extreme HALO skydiver wasn't a would-be murderer and he moved on, getting irritated. Maybe there were no murders planned for this event after all.

Remo had kept a close eye on these guys on the airplane and convinced himself even then that none of them were acting like executioners. They were nervous, sure—they were risking their fool necks for a huge cash prize.

But Upstairs was convinced this competition was going to be sabotaged. If Remo didn't double-check, Upstairs would nag him about it for days, maybe weeks. Upstairs was getting to be a real kink in the keister.

"How ya doin'?" he asked the next skydiver, who went into paroxysms that were quickly halted when Remo grabbed him by the harness. Their brief talk assured Remo this man was just another nonmurderer.

"Dammit!" Remo said. "This is a waste of time."

The skydiver, amazingly enough, saw something so shocking it distracted him from his unexpected visitor.

Many hundreds of feet below them, the first skydiver's chute deployed. It was way too early. The whole point of this competition was to get to the ground in the least amount of time, so the skydivers waited until the last possible second to release their chutes.

"Hey, you've got one smart guy in this bunch," Remo said, although he was already second-guessing himself. What if that skydiver was deploying early so he could gain altitude over the others and shoot them down?

But that thought vanished when the skydiver's chute collapsed, becoming a turquoise wad of flapping nylon.

"That can't be right," he told his companion, then steered himself away, cutting across a quarter-mile of open air to intercept the victim of the bad parachute. The chute was causing enough drag to lift the man toward him, and Remo snatched the lines in his fist.

Remo didn't bother asking the man for an explanation. The skydiver was already dead, with his head swollen and his eyes bulging against the transparent face mask. Trickles of steam issued from his mouth.

Another chute deployed below him and melted as Remo watched. Then another. He craned his neck, looking for the cause, but found the skies empty in all directions.

"Son of a bitch!" he told the corpse, turned it and yanked the emergency cord. The melted wad of the nylon emergency chute expanded and created more drag, and Remo allowed the corpse to fly away from him.

He had living people to worry about.

He became a raptor, or a swift, or a kite, whatever kind of bird could dive at unbelievable speeds, and below him he watched the sickly blossoming of melted parachutes one after another. The timing was consistent, exactly ten seconds between them, thanks to Remo Williams's careful jump coordination. Now his impeccable timing helped him decide what to do.

He knew how fast he could travel, relative to the falling skydivers, and knew exactly where he could intercept them before they were hit by whatever it was that was cooking them and killing them.

He cut through the air like a red-hot knife in cold water. He was in time to save the next man, but he hadn't been able to account for the nature of the killing weapon. The weapon had begun its work already, and the skydiver was being roasted by his overheated gear. It was the harness frame that was actually getting super hot, melting the nylon and cooking the competitors.

As he flashed by the screaming man, Remo snatched the cord for the emergency chute, which deployed at the same instant the primary chute burst open in a steaming, pungent mass. The two chutes tangled momentarily, then the emergency chute filled with air and carried the man high above Remo. The skydiver would make it to the ground without cracking up, but Remo didn't kid himself—he'd probably be dead of his burns by then.

Remo wouldn't allow this to distract him as he banked and steered up on an intercept course to the next skydiver, who was just starting to feel the heat. The man never saw Remo speed by, but he felt the sudden yank of the emergency chute, which carried him out of the hot zone. Remo moved on up the line, snatching rip cords until he was back to the first man in the line and the last one to jump from the aircraft.

"Hi, again," Remo called.

The skydiver had observed Remo in action and was speechless.

"I'll take you up on that offer now." Getting no response, Remo took it upon himself to buckle himself to the back of the skydiver, below the main chute, and reached around, yanking the cord.

He allowed his body to flow with the sudden jolt of deceleration as the canopy billowed above them, then he waited.

The smoking corpses of the first jumpers fluttered farther and farther below them on their ruined chutes.

Minutes later, Remo and his companion descended into the hot zone, but nothing happened. Below them the first jumpers began hitting the grassy plains of Montana with small bursts of dust. Remo was relieved to see that he had saved some lives. The jumpers he got to before they descended into the hot zone looked okay. The skydivers who left the plane first were hitting the ground like sacks of charred potatoes.

"Is extreme competitive HALO skydiving always this extreme?" Remo called up, making conversation.

"No," answered his partner.

"Well, it's still a stupid sport."

"Yes."

Five thousand feet later, Remo said, "I'm leaving before you talk my fool ear off." He slashed through his strap with his fingernails and plummeted the last several yards to solid earth.

The skydiver's parachute, freed of the extra weight, bobbed and lingered in the air for many seconds, then set the man on a hilltop near a small tree. He continued to sit there for a long time, thinking things over.

Remo snaked across the prairie until he found one of the dead victims. He gave the body a quick onceover, then relieved it of its equipment, wadding up the melted parachute and stuffing it back inside.

He had some phone calls to make.

3

It was amazing what a decent meal could do to lift your spirits. After they left the little Route 66 roadside store on that day weeks and weeks ago, Jacob Fastbinder made a meal from stolen groceries. Fastbinder's tastes were a little more cultured than those of his American son. Jack would eat nothing but lunch-meat-and-mustard sandwiches for days at a time and be happy. Fastbinder had been raised in a wealthy German household, and he opened a half-dozen tiny cans that had been stacked on the gourmet shelf at the market. Oysters, caviar, pâté, all of it went onto tiny slices of pretty good rye bread. Fastbinder ate until he was near to bursting.

Satisfied, he began noticing the control panel of Jack's Earth Drill. Various computers and gauges were bolted to a hastily constructed steel rack. There was a navigation system that, Jack explained, used what few digital seismological mappings were available for tracking their route in the subsurface. New features were mapped out in real time as Jack's Earth Drill pinged the underworld with ultrasound.

Fastbinder wasn't the genius his young son was, but he was still a brilliant, educated engineer. He read the data on the displays easily enough, and he was shocked.

"Jack, why are we so deep? Where are we going?"

The teenager grinned excitedly. "Big cavern I mapped out on the way over. The place is the size of the Mall of America, and it's like five miles down. Talk about a hideout. They'll never find us there."

"Five miles," Fastbinder breathed. "That's impossible."

"That's what the research says. I looked it up. The deepest mines are 12,700 feet deep, and that's not even 2.5 miles. We're going twice that."

Fastbinder spotted an external temperature gauge. They were up to 120 degrees Fahrenheit already. The interior of the mole was sixty-eight and holding, but Fastbinder started sweating anyway.

"Why are we doing this thing, Jack?"

"I told you, it's a good hideout."

"We'll burn up."

Jack's eyes sparked. "It's cool down there, Pops. That's why I found it. There was this cool place I passed through on the way over. It's a subsurface water shaft. Must come from some underground river closer to the surface. I figure an earthquake or something opened up a crack that went almost straight down, and the river started following it. It's like a twenty-thousand-foot waterfall. I put a drone down there and got enough of a reading to show me that it's a honking huge cavern system. The air-temperature reading I got was sixty-four degrees Eff. I guess the river cools it down."

But Jack Fast had a more compelling reason for wanting to see the deep cavern. He showed his father the photographs that his drone probe had transmitted back to him. Photographs of people.

JACOB FASTBINDER THOUGHT his son was joking, but that didn't make sense. Jack Fast had always been a straight shooter, always telling his father the unadulterated truth. He had earned Fastbinder's trust.

Still the elderly man experienced mounting fear as the hours stretched into a full day. Jack's Earth Drill crawled inexorably down at a steep angle, effortlessly forging its impressive and beautiful tunnel system. She seemed robust enough, and Jack's estimations of the tunnel strength were impressive.

Fastbinder hadn't known real terror as he lay dying in the old antique Mighty Mole, but now, even when his son assured him he was safe, Fastbinder grew terrified. His claustrophobia mounted as they stared at the darkness endless hours—the brilliance of the static electricity would have blinded them without a near-black shield over the front and back windshields.

Then the ordeal was over. Fastbinder sat up out of a fitful nap, roused by uncanny silence and stillness.

"We're here," Jack Fast said. Now that the blinding electric bolts were turned off, Jack shoved back the tempered-glass blast shield and they looked upon a new world.

Jack's Earth Drill had emerged atop a sand dune,

and below them stretched a plain of sand, rock and white slime. JED's spotlights revealed a wide river of crystal-clean water, and they could barely see the walls on the other side of it.

"It's a quarter-mile wide at this point," Jack said. "There's a mile of open space in front of us and look at this! There's not just one river coming in here, there's three rivers!" After checking the instruments he squinted into the darkness. "Two more rivers come into the cavern at the other end, plus the first one coming out over here, and they all empty into a big river that keeps going down. This is really amazing, Pops!"

"Yes." Fastbinder was thinking about it. "If the river caverns are traversable during the dryer months of the year, humans could come and go. But where are the people now?" Fastbinder's eyes prowled the high-contrast shadows for the freakish white faces from the blurry photograph.

"Hiding, probably. Check it out!" Jack placed the spotlight beam on a white, oily patch. "Let's get closer!" He engaged the battery dives. JED's treads rolled down the sandy dune at the speed of a leisurely walk, in near silence. The slimy patch began to look more like a pile of slimy things, then it became something recognizable.

"Fish parts," Fastbinder said. "Now we know what they eat."

"Yech."

"See the bones? They even strip off the ribs to eat. It has minerals the flesh doesn't have. They probably consume the organs, too, for the same reason."

"Hey, Pops, Jules Verne was right! 'Shrooms!" The rear of the hill-sized pile of fish scraps was smoothed over and fuzzy with thick mold and small copses of pale mushrooms, some of them knee high. A large quantity of them was scattered on the rock beside the hill. They looked fresh, as if someone had dropped them only minutes before.

Amid the fallen fungi were slimy, glimmering footprints.

"We must have drove the poor suckers off. But they're not getting far." Jack looked determined as he steered JED deeper into the cavern, following the footprints to a neighborhood of nests made from desiccated mushrooms.

"Zee two other rivers come into the cavern here, making it the coolest place in the cavern," Fastbinder observed, feeling energized and excited now. "Very cozy, eh, Jack?"

"Oh, yeah, looks great," Jack replied sarcastically, making his father laugh.

Then they saw them. People. Lots of pale, hideous people.

"Pops," Jack asked when he got his voice, "what're we gonna do with these ugly suckers? They look pretty low on the evolutionary scale."

"They will be good for many things, Jack," Fastbinder said, his mind spinning with new ideas as JED turned sharply around a protective outcropping and bore down on the terrified crowd of pale-skinned, white-haired people, now trapped against the back wall of the cavern system. JED blocked their escape route, and Jack Fast halted the earth drill. From a hundred feet away they observed the mob in fascination.

They were obviously albinos and they were all hideous, cadaverous creatures. They were pushing and shoving one another in terror, and one of them was wounded. Father and son saw the sudden spray of crimson, and with it the scent of fresh blood had to have wafted over the crowd.

Fast and Fastbinder witnessed their first feeding frenzy. The wounded creature—they didn't even have time to determine if the naked thing was male or female—was swarmed and dismembered by groping hands and gnashing teeth. There was meat enough for every albino to get a mouthful. The blood-smeared, nude, filthy albinos settled into unflattering squats to eat their lunch.

"Gross!" Jack chuckled. "Guess they'll eat anything that gets their mouth watering."

"Survival instinct will drive them to seek out any possible variety in their diet to get rare nutrients," Fastbinder agreed, nodding.

Jack nodded at the stacks of groceries and dripping foam coolers piled up in the rear of Jack's Earth Drill. "We're gonna be gods, Pops."

"Yes, Jack, my genius progeny, they will be ours to command, and they are the answers to all our troubles."

Jack ripped the pull-tops off all eight cans of Lil Wieners Hot Dawgs and tossed the fat rolls of Processed Meat Product across the sand. The aroma of meat fat in brine got the attention of the albinos.

They threw caution to the wind and scrambled for the hot dogs like starved Boy Scouts. The Lil Wieners vanished.

The blind, degenerate humans shuffled for the open hatch of Jack's Earth Drill.

"Now you are all very brave, I see, yes?" Jacob Fastbinder demanded. He flung Ding Dongs in every direction, creating a free-for-all. The pastries were consumed, foil wrappers and all, in a matter of seconds.

The albinos came back to Jack's Earth Drill expectantly. No, belligerently.

"Now that we have taught them we have wonderful gifts to give, we should teach them we are powerful deliverers of death, yes?" Fastbinder asked rhetorically.

"Oh, yeah, Big Daddy!" Jack excitedly dug into a steel locker bolted to the wall.

"You have firearms?"

"Yeah, but I have something better, Pops." Jack stood up with a red, white and blue cardboard box.

"Firecrackers. Big honkin' firecrackers. I brought them for stability tests on sedimentary deposits."

"Here comes a friendly sedimentary deposit, now, Jack." Fastbinder couldn't wait to see what Jack had in mind for the tall, tough-looking albino who was getting aggressive on them, obviously some sort of alpha male. Other males crouched and sniffed the ground at his feet as he muscled through the crowd. The big albino strolled this way and that, but came closer to JED than the others dared.

"You are a very ugly dude." Jack tossed the alpha male an M-80, which had about the same mass as a Lil Wiener Processed Meat Product and thumped on the ground with the same sound. The alpha male stuffed it in his mouth.

"Yikes." Jack slammed the hatch just as the alpha male's face splattered. The blood smell broadcast throughout the cavern and the albinos reacted.

Father and son had a front row seat for the second feeding frenzy of the afternoon. "Guess the wieners and Ding Dongs just whetted their appetite, huh, Pops? I thought they'd be a little, you know, terrified of the big bang."

"Yes, they will be, you will see. But they are driven by their instinct to feed, and always it will dominate them. We must use this to our advantage."

Soon after the last few fragments of the alpha male were devoured, the albinos became aware of how close they'd wandered to Jack's Earth Drill. They retreated until Jack tossed out the stack of thawed frozen dinners. After the dinners were gone, the albinos were in a state of agitation.

"They know we have more food. They are compelled to try to take it. Now they must learn we are their masters."

"Yeah." Jack said. "Big jerk albinos at ten, twelve and two."

Three more big adult males postured before JED, sniffing one another and engaging in brief wrestling matches to show their aggressiveness, until a temporary alliance was formed and they attacked JED with flat chunks of rock. No matter how much they pounded, they couldn't break the steel skin.

Jack opened the hatch and laughed harshly until the albino crowd joined in the merriment, shaming the three champions. One of them grew pink in the cheeks and grabbed for Jack, only to have both forearms crushed when the hatch slammed down on them. The next one shouted furiously at JED while Fastbinder taunted him in German through a narrow slot opening in the door. The brute eventually flung himself on the earth drill and tried to bite it open, breaking his teeth. Fastbinder moved the vehicle a few feet and caught the brute's legs under the treads, where he wriggled helplessly like a praying mantis freshly impaled on a collector's pin. Only one albino still had any fight left in him.

"Okay, I'll take care of that dude," Jack said, dragging on a big sweatshirt, but not before Fastbinder saw some sort of harness strapped beneath it.

"He is being cautious. He may be one of zee smart ones, Jack."

"Chill, Pops, he's already Purina Caveman Chow. But I got to show these shmoes that we're the baddest asses ever, even away from the big shiny thing we rode in on."

Fastbinder watched from the hatch, grabbing a pry bar from a tool chest to use in case Jack's judgment turned out to be faulty.

But Jack knew what he was doing, as always. The kid was some sort of a genius and played the scene just right. He yelled at the albino male until it was goaded into attacking him, then Jack's arm snapped out at the caveman, extended two feet too long and crushed his sternum. Fastbinder nodded with satisfaction—Jack had some sort of a mechanical arm under his sweatshirt.

The brute ignored the funny feeling of internal bleeding, instead staggering to his feet and charging Jack, only to be sucker punched in the hip. The caveman's leg bent an unnatural direction and blood spurted where the bone pierced the skin.

The blood smell got the albinos dancing and shrieking, but they wouldn't go any closer. Their greatest instinct had been subverted by fear of something terrible and supernatural.

Fastbinder and his son were now deities to the albinos. Being benevolent gods, they eventually allowed the albinos to feed on the trio of fallen heroes. The wounded brutes grunted and whined as they were ripped apart, and the last one, the smart one, even begged for mercy.

He begged in English.

4

The Korean man was so very old that his skin was like parchment. His flesh was nearly translucent, the wisps of hair over his ears were yellow-white and the threads of his beard were nearly invisible.

In the dingy office, he stroked the beard thoughtfully, then put his hand back into the sleeve of his pale gold Korean robe.

"I don't understand," said the man behind the desk in a pinched, sour tone of voice. "Does this have something to do with the succession?"

"It is a private matter, unworthy of your attentions, kind and generous Emperor," proclaimed the old Korean in a formal singsong voice. "It is between my pupil and myself."

"Master Chiun, I beg to differ," said the man behind the desk. "Anything that affects my enforcement arm is my business. Remo becomes more headstrong every day. He's never been the most cooperative man to manage, but now he's utterly unpredictable and belligerent. He is putting his own interests ahead of CURE's mandate."

The small Korean man, who was actually much older than the man behind the desk, wore a smile that wouldn't budge. The old man behind the desk, Harold W. Smith, director of CURE, glanced worriedly at his assistant. Mark Howard was at another desk, which looked out of place in the timeworn office.

"To be blunt, Master Chiun," Smith said, "Remo is failing to fulfill his contract."

"I assure you, Great and Humble Emperor of the North American Continent, Remo has fulfilled all your stated demands."

"You speak of his missions," Smith said.

"He has failed none of them."

"But he has failed to perform his most basic assignment," Smith said. "That is, to maintain the security of this organization. He exposed us all. The future of CURE is tenuous at this point, and that is because of Remo's reckless action."

Chiun tilted his head. "I fail to understand your meaning, O Emperor."

Smith long ago stopped trying to dissuade Chiun from calling him Emperor. Smith wasn't an emperor. He was the head of the most effective organization in the federal government: CURE. There was no government entity more secret, and there was none more illegal.

CURE was designed to protect the U.S. Constitution by violating the Constitution. The Bill of Rights was mincemeat when CURE got its fingers into it. But America would have fallen into anarchy without CURE's intervention in past crises.

"This Native American tribe out near Yuma, Arizona," Smith said. "All the people of this tribe must know about CURE by now."

"I cannot say, Emperor."

"How long has Remo been hiding Winston there?"

"I cannot answer that question, Emperor."

"And this daughter, Freya. Both have been there for years, from what I can tell."

Chiun was silent, his face a mask that could not be penetrated.

"And this man they call Sunny Joe Roam. Are you aware that he is Remo's biological father?"

Chiun's expression changed at that. Smith read volumes in it. "I understand, Master Chiun. You did know, but you did not expect me to know."

Chiun, Master of Sinanju Emeritus, trainer of Remo Williams, said nothing. What could he say?

"This is intolerable," Harold W. Smith declared flatly, and he turned in his chair to do something that was rare these days: he gazed out the one-way glass of his office at the pounding surf of Long Island Sound. He was troubled.

But Mark Howard, assistant director of CURE, didn't think his boss was as troubled as the old Master looked. Chiun's posture had become slightly more rigid, his brow stern, his childlike eyes intense. Still, Chiun said nothing.

"Remo has forced me into a very difficult position. I have never shied away from silencing those who could expose CURE." Smith rotated away from the view. "If this exposure had occurred ten years ago, I would have not hesitated to order—"

"Hold!"

Chiun's palm was toward Smith, who fell back in his chair as if shoved.

"Do not speak those words, Emperor," Chiun said. "Even as idle threat."

"I don't understand."

"And I shall not allow such things to pass my lips, even to educate you. Suffice it to say you tread dangerous ground."

"Dangerous to whom?"

"Dangerous to our continuing association," Chiun replied formally. "At the very least you risk forcing me to declare our contract void."

Smith's mind was spinning like an old-fashioned computer tape drive gone berserk. What was he missing? He personally hashed out CURE's contract with Chiun, every word of it an agony of negotiation. What stipulation was he close to violating and what was wrong with him that he didn't know it?

Mark Howard's wheelchair squeaked, bringing Smith back to the old office in the large private hospital in Rye, New York.

"May we then discuss the Remo problem?" Smith asked hesitantly.

Chiun smiled, so abruptly Smith didn't know what to make of it. "Remo has always been a problem, great Emperor of Puppets. What more can be expected of him?"

When the blue icon flashed on the computer screen hidden under his desktop, Smith was almost relieved for the distraction. He keyed on the telephone.

"Hey, Smitty, it's all messed up out here in Montana," Remo Williams said as soon as the line was opened. "Hey, Junior. Hey, Little Father."

"Can you be more clear about 'messed up'?" Smith asked. "Did you catch the killers?"

"Yes, explain this failure to your emperor," snapped Chiun.

"Well, if there was a failure, then I guess the blame ought to go to whoever gave me the lowdown on this fiasco," Remo said.

"Be polite, Remo," Chiun chided.

"Listen, Smitty, I came out here to look for a killer skydiver. Look for signs of tampering with the parachutes, you tell me. Look for a skydiver with a sniper's rifle. Well, I looked and I didn't find anything like that."

"Then what did happen, Remo?"

Smith listened closely to Remo's account of the championship round of the Third Annual Extreme Competitive High Altitude/Low Opening Skydiving event. He and Mark Howard simultaneously began combing the reams of information that was pouring into their data-gathering mainframes.

"You obtained a victim?" Smith asked.

"I obtained an equipment pack. That's what heated up. The problem is, there's nothing inside of it that could have generated that much heat."

"You should have acquired a cadaver," Smith said. "We can't be sure the heat didn't originate from something in their clothing."

"Yes, we're sure because I'm sure," Remo said.

"Even you'd be able to figure it out if you had a look at the guy. The heat starts inside the pack and works its way out. I think it's actually the plastic parts of the frame that get hot, but there's nothing inside the pack to make them get hot. Whatever started it came from the ground, but it got turned off or we drifted out of its range or something. You want me to send you the pack?"

"Remo, there might have been a radiant element hidden in the clothing of the competitors," Smith persisted. "It could have made the pack appear to be the heat source when, in fact—"

"You want the equipment or do I give it to Goodwill?"

"Remo," Chiun warned, "you shall treat your emperor with respect."

"Bring the equipment back with you, Remo," Smith said. "Get here as soon as possible."

"Hey, no, uh-uh, I'm going to the Middle East. Remember the mean old Mr. Senator who keeps doing bad things to the U.S. of A.?"

"We have not yet located Senator Whiteslaw," Smith said. "He's in hiding."

"Finding people is your specialty. You didn't even try, did you?"

"We made an effort to locate him, but we do have other problems vying for our attention."

"Yeah, like what? On second thought, don't tell me."

The click of the disconnect filled the office.

"Will there be anything more, great leader of the United States of North America?" Chiun was smiling as if he had no cares in the world.

When the old Master was gone, Smith turned to his assistant.

"Mark, what do you make of this contract-voiding business? For the life of me I can't figure out what he is talking about."

Mark Howard bit his lower lip. "There's an extended-family clause in the contract, isn't there?"

Dr. Smith frowned. "Yes. What of it?"

"You would ask him to assassinate members of his own family," Mark said. "That's so forbidden it is like…blasphemy."

"I did not say that I would, and regardless, I would have made the request of Chiun, not Remo. Despite their relationship, Chiun and Remo are not related by blood."

Mark just sat there. Smith suddenly understood that what he had said was dead wrong.

"How can this be?" he asked. "How long have you known?"

"A few weeks. Since I went to Yuma to get him. Remo's related by blood to the entire Sun On Jo tribe, and the tribe, from what Remo says, was founded by a pre-Columbian Sinanju Master."

Harold W. Smith turned again and stared out at the Sound. The waves were mighty today, like powerful fists battering the land, but they were fragile compared to the realization that assaulted Smith's mind.

He had seen much that was illogical during his tenure with CURE. He had witnessed amazing things, and yet his mind rebelled against what he had just learned and all that it implied.

Remo and Chiun, related by blood.

Remo and Chiun, distanced by fate.

Remo and Chiun, rejoined by CURE.

The odds against it happening by chance were incalculable, but the alternative was unthinkable: Remo and Chiun brought together by CURE, which was under the control of something else.

Smith felt his chest become heavy. The question that remained, the unanswerable mystery, was what or who had manipulated CURE?

CHIUN STOOD in the hall, out of sight of Emperor Smith's well-meaning but doddering secretary, and eavesdropped as Mark Howard confirmed what he knew of Chiun and the Sun On Jo tribe. It was a secret best aired, Chiun considered. Too long had the truth remained unspoken to their employer.

Smith was a ruthless man, willing to make any sacrifice to continue the work of his hidden power base. Chiun learned years ago that it was best to keep quiet to the Emperor about the true extent of the fame and glory of Sinanju, and yet Remo was not so skilled at masking the truth. That he had kept the secret of the Sun On Jo for all these years was tribute to his patience, if not an indictment of his stubbornness. This subterfuge had been necessary once, lest the emperor view the existence of this tribe and Remo's offspring as a threat to his power, and order their destruction.

That would be a foolish act, brimming with ruinous consequences, and Chiun did not think Smith would make that misstep. Still, he would keep a wary eye on the emperor in the coming days.

The emperor, after all, was old and set in his old ways, and had always been prone to episodes of insanity.

Chiun extracted a white electronic device from his sleeve as he strolled the hall of the rarely used wing of Folcroft Sanitarium. The private hospital served the wealthy and the special cases—this was the front for CURE. Chiun and Remo had for years maintained a suite of sparsely furnished rooms here. Their current stay was now stretching into weeks, since Remo had been struck down by a grievous wound that kept him comatose for days. He had recovered....

Chiun preferred not to recall the episode.

Now Remo refused to return to their proper home until he satisfied his current infatuation with the annihilation of a puppet senator. Chiun was tired of Folcroft, but also was he tired of the drab two-flat in which the Masters dwelt in Connecticut.

Chiun had his interests to distract him, and as he touched a button his device blinked happily to life.

The device allowed him to read the Internet-posted journals of people from around the world. Today, the Mississippi Trollop had updated her diary. The first words hinted at much juicy debauchery and amoral activity. This promised to be fine reading.

A lovely young woman emerged from one of the

rooms and gave him an enchanting smile. The old Master stopped and bowed, a refined, rare display of respect.

"Chiun, I told you to stop that." She kissed his cheek, then she locked her arm in his and dragged the beet-faced Master of Sinanju Emeritus into her own suite.

5

"It's a beautiful day in the Underworld, Pops." Jack Fast stepped aside to exhibit a color television screen—with reception. "This neighborhood officially has broadband!" He started flipping through sitcoms and home-decorating shows. "I tapped into satellite TV, digital TV, Internet, phone, everything!"

Jack's mobile phone rang.

"That would be Herbie, yes?" Fastbinder answered it. "Right on time, Senator. We just went on-line."

"Jacob, you did it! I knew that kid would get to you in time. He's a sharp one, isn't he?"

"How's Cairo, Senator?"

"It's a hundred degrees and there's sewage in the streets."

"How are your feet, Senator?"

Senator Herbert Whiteslaw's feet were severely burned in an assassination attempt in Washington, D.C., months before. He had done a poor job of taking care of the wounds, and they hadn't healed well. "Still hurt like hell," Whiteslaw complained. "I don't even get full credit for getting them fried. Every politician except me gets big bonus points from an assassination."

"Unless the attempt was successful," Fastbinder added.

"Yeah. Just my luck I get bombed the same week the damn Senate building gets bombed!"

"But you were a victim in the Senate attack, as well," Fastbinder reminded him.

"Yeah, but so what? I was still second fiddle to that right-wing wacko Orville Flicker in the press coverage."

"He was killed, however."

"He still got the best press!" The senator was losing his cool. He'd been under a lot of stress in recent months. Fastbinder knew it and truly enjoyed pushing the senator's hot buttons. "Listen, Fastbinder, you gonna help me do this thing?"

"Not yet."

"Come on, Jacob, I don't have time to fart around here! This opportunity only comes around once every four years, you know? And you owe me—I supplied you with some Grade A intelligence. You must have made millions on all that great stuff you stole."

Senator Whiteslaw, by virtue of his access to Defense Department secrets, had provided Fastbinder and his son with intelligence about some of the U.S.'s top-secret military technology, which the Fastbinders then stole. Fastbinder had indeed made millions, but arms sales were more of a hobby.

"If we're talking about who owes whom, keep in mind that we lured your secret assassins into the open," Fastbinder said. "We got you the evidence, but you failed to warn us sufficiently about their capabilities to do us harm. Both of us, my son and myself, nearly died at their hands."

"And they stole our 'bots," Jack Fast added.

"Losing Ironhand was like losing a member of my family," Fastbinder lamented. "Our agreement is null and void, Senator. My son and I never intended to pit ourselves against these insane killers. Now we must wage war against them and strike them down. Until we do, all other matters are secondary."

Jack Fast nodded encouragingly. His dad was playing the dweeb senator perfectly. Whiteslaw whined and begged and threatened, until finally he allowed that he would be willing to come up with more good intelligence—a lot more.

"We're not looking for weapons any longer, Senator," Fastbinder said. "We need people."

"People? What kind of people?"

"The smart, well-educated kind."

"Like, you want to kidnap all the grad students from UC San Francisco?"

"Nothing so simple. We need professionals from many occupations. Engineers, machinists, geologists, electricians, carpenters, city planners."

"City planners?"

"We will need professionals who are in very specific regions of the United States."

"Huh?"

"I'll e-mail you our shopping list," Jack said, leaning into the phone. "We need healthy folks without fish allergies. They have to be the best in their fields. Get into the DOHS databases."

"How'm I supposed to get into the Department of Homeland Security?" Whiteslaw demanded. "Not only am I in Egypt, I'm being investigated for high treason! Under the circumstances I bet my security clearance is downgraded."

"I don't care how. Get your people working on it," Fastbinder said.

"Like I still have people. What's all this for, anyway?"

"Call back when you have good news, Senator."

6

Jack Fast waited until his father was on the far side of the cavern, supervising the albinos on rock-hitting duty. They couldn't seem to get the hang of using sledgehammers to break stone—but somebody had to hollow out the sixty-foot boulder that was destined to be their new headquarters.

Fastbinder demonstrated an overhead swing that chopped a hefty shard of stone from the boulder. The albinos stood groping for Fastbinder, trying to feel his demonstration.

The workers became excited, as if they understood now what was required, but on the first swing one of them smashed his own foot and started howling. There was no blood, thank God. Another feeding frenzy would have delayed the work for hours.

Jack kept an eye on his father as he dialed up the hotel in Cairo. "Hey, Senator, it's me. Jack. Yeah, we've got a few more items to add to our shopping list."

WHO? OR WHAT?

Those were the only questions that remained after all the other facts settled into their appropriate slots.

Dr. Smith saw perfect logic in the fact that Remo and Chiun were related by blood. Remo's aptitude for Sinanju training had been extraordinary from the beginning—so much so that Chiun had acknowledged Remo as being the fulfillment of Sinanju prophesy, destined to be the greatest of all Sinanju Masters. Therefore it made sense that Remo would have Sinanju blood in his veins. Chiun had mentioned that Remo's skills had to mean he had Korean ancestors—but Smith hadn't taken the comments seriously. Just like Remo's comments about visiting his family out west—Smith always assumed that much of what came out of the Masters' mouths was just rambling.

Somehow the ancient deviation in the lineage, after hundreds of years of separation, intersected again via CURE, and this one fact troubled Smith deeply. The events that brought it about had to have been engineered.

Was Conrad MacCleary responsible? MacCleary had worked with Smith in the CIA, and in the early years CURE *was* Smith and MacCleary. MacCleary hand-picked Remo to be CURE's enforcement arm. Mac-Cleary had been the one who urged Smith to hire a very old North Korean man to serve as one of Remo's trainers.

Yes, it made for a neat little package, but this explanation had a fatal flaw: Conrad MacCleary could never have pulled it off, even if there was a reason for him to do so. Smith and MacCleary worked closely together for years. They were friends, die-hard compatriots with a mutual love of country. MacCleary would have had no patriotic reason for pulling off the scheme without telling Smith, and however skilled he was, MacCleary was still an old drunk. Smith wouldn't have been deceived.

Smith looked deeper. Could anyone have influenced MacCleary to choose Remo and to recommend Chiun, without MacCleary or Smith ever being aware of the manipulation? Not possible. The events that influenced MacCleary occurred over decades.

Which left the option of a nonhuman entity.

Smith didn't like the looks of the ice under his feet, but it was impossible to stop walking.

Had a nonhuman entity manipulated CURE and brought about the pairing of Remo Williams and Chiun, Master of Sinanju. Was it God? Was it some Sinanju deity, seeking the reunification of an ancient Sinanju bloodline?

"Dr. Smith? Are you okay?" Mark Howard asked.

"I'm fine." Smith had forgotten the young man was in the office with him.

But five minutes later, Smith was still staring out the window at the pounding surf of Long Island Sound while a growing list of records waited, ignored, on his computer screen.

WHEN MARK HOWARD CAME into the suite he found the young woman and the Korean Master, several times her age, huddled together on the mats.

Sarah Slate was giggling.

"Good evening, Prince Mark." Chiun reluctantly rose to his feet. "I fear I have usurped this young woman's attention. Do not hold her responsible for failing to fetch you."

"I asked Sarah not to come up to the, er, offices," Mark said uncomfortably.

"Ah." Chiun nodded as if he did not understand and was marking it up to the eccentricities of the Prince Regent, heir to the American Emperor and Master of Puppet Politicians.

"Chiun, you know Sarah must stay isolated." He looked at the young woman helplessly.

Sarah rolled her eyes. "Oh, relax, Mark, we were just blogging."

"Yes," Chiun agreed happily.

"That's a relief." Mark rolled to his hospital bed, using the arm grips to hoist himself out of the wheelchair. Sarah went to care for him and Chiun left them.

SARAH SLATE WAS BORN RICH, but she was born with a heart. Mark Howard liked to think he sensed the goodness in her soul; that was what he found so attractive. The fact that she was beautiful…well, it helped.

But she was good, full of kindness and inner strength. She stayed with him when she didn't have to stay, doing everything she could to make his life easier as he recovered. The torn leg muscles were healing slowly, and he'd start trying to walk again soon. But he was bone-tired so much of the time.

"What would I do?" He sighed as she inspected his leg stays.

"Without me?" she asked.

"Yeah."

"You'd have your brace checked by Nurse Escobar."

"Nurse Escobar smells weird," Mark said, eyes drooping.

"That's my main advantage over Nurse Escobar?"

"You're a *lot* better looking, too."

"Gotcha," Sarah said. "Eye candy, no stink."

Mark couldn't tell if she was being sarcastic or not. "Well, you must admit, Nurse Escobar is twice the woman you are."

"Maybe more than twice."

"That's a lot of woman to love," Mark said, then regretted it. He met her eyes.

"How would you know?" she asked. "Have you and Nurse Escobar…?"

"Maybe."

"I see. The truth is, Mark Howard, that sometimes more is *not* better." Sarah brought her face so close her nose almost touched his. "If you say 'prove it,' I'll slap you."

Mark Howard mimed locking his lips and tossing away the key.

"Still, I guess I'd better prove it," Sarah said, slipping off her sweater.

7

Neil Velick was on day six of his seven-day rotation in the Pit, and he was counting the minutes until the long, long elevator ride back to the surface. This time, swear on a stack of bibles, he was never coming back. Even the great paychecks weren't worth it.

Then Neil thought about the house. It was way more house than he could afford, but it was the house that his fiancée had selected as the one and only suitable dwelling for her and her children. Never mind that the house was five bedrooms, never mind she wasn't even pregnant, never mind the wedding was still twenty-one months away. Melody Toped had made her decision.

Neil had wondered what would happen if he put his foot down. All it would take would be a quick "I quit" to his boss. The salary would vanish. The house would go with it. Would Melody vanish, as well?

Good chance.

Neil tried to picture it in his head. Melody would throw a big crying fit, then she would beg him to try to get his job back, and when she knew it wasn't going to happen—well, she'd be history. No doubt about it.

And then she would walk out the door, sobbing, and Neil would be standing there and what would he do?

Neil saw himself wearing a big grin as imaginary ten-ton weights were lifted off his shoulders.

He hadn't even realized he was toting those weights around with him, but damn, now he could feel them. Wouldn't it be great to get rid of the weights and job and, yes, Melody, too. She was nice and all, and a hell of a body, but it wasn't as if she was all that nice to Neil, come to think of it, and it wasn't as if she let Neil make use of that nice body very often, right?

Neil's endless hours of boredom at the bottom of the old mine shaft had finally paid off. Enlightenment had come to him. He knew what he wanted, he knew what he sure as shitting did *not* want, and he knew how to make it all come about. His future was planned, and it looked real good.

Neil did not know that his life was going to be far shorter than he ever imagined, and none of the next few minutes would be anything like he planned. Or imagined. Or dreamed in his worst nightmares.

When he heard the skittering he ignored it. It was down Shaft C, and Shaft C didn't go anywhere. Shaft A and Shaft G, those were the ones he had to keep an eye on. If the place was infiltrated by terrorists, they'd come at him from Shaft A or Shaft G.

More skittering. Neil Velick put his feet on the desk in the dimly lit roundhouse of rock known as the Intersection.

It was an old wooden desk, and how it got down into this godforsaken hellhole was a mystery. Some said it was brought down a hundred years ago by the miners. If that was so, it had to have been stored in a dry place, away from the eternal seepage of the Pit. Anyway, the antique desk was now put at the intersections of the seven primary corridors, or shafts, and that's where the guards sat, on an uncomfortable folding chair.

The skittering became constant and Neil's curiosity was aroused. There were always rats, but this sounded like a lot of rats. Maybe a hundred of them.

Neil got to his feet and went to the rotting wooden boards that partially obscured Shaft C. The boards were older than Neil was. The paint strokes of the white Danger! warning were gray with age. Neil heard tell of some sort of unexpected drop-off down Shaft C, where lots of miners died in the old days. At least two company guys had slipped through the old boards and gone exploring, looking for forgotten gems, and didn't come out. Talk was the company hadn't even bothered to fish them out again—the Shaft C drop-offs went way down and the cost would have been far too high.

Neil flipped on the flashlight. The beam penetrated maybe fifty feet before getting lost in the tumbling rocks and the curvature of the corridor. Something disappeared behind a boulder. Something pale.

Cave rat. Neil had seen albino cave rats, and they weren't pretty. Maybe he ought to try pegging a couple of them.

The company stipulated there should be no weapons fired in the subsurface except in the face of immediate threat. Violating that rule was a serious offense. A guy could get fired, Neil thought with pleasure as he switched off the safety.

He poked the assault rifle through the wooden slats and flipped on the barrel-mounted light. There was another flicker of movement, and he shot at it. The burst of fire echoed away into the shafts and corridors.

Something squealed, but it sure didn't sound like a rat.

Neil watched the corridor. "I know I shot *something*," he mumbled.

Then he saw what the something was, as it came out of the rocks on wobbly legs. He saw the something fall dead in a pool of blood.

He still wasn't too sure what that something was.

Another one appeared, sniffing, crawling along the floor, until it was sniffing at the corpse's bullet wound.

The creature snarled with a mouth full of yellow teeth. It raised its head, sniffed the air and turned to Neil. It rotated its head as if transcribing a circle in the air, reminding Neil of a bird of some kind.

It was human, more or less. Mostly less, and its flesh was pale, like death. Its eyes were closed. No, Neil realized, its eyeballs were grown over with a transparent cover of skin, with a web of blood vessels visible beneath the translucent skin.

Neil had never seen anything more repulsive in all his life.

He was about to run, he was about to radio for help, when the cave thing did something that made it even more repulsive.

It started eating, voraciously. Huge mouthfuls of flesh were ripped off the corpse and swallowed.

Whatever that thing was, it shouldn't be. Neil could not suffer it to live. He stitched it across the chest with a quartet of rifle rounds. It was still chewing as it died.

Then other creatures arrived and began feeding on the first two bodies, and Neil shuddered. He shouted briefly into his radio, tied into the wire-linked transceiver on the desk, then began the task of exterminating the subhuman vermin. He never doubted that he was doing the right thing as he slaughtered the creatures in Shaft C.

He had a magazine in the rifle and a spare in his belt, and both mags were emptied in two minutes. By then the shaft was a madhouse. The creatures were thrashing at one another, sniffing for wounds, scampering to and fro to escape the mysterious cause of death. And all the time they were eating, burying their razor fangs into any bloody flesh their sense of smell could locate, tearing it off with shaking heads and chewing fast. But the most horrible thing to see was the wounded victims being eaten alive. Neil would never forget that, even if he escaped this hell and lived to be a hundred.

When the gunfire stopped, the creatures calmed themselves and started sniffing the air, bobbing their heads and coming for Neil Velick.

Neil's gun was dry. The armed response to his distress call was at least ten minutes away. He wasn't going to last ten minutes.

Neil started running. He chose Shaft E, where maybe he'd meet up with the reinforcements. It was an uphill run and he ran fast.

The slapping of their feet told him the creatures were coming after him, and getting closer. He wasn't going to outrun them! He found a crevice in the wall where he could make a stand. They were eyeless. He could hold them off with his bayonet.

As he took up the position, his sweeping light caught two or three of them in its shine, but then they were gone, into the darkness. They were just like the colorless salamanders that skittered around some of the cave pools.

Neil tried to control his heaving breath, which sounded like a rushing windstorm. He couldn't hear the creatures anymore. Maybe they had been scared off.

One of them came out of the blackness, and Neil didn't see it or hear it until the death-white hand closed on the barrel of his gun. It started to pull, then whimpered and let go, flesh burned by the heat of the metal.

Neil pulled the rifle closer into his coffin-sized crevice, and when the next creature came to grab his gun barrel, he gave it a shove, twisting it, and the fast-moving creature ran into the bayonet. Its gut opened up in a flash of brilliant red before it disappeared into the blackness, whimpering. A moment later there was another brief scream and the liquid, rending sound. Neil was now very familiar with that sound. It was the sound of feeding.

They came again and again for the gun, and they received more burned hands and more sliced abdomens. But there were a lot of them out there. Neil wondered how long until the electric cart arrived, and if he could really last that long.

The answer came soon enough. The next time two creatures rushed out of the blackness together and snatched the rifle, whisking it into the blackness.

Neil knew he would never see them when they came for him. He would never see anything again. He resigned himself to death, as easy as that, but he couldn't endure the horror of being eaten alive. Far better to spill his own blood first. He wrenched the snaps off his utility knife sheath, then felt something cold take hold of his wrist.

He grabbed for the knife with his free hand, pulled it out, then felt his hand get pushed into the rock wall. Some hand bones broke and the knife fell. It clattered on the cave floor next to his foot, but it was as irretrievable as if it were a hundred miles away.

"Do it fast do it fast do it fast."

They didn't do it fast. They took him along, gathering their dead and feeding off them. Neil was dragged deep into Shaft G.

The creatures ate frequently, until the corpses started to stink. Even then the bodies were carried along with the band of creatures as they traveled through utter blackness, deep into the earth. The warm caverns became hot.

Neil didn't know how far they went, but it was a long distance. Impossibly long. Not that he cared. What did he care about some deep caves? He was going to die, and he was going to die horribly.

He tried to crush his own head against the cavern walls and only succeeded in giving himself a headache. After that the creatures kept him firmly in hand.

They marched through hot streams and ice-cold waterfalls. He began to starve. How many days was it? Five? Seven?

One day he saw a light ahead.

He heard human voices, speaking English, and he dared to hope that he might be saved.

NEIL VELICK WAITED at the entrance to the cave where the light was. There was a creature there, like the ones who captured him, but different. He was talking. He made the same creature sounds as the others, but these sounds came together in a way that made Neil Velick know it was intelligent speech.

The creatures, and Velick, stood at the gate while the speaking one went through the entrance. Inside, in a dim glow that was brilliant as the summer sun to Velick, he saw structures. He saw a machine.

Then he saw a human man. The man was wearing clothing. The man had hair. And truth be told, it was just a teenager.

"Hey," the kid said by way of greeting. Neil Velick tried to say hello and only croaked.

"What do you do?"

"What?"

"Job. You worked in the Pit, right? You a radiological expert? Nuclear-materials handler? What did you do there?"

"Security," Neil said, very confused.

"Security guard?" The kid turned on the talking creature. "You worms went all that way to the Pit and came back with nothing but one security guard?"

"I sorry," the talking creature said in English so guttural it was like listening to someone choke.

"Waste of time," the teenager said.

"Please, let me go," Velick pleaded.

"Dude, you couldn't find yourself topside again in a million years. You're food. Deal with it." The kid said to the talking creature, "Send 'em back to the Pit and tell them not to come back without five prisoners. This many." He held up his hand with splayed fingers. "Got it?"

"Yes, got it."

The kid stepped through the door and was gone.

"Where are you taking me?" Velick asked the talking creature.

"To the feeding," the creature answered.

"Kill me first."

"No. You must stay fresh. We like fresh."

When Velick finally was eaten, he was still quite fresh. The band that had gone to all the trouble of bringing Neil fresh from the surface never got their teeth into him. They were on their way back to the Pit for more prisoners.

This time they came back with five struggling hairy things, and, to their amazement, they didn't get to eat any of them. Not one.

8

When Harold Smith gave Remo a picture of a bloody cave floor in Kansas, he wanted to know what it had to do with finding and delimbing United States Senator Herbert Whiteslaw.

"Nothing."

"Then I'm not interested."

"People are being killed on the site of the biggest commercial radioactive waste storage facility in the United States. That doesn't interest you?"

"Real world to Smitty, we have a rogue U.S. senator to deal with."

"Remo, hush," Chiun insisted.

"Remo no hush. Remo mad. Remo go berserk maybe." He said to Smith, "I want Whiteslaw. If you had your priorities straight, then you'd want him, too."

"I am not certain how you rationalize putting Whiteslaw ahead of the perpetrators in Kansas," Smith said sourly. "Whiteslaw is powerless. His support system no longer exists. The fact that he vanished in the Middle East means he's aware that he's being investigated for treason."

"He wanted us. Remember, Smitty? CURE. He got damn close to getting us, too."

"Jacob Fastbinder was the real threat, and Jacob Fastbinder is dead. Senator Whiteslaw had nothing except a few ideas for drawing yourself and Chiun into his traps."

"His traps almost worked."

"I doubt Whiteslaw has another source that can support him in further efforts to expose CURE—a task we seem quite capable of handling internally."

"Oh, man, not that again." Remo got to his feet. "Smitty, we've been through it all."

"On the contrary, we have not yet started going through it," Smith said. He was at his calmest and sourest.

"What more is there to talk about?"

"Your commitment to CURE. You have a contract with this organization. You violated that contract. You, a Master of Sinanju, are in breach of contract."

"When?" Remo demanded, noticing Chiun's brows knitting.

"The most egregious example comes in the form of your violation of CURE's status as a secret entity. You told the Sun On Jos about us."

"I didn't tell them anything about CURE. Winston knows who you are. Any other knowledge they may have came from when you tracked down Sunny Joe and started phoning the place and sending Junior visiting. You did it, Smitty, not me. You are a dangerous security leak that needs to be plugged ASAP."

"Remo!" Chiun barked.

"You've been generally careless and unavailable," Smith persisted. "This is not exactly a nine-to-five job."

"This job is not the reason for my existence, either. I usually jump through every damn hoop you hold out for me, but you can't expect me to be at your beck and call 365 days a year."

"I do expect it."

"Then you're setting yourself up for real disappointment."

"And you are obliged to meet my expectations."

"Says who?"

"This is stipulated in your contract with CURE."

"His contract with CURE." Remo gestured carelessly at Chiun.

"Remo, your temper tantrum is out of hand," Chiun declared. "This behavior is childish and unbecoming."

Remo flopped in a chair and glared at Chiun, who was uncharacteristically reserved through all of this. The old Korean liked his gold, and Smith paid them plenty of it. So why wasn't he going ballistic about now?

"I want the contract rewritten," Remo said.

Chiun's lips were a hard white line.

"The contract will not be rewritten," Smith replied, full of condescension. "Let's learn to live with it the way it is."

"No."

"The contract is written, signed, sealed—there is no need to change it. Can we please discuss the killings in the mine in Kansas?"

"No. I want Whiteslaw."

"Whiteslaw is not a threat."

"Bulldookey."

"Also, he has vanished."

"And you aren't finding him."

"We're scanning the global nets constantly." It was the first comment Mark Howard had dared make. "He's gone deep undercover, and he knows how."

"Junior, I've seen you guys really looking for somebody, and you aren't doing that now."

"Remo," Smith said abruptly, "how positive are you that Jacob Fastbinder is dead?"

"Why do you ask about him?"

"I am uncomfortable raising the subject. I feel it is wildly speculative, but so is your contention that Whiteslaw remains a threat."

"Not following you."

"Okay. You want Whiteslaw. You had him in your sights once but never had the opportunity to remove him. He remains a threat, maybe a direct threat. So you see a need to deal with him as soon as possible. Am I correct so far?"

"Yeah," Remo admitted.

"What if the Kansas mine killings are the work of Jacob Fastbinder?" Smith posed. "Another of your targets at work, only this time there's tangible risk. People are dead."

"Why would you pin it on Fastbinder?"

"He had an earth-drilling device," Smith said with a shrug. "The murders were in some of the deepest places man has penetrated the earth's crust, and nobody knows how the perpetrators got down there. Maybe the earth drill is how. We just don't know."

"So you think Fastbinder's drill wasn't really broken and he burrowed away into the earth and, by the way, went down into this deep mine shaft for a little kidnapping?"

"No, I do not think that, but I think it is just as likely as the eminent danger from Senator Whiteslaw. Both perpetrators are linked to you. I don't believe it, but you should."

Remo blinked. "So, if I have this straight, you're playing mind games with me and you're trying to explain just how you're playing mind games with me."

Smith nodded. "Exactly."

"But the Fastbinder threat is real?"

"Just as real as the Whiteslaw threat."

Remo looked at Chiun. "Little Father, is my chain being yanked?"

"Quite adeptly."

"So why don't I have any idea what's going on?"

Chiun said with a shrug, "What is going on is that we are going to Kansas."

9

"I was had," Remo announced as he steered the Hyundai through endless cornfields.

"Yes," Chiun replied.

"Thanks for being supportive."

"You deserved no less than a comeuppance, Remo Williams. Your behavior insults the Emperor and shames the Masters who came before you."

"And then there's you."

"Yes. There is me."

"You're acting like the Reigning Master of Weirdness Emeritus."

"Call me names if it eases your guilty conscience." Chiun's eyes were riveted to the screen of his plastic white gizmo.

"Look at all that corn," Remo said eventually. "Makes my mouth water."

"You are trying to make me pay attention to you and succor you with pity."

"I just have a hankering for nibblets."

"Slaver in silence. I am trying to read."

Some time later, Remo said, "You know, at first I thought the Eye Booger was a good idea."

"It is an iBlogger, dimwit."

"Whatever. I thought it'd be better than those horrible, awful soap operas. At least you're not getting square-eyed from watching the tube. And at least it's real and not a bunch of fake tears and fake boobs and fake hair. But then I did a little investigating into this blog thing."

"Really?" Chiun asked. "What did you learn?"

"Well, I had Junior tell me more about it, you know, show me some of the blogs on the computer. I was a surprised at how many there are. Junior said he found something like ten million."

"Yes, there are many. It is a great step for mankind to be able to share its joy and sorrows in this way."

"Yeah, well, Junior pulled up some of those blogs for me, and joy and sorrow weren't what I saw. More like kink and sleaze."

Chiun nodded. "Yes, if the Internet has proved one fact irrefutably it is the base nature of mankind. With each technological achievement the human animal says, 'How may I use this innovation to further my mating adventures?' But this is only a part of the story."

"That's the only part of the story I saw," Remo said.

"You did not look hard enough. Once you learn to filter through the monotonous and pornographic blogs, you find blogs of great variety. Some are touching and some are intriguing. Just now I am reading the entries of an extended family in Brooklyn, in New York. Six of the children and grandchildren in the family are entering their journals, each with his own perspective on the challenges the family faces. It is fascinating. Listen to an entry from the son, who is a college freshmen."

Chiun held up the device and touched something on the front, and the iBlogger began speaking in a deep digital monotone. "Today Dad went to the Turnpike Suites again but get this—met a totally different babe. I had Buck with me and we passkeyed into the room next door and got great video through a hole in the wall."

The voice changed to a breathless young woman. "All my men shop O-Buy, the on-line auction house. You can buy anything on O-Buy—and I mean anything."

The robotic male voice came back. "So me and Buck found the best five-minute clip for your viewing pleasure."

"Hold on a second," Remo interrupted. "This kid videotaped his dad having an affair? It's kinda sick, isn't it? Isn't this the same kinda crapola you complained about on the soap operas?"

Chiun gave him a pitying look. "If it is real, it is not sleaze. Try to see this for what it truly is, Remo—a son attempting to come to terms with his father's frequent infidelities by sharing his feelings in his public journal. Others in his family also post their journals. Although they may feel uncomfortable sharing their anger through conversation, they can do so through a sincere, heartfelt blog."

"So the dad doesn't know anything about it."

"Of course not."

"And the mother?"

"She has her own problems, including compulsive thievery. Would you care to observe an electronic film clip of her shoplifting veal?"

"So they spy on her, too, huh? But does anybody bother telling her about her husband? Or vice versa?"

"That would be unnatural," Chiun explained sincerely. "Better to let the relationship take its natural course and let her find out in her own way."

"But when they find out, then the blog is over, right? I mean, the dad's probably going to be a little more careful, huh? And what's with the commercial? The bloggers get a cut, right?"

"I believe I see the direction in which you head, Remo Williams."

"They're making a profit by exploitation of their family problems. What a bunch of sickos."

"Stop the car, please," Chiun said.

"Why? This isn't the mine."

"Over there." Chiun nodded at the high fences. Beyond it they could see a junkyard with the peaks of mechanical corpse piles visible over the top. Next door, gleaming in the sun, were five rebuilt recreational vehicles from decades past.

"Can't stop," Remo said. "No time. Don't want to be late. Wouldn't be professional."

Chiun said, "There," and indicated the spot on the roadside where Remo should stop the car. Remo pulled over reluctantly.

"Chiun, I don't want…"

Chiun was gone.

10

Breck Kasle took one look at you and he knew if you were a buyer, a browser or a sucker. Buyers got his attention. Browsers were ignored. Suckers got the hard-sell, because sometimes a sucker could become a buyer, if you worked him right.

Charlie the finance guy pointed out the window of the office RV and asked, "What is he?"

"Damned if I know," Breck Kasle said.

"Come on! Admitting defeat and he just walked onto your lot? I say he's a sucker."

"Maybe. When in doubt you treat 'em like suckers." Breck tightened his polyester garage-sale tie and went to greet the new arrival.

The little Jap in the girls' clothes was evaluating the lines on the 1961 Airstream. He was older than Methuselah but damned if he didn't have the straightest backbone this side of the Mighty Miss.

"Morning."

The old man didn't notice him. Probably deaf. "Morning," Breck said to the younger man, in an ivory T-shirt and Chinos. He was another unsettling character, what with extrathick wrists and eyes like one of those biker dudes who'd kill you just 'cause he didn't approve of your hair plugs.

Still, the younger man had a tolerant, resigned look, and Breck got the picture. Young man taking care of an old man who's prone to impulsive acts, and the best thing was to just go along with it. These two were browsers.

"This caravan is outfitted with a working cookstove?" the old man squeaked.

"Yes, sure." In a twinkling Breck's assessment changed. That wasn't the kind of specific question a browser asked. These were definite suckers.

"Not electric, I hope?"

"Propane. You hook up the tanks in the back. How would you like to see the inside? This is a real work of art."

The old man turned away from the Airstream and seemed to glide away. He was heading for the '46 Spartan. Breck Kasle followed behind him, trying to stay casual. You never wanted to look like you were trying to make a sale.

"That's a 1946 Spartan Manor," he said. "Man, that one's a real gem."

"This caravan has been fitted with nonoriginal components," the old man announced, and he speared a rigid finger at the undercarriage of the Spartan, where a bright yellow metal piece was visible.

"Oh. Yeah. Well, we do take liberties with the mechanicals," Kasle admitted, and now he was mentally salivating. These were buyers! Definite buyers! The old man knew his stuff, and now Breck saw that the old man's robe was some sort of hand-stitched original artwork all on its own. Valuable. These folks had cash! "You see," he continued nonchalantly, "we don't make museum pieces—we rebuild vintage RVs that people can use. We install new brakes, new electricals, various safety features. You want an RV restored to *original* condition, well, those'll cost you about twice as much and you can't even drive it. Nobody will insure it for road use."

"You work on these things?" asked the young man, but he didn't really seem to care.

"Naw. My brother does all the labor. Hard to believe what he can do with some of these old hunks sometimes. Takes a lot of love and a lot of elbow grease."

The old man flipped open the door of the Spartan and skipped inside. Breck was sure it had been locked—every RV on the lot was kept locked. The younger man sighed and followed the old man in.

"I THOUGHT YOU WANTED to live in a jet," Remo said, ignoring the salesman who followed them in.

"A jet must always stay at the airport," Chiun replied. "A jet that is sufficient in space would be too large for the small-town airports to which we are often dispatched."

"Yeah, and Smitty would freak out if we started traveling around in our own 777." Remo hadn't wanted to live in an airplane anyway. But he wasn't into living in a camper trailer, either, even a nice one.

Chiun was examining every aspect of the pristine RV interior, which was stifling in the heat and thick with the smell of new plastic and fresh-cut plywood. Someone had done a good restoration job. The interior was narrow, but one end opened into a massive wraparound kitchen with a vast expanse of brand-new, salmon-colored countertop. The only thing that broke it up was the sink and a decorative pair of pink champagne glasses on a white doily. Above it was a huge, three-segment picture window that offered a 180-degree view.

"Man, imagine backing that up to the Grand Canyon," Remo said.

Chiun furled his brow. "Why do such a thing?"

"Just think of the view you'd have while you heated your franks and beans."

Chiun didn't dignify the comment with an answer.

"Quite a kitchen, isn't it?" the salesman offered.

"You could do an autopsy on that countertop," Remo said.

Breck Kasle didn't have a ready response to that.

"So what about the tour bus idea?" Remo asked Chiun.

"What tour bus?" Chiun turned on the propane stove. An automatic igniter clicked and produced a small blue flame. Chiun looked at the salesman significantly. The salesman struggled to come up with an affirmation about the stove; Remo could see the effort in his quivering cheeks.

"You remember the tour bus that those idiots from Union Island drove to Mollywood? You fell in love with it. And before that you were all gaga about a yacht."

Chiun tapped the polished, salmon-colored countertop experimentally like a skater testing the ice. Remo knew from the sound that the cabinets were solid and well-constructed, probably more durable than the original equipment. But, man, that sure was a lot of salmon-colored Formica.

"Well made," Chiun announced in Korean.

"So?"

"This craftsman succeeded in recreating the original lines and palette."

"Why am I not surprised that you're an antique RV buff?"

The salesman—who was sweaty and had the sporadically racing pulse of the meat-eating, habitually deceptive type—was almost in tears. Remo guessed he was profoundly disappointed because the Korean conversation kept him out just when he needed to exploit a weakness.

Breck, whose name tag read Hi, The Name's Breck!, perked up and nodded at the English word "RV."

"What power level?" Chiun demanded as he turned the stove on again to its highest setting.

"Power?"

"Power! How high does this get?"

The salesman fussed over the stove until he got the grate out of a front burner and discovered a label. "Eight thousand BTUs."

"And this means what?"

"It's a nice little stove…."

"It is *too* little to be nice! And what fool requires four feeble burners? Why was it not installed with two adequate burners instead? How can water be heated to steam on such a pathetic flame? What sort of rice would come from this butane lighter?"

The salesman was in a rare state. He'd never quite had a sale go this way before.

"We could always put in more powerful burners."

"How powerful?"

"I think we can get something at about fifteen thousand BTUs, maybe even higher if we go to a commercial kitchen supplier. I'll need to talk to my brother—"

"The bunks—how much time would it require to have them removed?"

"Removed? I'm not sure. We've never had that request. I can find out—"

"The carpet?"

"Very plush, isn't it?"

"It is hideous!"

"We'll rip it out in no time."

"And replace it with what?"

"How—how—how about a linoleum that matches the original equipment?" The salesman's heart was racing, stymied at every turn but convinced he was close to a big sale.

"What would be put in the place of the master bedroom bunk?" Chiun demanded.

"What would you like? Storage closets? Library? Meditation room?"

The vintage RV with the new-car smell went quiet as a tomb. The salesman didn't know why. Had he in-

sulted the old man with an Oriental stereotype? Had
he cost himself a sale?

"Remo, a meditation chamber!"

"Be kind of squeaky for meditating." Remo knew
that resistance was futile, but he had to put up a token
fight.

"Why squeaky?" Chiun chirped.

"Yes, why would it be squeaky?" the salesman
asked, sincerely not understanding.

"This thing's solid as a New York City bus, Chiun,"
Remo pointed out. "It's got a thousand bolted-together
parts that will be creaking and settling and moaning
even when it's standing still. How are you gonna meditate in all that racket?"

"A house does the same thing—the two-flat settles
constantly," Chiun argued.

"Yeah, well, imagine the two-flat if it was made
from an Erector set by a kid who can't get the screws
really tight—that's what it would be like trying to
meditate in an RV."

Chiun glared. "You want to deny me a proper home."

"The two-flat's proper."

"Look at me," Chiun said to the salesman. "What is
wrong with me that I should be treated with disrespect?"

Remo jumped in before the salesman even hinted at
an answer that could get him killed. "There's nothing
wrong with you, and you can have any kind of house you
want. So why not a house with room, something solid?
Maybe a mansion. Hell, we're just a stone's throw from
that Victorian bed-and-breakfast that you liked in Oklahoma City. Let's go buy it and have it moved out east."

"Fah! Victorian is unsightly as that junkyard beyond the fence."

"You told me you liked that place."

"You are mistaking me with someone else."

Remo sighed. "How about another church? I mean, another Castle Sinanju. In Boston, even. The Boston Catholic franchise must be having a fire sale these days to pay off the lawyers of abused kids. We'll go make them an offer on the biggest, god-awfullest piece of Christian architecture we can find. Then we'll rip the insides out. Wouldn't that be fun? And we'll redo it however you want."

Chiun considered it. "You would be amenable to such a home?"

"Yes, of course."

"I seem to recall you mentioning, once, a dislike for the Boston castle."

"No," Remo said sincerely. "You are mistaking me with someone else."

Chiun nodded, then turned on the salesman. "Remo is right."

"He is?"

"I am?"

"This dwelling is not sturdy! I need one built to a higher degree of strength."

Remo gave up and slumped on the plastic sofa, trying not to breathe its particles.

"Sir, I assure you this is a finely rebuilt camper, and my brother puts in extra reinforcements to make it extrastable." The salesman placed his hand on the wall and shoved. The wall didn't budge.

"It is flimsy!" Chiun stamped his foot. The Spartan trembled and rattled as if it were in the midst of a tornado. The pink champagne glasses toppled and shattered.

"We could do better!" the salesman pleaded. "Extra reinforcing foam in the walls and triple-paned windows and we'll weld steel reinforcement bars under the floors!"

Chiun glared around him. "Too small. Show me another."

"This is the largest model we have complete at the moment…."

"What caravans await refurbishment in your scrap heap?"

"Oh. Uh. I would have to ask my brother—"

"Take me to him!"

THE BROTHER WAS a night owl who had to be prodded out of bed, and he came outside with wild hair and one unbuttoned flap on his overalls. He started out peeved, but became excited as he showed the old Korean the ancient hulks strewed about the salvage yard.

"He's an intense gentleman," the salesman mentioned to Remo as he glugged a can of lemon-lime Fanta and sat on the stoop of a rusted-out GMC camper trailer that stank of mouse droppings. The salesman had been excused from Chiun's presence. "I admire a man who knows what he wants," he added hastily.

"He knows what he wants this afternoon," Remo

clarified. "Tomorrow he'll want to live in an Austrian sod hut or some crazy-ass thing."

Two hundred feet away, Chiun paused midsentence and looked at Remo balefully, then went back to his conversation.

"He actually have enough money for this?" the salesman asked, finally getting the nerve.

"Unfortunately, yeah."

"He rich or something?"

"Theoretically, it's me who's the master of the money, not him."

Chiun glared again, and Remo could swear his flesh started to singe. He added, "But that's only a theory."

11

When Senator Herbert Whiteslaw had embarked on his recent excursion to the Middle East, it was ostensibly under the authority of the President of the United States, who asked him personally to continue the undercover work he started years ago, before the last Iraq war. The President had sent him on that first mission, too.

But on his first mission, Whiteslaw had turned traitor. He sold highly sensitive war plans to one of the region's worst dictators. Amazingly, somebody had gotten hands on first-rate incriminating evidence against Whiteslaw. Even more amazingly, the evidence had been doctored by somebody as a tool to use against the meteoric rise of presidential contender Orville Flicker.

After Flicker's messy demise, Whiteslaw knew that *somebody* knew the truth about his guilt. When the President ordered Whiteslaw back to the Middle East for further intelligence gathering, Whiteslaw assumed he was being set up. He kept his nose clean in the Middle East.

Soon enough, the grapevine was ringing with the

news that a federal indictment was being prepared against Whiteslaw, and he went into hiding.

But Whiteslaw wasn't waiting around to see what happened. His political machine was hard at work, putting together a political campaign unlike any other.

Herbert Whiteslaw was going to be President of the United States, and soon. The election was approaching. The candidates were campaigning. Senator Herbert Whiteslaw was not looming large in the consciousness of the American people. But soon he would be the only popular electable face in the race.

First he would convince the two big political parties to yank their candidates. Then he would get their endorsement—both parties, behind the same man, and he'd be a sure winner.

There would be an outcry, of course. The partisans would hate him, even the partisans in his own party. How could you be on the right side when the wrong side endorsed you, too?

Whiteslaw knew just how to handle that: he would promote himself as the one President who could really, truly, finally work through the incessant party bickering and actually get something done. That would take the wind out of their sails.

Not that he cared what anybody actually thought of him. Sincerity wasn't his strong point. He would have promised every American a new Chevrolet if that's what it took to get elected.

The truth was he wouldn't need to promise anybody anything. If he was the only viable candidate, he'd be elected, simple as that.

The people who were going to make it simple, however—Jacob Fastbinder III and his American son, Jack Fast—had turned out to be an eccentric and unreliable pair.

"But we did get the job done," Jack Fast said without concern. "We gave you exactly what you asked for—evidence of a great scandal."

"True, but—"

"And it wasn't exactly easy, either, Herbie," Fast said. "Almost killed Pops."

"I appreciate the danger it has put you in…."

"But I can't complain. Look what we got out of the deal!" Jack pointed out the front window of the vehicle. All Whiteslaw could see through the black-tinted glass was the glimmer of frantic bolts of electricity. How did the kid see where he was going?

Maybe visiting Fastbinder wasn't a good idea.

You couldn't have lured Senator Herbert Whiteslaw into a cave for love nor money. But that old man Fastbinder and his punk kid had something even better. They had the power to make Whiteslaw into the President of the United States of America, and they had the power—he hoped—to get rid of the one threat that might strike him down before he achieved the office.

So when Fastbinder summoned him to his coronation ceremony, Whiteslaw agreed to take a ride down into the earth's crust.

It should have been an adventure, but Whiteslaw didn't feel adventurous when they reached their destination.

"How far down are we, anyway?"

"Three-point-six miles," said Jack Fast with a grin. "You'll be safe. Chill, Herbie."

"Chill?" Whiteslaw didn't think it was funny, but the Fast kid was showing every tooth he had. "How can I chill when it's more than a hundred degrees?"

"Aw, you're exaggerating." Fast looked at his watch, which seemed to be some sort of a superhero utility watch with all sorts of gizmos built in. "It's ninety-three and the humidity's only thirty percent."

"I don't care! I'm uncomfortable as hell."

"Yeah, it's always hot at this end of the cavern. It's farthest from the water. At the other end is where two of the rivers come in and they keep it at exactly sixty-four degrees. But this is the only place where we can gather all the mole people for a proper ceremony."

That's what the kid called the cavemen, mole people. Whiteslaw wasn't looking forward to encountering them. He pictured savages, monsters. Whiteslaw liked to keep his world civilized. He fidgeted nervously on his too-hot stone seat. "Yeah, okay."

Senator Whiteslaw was still not sure what the purpose of this crowning ceremony was. It was ludicrous, silly, even. It was out of character for Fastbinder and Fast. Why were they doing it?

"Stay put, Herbie. We're about to begin." With that, Jack Fast left the senator alone in the vast cavern.

The albinos arrived.

They were hideous, putrid creatures, as pale as walking cadavers. They were nude and filthy, and worst of all were their bulging heads where the eyelids had grown over their eyeballs.

They had weapons. There were spears with worked metal points, and swords of scrap metal with edges made deadly by pounding them into jagged saw teeth. Crude but doubtless effective.

The albinos came in small family groups, then in larger tribes. Whiteslaw was on a seat of honor in the center of the cavern on a carved bench atop a large stalagmite, where he was soon surrounded on all sides by the mole people.

He was helpless. Any one of them could ascend the steps behind him and rip his throat out with one of those saw-toothed swords. Even if he heard them coming he couldn't run away—he could barely walk on his sensitive feet with their fresh new skin.

Would the albinos never stop coming? How many were there? How could there be so many? Whiteslaw tried estimating their numbers and came up with something like a thousand.

And more poured in every second.

They were haggard, road weary. Fastbinder had summoned his mole people to attend the event from miles away, and for some reason they had heeded his call, despite the danger of the journey. After all, this was a once-in-a-lifetime event: the crowning of the new king.

Jack Fast appeared on the stage, a flat slab of limestone at the opposite end of the cavern.

"Silence."

The grunts and growls, the arguments and bickering, continued. Jack Fast gave Whiteslaw a wink across the sea of blind faces, then lifted a megaphone to his lips. "Silence!"

The sound was deafening in the chamber and the albinos quailed, some collapsing under the weight of the sound.

"You shall obey," Fast thundered.

The albinos trembled, and Whiteslaw was fascinated by the performance. He had to remind himself again that the kid with the idiot grin was no idiot. Jack Fast knew how to work things.

So what was Fast doing now? Whiteslaw wondered.

Fast had a Peavey amplifier sitting on the stone stage next to him. He spoke into his microphone, loud, but less abrasive than the megaphone. "Meet your new king."

Fastbinder walked on stage. From the hips down he was encased in a steel framework of anodized steel tubes and pneumatic cylinders. It was some sort of bionic thing, like the loader robots that people used in science fiction movies. But without the mechanical arms, what good was it?

Then Whiteslaw felt the footsteps vibrating the ground under his rump, and he understood. The albinos were blind—or as good as blind, according to Jack Fast. A light show or a fancy uniform wouldn't impress the cave people since they couldn't see it, but footsteps that shook the very rock—now that was something an ignorant mole person could understand.

Tides of fear and awe rippled through the albinos. Fastbinder stood at the edge of the rock, where the audience could feel his towering presence. "I am now your king," he said. "Bow down and obey your king."

According to Fast, some of the albinos could speak rudimentary English. Apparently, generations ago, these people dwelled on the earth's surface. They had all been taught to understand some basics of the language. Many of the albinos obeyed at once.

Fastbinder spoke into the microphone, and his voice came from an amplifier on the wall in the back. "Obey your king!"

The albinos in back squealed at this display of great sorcery and prostrated themselves.

"Obey!"

This time his voice came from a speaker in the ceiling overhead. A crater appeared in the middle of the crowd of the albinos as they sought to mash themselves into the floor under the weight of the sound.

Whiteslaw was impressed. What power. What fear Fastbinder evoked from these miserable troglodytes. But the credit went to Jack Fast. He had turned his father into the new king of the Underworld with nothing more than a few loudspeakers and some cheap factory equipment.

The kid was loving it, too. His eyes were glittering in the light of a few strung-up bulbs, and his face shone with pleasure.

Jack Fast practically started bouncing with excitement when the resistance movement showed itself. A tight knot of powerful albinos was pushing its way through the obedient subjects. Whiteslaw knew them for what they were at once. Tough guys. Bullies. Their leader was a pale-skinned bulldog. Part of his upper lip was missing, giving him a permanent sneer. He trudged to a halt before the stage, lifting his scrap-metal sword defiantly.

"No king. No obey."

The bully's men were on the move, moving carefully through the crowds, not pushing now as they approached either side of the stage. They were going to make an assassination attempt on Fastbinder and Fast!

Which meant—Lord in heaven! If those two got killed, Whiteslaw would never see the surface world again.

"Obey!" Fastbinder shouted, amplifying his voice into thunder.

"No!" the bully bellowed.

"Fast, look!" Whiteslaw squealed and waved wildly at the sides of the stage. The idiot kid gave him a big smile and a thumbs-up, but never even glanced to the side. There were four on one side, two on the other, and they were going to chop Fast and Fastbinder into bloody pieces and all Whiteslaw could do was watch.

The attackers came to a halt, made surprised sounds and began struggling oddly. There was something sticking to their feet. One of them bent down and grabbed at the thin rug covering the stage, only to find his hand adhere to the stuff. Then his other hand.

Jack Fast wasn't even looking, but he gave Whiteslaw another thumbs-up, then reached for his lighter fluid.

Whiteslaw watched the attackers wad themselves up in the sticky material, which was the human equivalent of flypaper. Before long they were enmeshed. They had no understanding of their predicament, only that they were helpless and vulnerable and they hooted in terror. The bully called to his men and got grunts in return that may or may not have been words, but the bully knew his men were in trouble. *All* the albinos knew it.

Jack Fast spritzed four of the attackers with Kingston Charcoal Brand Lighter Fluid and announced into his microphone, "They would not obey."

He struck a fireplace match and tossed it on the helpless attackers, who burst into a white blaze of screaming flame unlike any stack of charcoal briquettes Whiteslaw had ever fired up. The light was brilliant and the heat wave was intense, but not as intense as the sound the victims made before they died.

The albinos shrank back, and they looked up.

Yeah. Fast said they had some vision. They couldn't see much, but they could see his blaze, and they saw Jack Fast silhouetted in front of it with both hands raised. Even with atrophied eyeballs and a coating of skin, they saw that much!

The fire faded in seconds to an orange glow, and Fast moved across the stage, talking, keeping the people trained on him. He came to the other pair of attackers, who were just as glued together as the first group. They wriggled as he spritzed them. "They would not obey. They would not obey," Fast intoned from the speakers mournfully, and struck another match.

The albinos watched, and Whiteslaw marveled at the brilliance, literally and figurative, of the young son of Jacob Fastbinder.

When the second white blaze diminished, Fastbinder stomped his feet, shaking the rock floor, and commanded, "Obey!"

The albino bully collapsed, whimpering in subjugation, and the others—every last one of them—followed his example.

Fastbinder seemed pleased with himself, and Herbert Whiteslaw wondered if the old kraut had any clue what just happened. Oh, sure, Jack's stage show had firmly convinced the cave people that Fastbinder was their lord and master. None of them would ever think of disobeying him.

But Jack himself made a stronger impression. If Fastbinder was their new king of Hell, then Jack Fast was their new god of Hellfire.

The new king of Hell stepped off of the stage. The bottoms of his bionic boots landed on the bully and splattered him in every direction. The blood lust infuriated the albinos, but Fastbinder said, "No!"

Whiteslaw watched the people quivering with their need to feed. Fastbinder strode away, the crowd parting before him, and nobody moved until Fastbinder announced, "Eat."

They ate.

WHITESLAW WAS AS WHITE as one of Fastbinder's albinos, and his lightweight shirt was drenched with sweat.

"They do enjoy their chow," Fast said, escorting the senator down the steps and into a small side chamber, which was covered with a fabric door with clear plastic windows. When Senator Whiteslaw felt the air-conditioned air he nearly fainted with relief. Fast nudged him into a folding director's chair and waved at a wheeled catering cart. Inside was a mountain of ice and bottles of water.

Whiteslaw snatched one of the bottles and drained it in four great gulps. He didn't even mind the painful bout of brain freeze that came and went as a result, just grabbed another one.

"Good?" Fast asked.

"Best water I ever tasted."

"It's from a rare desert spring in New Mexico," Jacob Fastbinder announced happily. "I recently purchased zee bottling plant and zee store that sells it."

"Good investment," Whiteslaw said when he finished his third bottle. "I'm gonna have nightmares about those cave people for the rest of my life. Is this where you people live?"

Jack sprawled in a chair. "You kidding me, Herbie? This is just a sort of green room, for you to relax in after the show. I think it's time we took you on the tour."

Whiteslaw became distressed at the thought of leaving the air-conditioning. "Can't I stay here until it's time to leave?"

Jack laughed. "You came all the way down, you gotta see the city, Herbie! First, though, some lunch?" Jack pulled a deli tray of cold cuts out of the refrigerated cart.

Whiteslaw shook his head and plucked his soggy shirt from his chest. "What's so important about my being here?"

"We wanted to make a demonstration," Fastbinder said matter-of-factly. "Not just for the cave people, but for your benefit, too."

"After all, Herbie, the next President of the United States needs to know what kind of an ally he'll be getting if he decides to be friendly with the Federation of United Subsurface Tribes," Jack said.

"And what kind of enemy he'll have on his hands if he decides not to stay friendly," Fastbinder added. "That is zee reason for bringing you here."

"Well, I am certainly impressed."

"You are being disingenuous. Come on, Senator Herbie."

There was a rear exit, leading to a golf cart, which wasn't air-conditioned. Whiteslaw couldn't stifle a groan.

"You'll be perfectly comfortable in just a few minutes," Fastbinder promised. He drove the cart between a pair of boulders and down a long, rocky incline, and Whiteslaw felt the temperature grow more bearable by the second.

"It's twenty-five degrees cooler at the city level," Jack Fast said. "There it is."

Whiteslaw no longer noticed the temperature as he took in the "city," where hundreds of cave people were returning to their work. They chopped doors and windows and rooms out of the rock. There was a turbine whining against a far wall, and a generator sprouted electrical cables that snaked across the ceiling. The generator powered a web of lights attached to the cavern's roof.

"See the water? That's what makes this place work," Fast said, waving at two black sockets in the distant wall. Rivers emerged from both mouths and quickly merged into one strong current.

"The rivers come from way up, and they channel lots of air down with them," Fast explained. "They keep the city cool all the time. The channels are partially dry, at least this time of the year, and the river eroded a natural deep channel in the center, so you've got easy walking all the way up."

"They give us access to zee world above. One goes east, one goes northeast. Add to that river from zee southwest, which led Jack here in zee first place." Fastbinder nodded to the third river, the largest of them all, which cascaded from an ugly black pit in the wall and piled on top of the water from the other rivers.

Whiteslaw was lost in his admiration when the explosion came. Shattered rock poured from the roof above the river and slammed into the water. Whiteslaw shouted.

"It's cool," Jack said.

"We're being attacked!" Whiteslaw blurted.

"It is only zee afternoon blasting," Fastbinder said. "We're damming zee water. See?"

Whiteslaw watched the strong river flow widen as the shattered rock continued tumbling into it. He was shaking too hard to ask why.

"See, the rivers bring us stuff," Fast explained. "The dam is being built like a big shallow sieve to catch shipments and seafood."

"Any fish bigger than zee bluegill will find itself stuck here for us to harvest as we see fit," Fastbinder said. "Zee mole people see the new abundance of food as a gift from zee God Emperor Fastbinder."

"I'm also working on making special containerized transport barges," Fast enthused. "No steering needed. Just load your stuff, toss them into the river source near the surface and it'll make its way here. Automatic speedy delivery."

The older man was frowning as he started the golf cart again. "And too risky. I predict our cargo will be damaged beyond use."

"Hey, Pops, you said I could give it a try."

"And you may. Then you will see zee results and can set about building me barges that can be controlled. I don't care if they will be too slow."

"You wait, Pops. My transport pods are gonna work."

"We shall see."

After a disgruntled silence, Jack got his verve back and waved at the roof.

"See all that wiring? We've got fixtures for a thousand floodlights just in phase one," Jack Fast said. "Our shopping trips have only netted us a couple hundred so far, but when we're fully operational it will be bright as day in here. The electrical grid also powers our machine shop."

Fast steered the little cart through a narrow gap in the rock, and Whiteslaw found himself looking down a sheer drop, just inches from the cart's balloon tires.

"Relax, I'm a safe driver," Fast said. "This is where we make stuff."

"Those are people," Whiteslaw said, as he realized he was looking at regular human beings. They were dressed in normal human clothes, and they looked up at the cart with stricken, but normal, human eyes.

"I wasn't about to try to train the mole dudes to work sheet metal," Fast explained. "Mechanics, heating and ventilation engineers, electrical guys, refrigeration guys. Even got a few plumbers. It's gonna take a lot of work to get this city up to our standards, you know. This bunch we nabbed mostly from a nearby subterranean construction project."

"And that's not even half of them," Fastbinder said. "Let us show you other grottos."

It turned out that there was a series of grottos—stone pits with concave walls. The senator was startled when the words Grotto Number Two—Best Food In Earth appeared in buzzing blue neon letters. In the dismal cavern it looked utterly foreign.

"We made an experimental expedition to the surface one night last month. Those morons brought down a sign maker by mistake," Fast said with a pleasant shrug. "So I thought, what the hell?"

The blue letters flickered, then blazed to life again as Whiteslaw peered down into the catering operation. There were stone tables and stone coolers with heavy plastic sheeting for doors, and everywhere was fervent activity. It could have been the kitchen of any big-city hotel.

"There's our dumbwaiters," Fast said. "That's how we get stuff in and out." Whiteslaw saw albinos on the edge of the grotto putting supplies into small baskets, then lowering them on booms to waiting kitchen staff below. The basket chains were small gauge. Fast explained that the winches were fitted with governors that were activated if the load was more than forty pounds. "Nobody is gonna get out that way."

It dawned on Whiteslaw now that the grotto dwellers were imprisoned in their workplaces. The dark windows in the rock walls had to be where they slept.

"How do you keep them motivated?" Whiteslaw

asked wonderingly as a man in a chef's hat gave Fast-binder a subservient smile and gestured at the meal he was preparing.

"That is Horst. He makes lousy sauerbraten," Fast-binder explained quietly, but smiled and waved back. "Jack, we need a cook who makes good German food."

"Adding it to the list," Jack said, tapping on the keys of his PDA with one hand as he steered the golf cart along the edge of the grottos with the other.

Whiteslaw couldn't help but notice that his question had been ignored.

The words Central Processing blinked on in orange neon, but the grotto's handful of inhabitants were just sitting around. They were taking turns at a single computer terminal.

"Our next big excursion, we're gonna get lots of PCs," Fast said. "I want my own intelligence center to keep watch on the outside world."

Whiteslaw stuttered. "You're go-going to let them go on-line? They'll call for help!"

Fast grinned. "Maybe. But I'll know about it. And if they do, well…"

Whiteslaw waited. "Well what?"

Fast grinned. Fastbinder nodded, and they drove away from the grottos to the cafeteria. It was the albinos' cafeteria.

"See that guy?" Fast asked. How could Whiteslaw not see the man dangling over the gathering lunchtime crowd? The obese man was held teasingly high over the albinos by a pair of chains. "See the lights? See the cameras?"

Whiteslaw did indeed see the lights and the wall-mounted video cameras. Jack did something on his PDA and the lights brightened on the prisoner. Small red indicators showed that the cameras were now working. The chain clanked as the prisoner descended.

"Big-screen monitors in all the grottos," Jack shouted over the joyous grunts and growls of the albinos. "Everybody gets to watch what happens to prisoners who don't behave themselves."

"This is an effective method of motivation." Fastbinder beamed. "You agree?"

"Yes," Whiteslaw said. "Can we go now?"

"No. See who is zee main course?"

Whiteslaw realized that he knew the entrée personally, as did any American who paid attention to the gamut of elected federal officials. Cecil Luigi was a six-term senator and chairman of the Senate Ways and Means Committee. Luigi and Whiteslaw were bitter political opponents. The feud had become personal. If there was anyone who would fight hard to oppose Whiteslaw's rise to the presidency, it would be Senator Luigi.

Luigi recognized Whiteslaw, too, as his corpulent, nude torso descended on the clanking chain connected to manacles on his ankles. The Ways and Means chairman pleaded loudly, "Whiteslaw, please have mercy!"

Fast thumbed his PDA and the chain clanked to a halt. He looked expectantly at Senator Herbert Whiteslaw.

"You want to give him mercy, Herbie?"

"It's not in my nature," Whiteslaw said with a mixture of revulsion and elation.

Jack grinned. Fastbinder clapped the senator on the back. The Ways and Means chairman descended again, until he was within reach of the lunchtime crowd, which was still famished, by all appearances. The half-dozen rebels at the coronation ceremony hadn't been enough meat to satiate a thousand hungry mole people, after all.

They had tea on the veranda. Fastbinder spent fifteen minutes relating his struggles to teach the albinos the art of rock breaking and how, after a week or so, they learned it well enough to hollow out the massive granite boulder that was now the palace of the king.

"I don't get it, Jacob," the senator asked finally. "It's fantastic, sure, but what's the point of all this? What's in it for you?" Whiteslaw sneered at the filthy albinos working below them. "They're just ingrates. They're useless."

Fastbinder was wearing a tight smile. "On the contrary, they are very much up to zee tasks I need them to do. They are loyal to myself and Jack. They will do whatever I ask, even march to their deaths. This advantage you will not enjoy as President. Even when you are President you will be struggling, day after day, to legitimize your hold on power, and you will be compromising with the other wielders of power. But see, I have already attained a status that is all-powerful, eh?"

Whiteslaw had to concede the point. "Still…"

"And as for the albinos, they are my muscle and my workers, but soon I will have a population of civilized human beings large enough to satisfy my social needs. Loyalists, I mean."

"I see," Whiteslaw said.

"I see you are beginning to see. The reach of my

power is not yet known in geographic terms, but the albinos have legends of their previous generations exploring as far as the land of permanent snow, and as far east as the sea, and as far south as the sea."

"What south sea are you talking about, exactly?" Whiteslaw asked.

Fastbinder shrugged. "A mystery. Probably the Gulf of Mexico. Regardless, it is a vast territory."

It was indeed vast. It was the entire North American continent. After their stiff and polite replies, and during the first few hours of the journey back to the surface, Whiteslaw thought about it. He tried to put it out of his mind, but he had forgotten to bring any magazines or books. His mind kept pondering what Fastbinder had said. Could it be true? Was the belowground population really that big?

JACK COCKED HIS HEAD, staring into the mirror of the near-black windows of the interior of Jack's Earth Drill. JED rolled along smoothly, with the heavily shielded lightning flashes and the muffled noise of frying rock giving its occupants a distant perspective to the violent activity outside.

"Lots of ways my dad could help you out," Jack was saying. "His albino army will be able to go just about anywhere, including most of the places the U.S. government thought were its best-kept secrets. Anybody gets in your way, we'll be able to get at them and, you know, take them out of your way. Trouble is, my dad doesn't think you'll be able to do much in return."

"Well—"

"I mean, whatever we need, we take. No problems."

"I can keep you from being harassed by the military," Whiteslaw said, trying to sound confident. Jack was tedious company.

"Well, that's a so-what in my dad's book. The military's doing its best already and they're getting squat for it," Jack pointed out. "You know we've only been down here a couple of months. Just think how much stronger we'll be when we consolidate, bring more albinos into the fold."

Whiteslaw felt ice in his veins.

"We're not sure how many there are, mind you," Jack added nonchalantly. "Maybe a thousand more. Maybe ten thousand."

"Impossible!"

Jack clammed up for a short while, then turned off the tunnel into a side tunnel and brought the mole to a quick stop. Outside the black glass the frenetic sizzle of lightning vanished. The mole rocked gently forward, then back.

Jack raised the shaded glass, and they looked out into a cavern too big for the headlights to see across. The mole had emerged nose first from the cavern wall, and as they nodded gently, Whiteslaw looked down in horror at the cavern floor far below.

"It's safe—I welded an anchor on the fly so we wouldn't drop," Jack said. "See 'em down there?"

Whiteslaw saw people down there. More albinos,

but different. It was hard to tell what was different because they were scurrying around in a blind panic.

Well, no, the senator thought, not a blind panic at all. "They have eyes," he observed. "Exposed eyes."

"Cool, huh? I stumbled across them accidentally on one of my trips. Saw the big open place show up on my mapping system and I checked it out and here they were. There's a couple hundred of them, and I'm God to them now. Watch." He maneuvered a searchlight on the exterior, revealing a ten-foot high drawing of a toothy worm with lightning coming out of it. It had the head of a man.

The drawing was done in blood. Underneath the drawing was the name of the god, in very crude but antique-looking letters.

The wall read, "Jack."

"I told them my name," the kid admitted sheepishly. "They think I'm the greatest. Always making me offerings, see?"

A trio of men emerged from the terrified mob, leading one of their tribe on a leash. They led the prisoner into a stream of water that fell from the ceiling far above. The caked mud sluiced off, revealing a female albino.

"They give you women?" Whiteslaw asked incredulously.

"Yeah, and these are some hot cave-babes. Way nicer looking than the blind ones down below. And when you're a god they do anything you tell 'em. Want one?"

Whiteslaw thought about it, then decided finally, "I'd have no place to keep it."

Jack shrugged and announced on the loudspeaker, "Hey, people, I shall return in less than one sleep."

They backed out of the cavern and continued on their journey to the surface in silence. Whiteslaw found the image of the cave girl stuck in his head. Once she was showered, she had turned out to be a porcelain-skinned, pink-eyed young beauty. She had gazed up at the earth drill with a mixture of adoration and excitement, eager to be of service to her god—or any other deities he hung around with.

"So, anyway, I just found them. Haven't even told Pops yet," Jack explained. "The point is this—think how many I might find if I start really looking. Couple hundred here, couple thousand there. The population adds up fast that way, Herbie."

"Will you tell your father about any of them?" Whiteslaw asked, just for something to talk about.

"Maybe. Maybe not. Pops is being kind of a wet blanket these days. Keeps giving me the cold shoulder 'cause I haven't solved the assassins problem yet."

"The assassins can be dealt with," Whiteslaw said, as if they were of no consequence. "You've done spectacular work as far as I'm concerned."

"Very upstanding of you to say so."

"You're welcome. You know, Jack, your father has been tremendously useful, but it's pretty obvious that you're the real brains of this outfit. Without you, Fastbinder wouldn't keep his hold on the albinos. He couldn't execute raids of the surface. All his accomplishments are really because of you."

Jack beamed. "I got news for you, Herbie. Without

me, my dad couldn't even get out of his cave! Only I can make JED work."

"You're *really* the king of the Underworld, Jack," Whiteslaw observed.

"Tell me something I don't know," Jack Fast said.

12

Breck Kasle and his brother, Jeremy, waved goodbye to their new best friends. As soon as the old Asian and the mean-eyed Gloomy Gus drove off, Breck scrambled for the phone and rang up Trina over at the Bank and Trust.

"Is that money really there?" he demanded.

"Yeah, Breck, 'course it's there."

"I mean, they can't cancel the payment or anything, right?"

"Naw, Breck, it's not like they charged a purchase, see. They actually got cash from their credit card and had it put in your account, see? So they can't be taking it back." She whistled appreciatively. "Mother of pearl, Breck, what're you two crazy bachelors gonna do with that kind of money?"

Breck was all smiles as he thumbs-upped his brother, who showed all his teeth. "I'll tell you what we're gonna do—Jer's gonna build the solidest vintage recreation vehicle that ever was or ever will be."

"Sure, but what're you gonna do when you're not making the RV? Like tonight, for instance? A celebration is in order when you come into cash like that."

"Well, now, Trina, you got a good point."

"My sis and I are free if'n you boys would want to have a little party an' celebrate your newfound wealth. You know my sister, Sophie? Sophie's always saying what a cutie Jeremy is."

They made a date for dinner and dancing at the Four Corners Restaurant. So what if them girls was going after him and his brother for their money? It was just Sophie's bad luck that she wasn't in the right place at the right time to take this opportunity. Then she'd have been the one to get stuck with the ugly brother. But Breck did know Trina and Sophie well enough to be sure they weren't gonna let a money-grubbing opportunity such as this one slip away, even if poor Sophie got stuck with gross old Jeremy.

Trina was a lucky gal, Breck thought, seeing as how he had the cleaner fingers and the more complete set of teeth and even some culture under his belt.

That was why he was the one who dealt with the public and did the RV selling, except for today. It was an unspoken understanding that Jeremy was, well, not a people person. Repulsive, in fact, but also an artist. Still, Jeremy's skills would have never seen the light of day if it weren't for his handsome, smooth-talking brother selling his creations.

Everybody he knew, Breck Kasle thought, was lucky to have Breck Kasle in their lives.

REMO TRIED FINDING OUT what exactly Chiun had contracted the grease monkey to do. It cost a lot of cash. Not that Chiun couldn't afford it, and not that it mattered at all anyway since the entire sum was electronically transferred from the credit card account of one Bucky Chang, a sixty-seven-year-old podiatrist from Madeira Beach, Florida, who did not exist. CURE would pay the bill, but Remo wanted to know what the money was actually for.

"I have a feeling I'm gonna be living in it, whether I want to or not," Remo complained. "I have a right to know, don't I?"

"No."

"Why not?"

"Keep your eyes on the road."

"I keep getting distracted by all that yummy-looking corn they grow around here."

"Don't bother trying to raise up my goat." Chiun turned to his iBlogger for the next twenty miles.

"Hey, Chiun," Remo said then, "you think Smith was on to something about these mine shaft killings?"

"You mean about them being possibly the work of the earth-drilling German from New Mexico?"

"Yes."

"No."

"Why not?"

Chiun looked up. "Remo, it was you who disabled the tunneling machine. Do you doubt that you did so effectively?"

Remo had been worrying about that very fact, but had also come to a conclusion. "No. It was broken."

"Then you have your answer."

"Not only did I break the hydraulic earth flattener, but I locked it up so bad it froze the engine. Then we buried him under sixty feet of soil."

"Exactly."

"He might have, maybe, been able to dig his way out of the hatch and then clear enough dirt to work on the hydraulics, but I don't see him having a lot of spare parts. It would have been nearly impossible to make the thing run without the smasher to compact the earth he dug up. And anyway, there's no way he was going to rebuild the engine on the driller, even if he did have access from the interior of the thing. Right?"

"Precisely." Chiun wasn't paying attention.

"So what if he was rescued."

"By whom?"

"Whiteslaw?"

"Herbert Whiteslaw is a manipulator. He is in government because he is skilled in the art of influence and because he has not the desire or ambition to achieve his own goals. I do not believe he would take the initiative to rescue his trapped coconspirator, even if he did know what had become of the man."

"He could hire someone to do it," Remo suggested.

Chiun waved the idea away.

"He had help from somebody else, right? Whoever was handling the operation in D.C."

Chiun shut down the iBlogger with a sigh. "The one on the airplane went into the ocean."

"So the Air Force claims. Did you see it happen?"

"No."

Remo Williams was thinking about Chiun's reaction. Had he just stumbled across something? "What's with the weird vibes, Little Father?"

"It is the effect of the corn pollen, intoxicating you and dulling your senses."

"No," Remo said, "that's not it. It's coming from you."

"Corn pollen?" Chiun demanded.

"You know what I mean. You've been, well, not quite right."

"You believe you have the exclusive right to be the one who is always behaving improperly?"

"See, even that insult was halfhearted. And in the office with Smith, I was causing all kinds of bad trouble and you were just letting it roll off you."

"I controlled my temper in the presence of the Emperor. This is a skill you would do well to learn. It is foolish to become hysterical in the presence of the king who provides our gold."

"You usually don't let me get away with it, either," Remo said. "Are you becoming more tolerant?"

"I am weary."

"Bulldookey. Are you giving me less grief because you've accepted the fact that I'm supposed to be the one calling the shots anyway?"

"Of course not."

"Then what?"

Chiun turned on his iBlogger again.

"Fine," Remo said. "Forget I brought it up. Keep acting weird. It's kind of a novelty, you know, having a slightly new kind of weird. Not that's it is better than your old weird. Just different. Sort of a lateral change in the quality of your weirdness. I'll just keep talking like this all the way to the mine because I've got nobody else to talk to, and if I don't talk then I start thinking about sweet, luscious, beautiful yellow corn."

But Remo couldn't keep it up and the filibuster faded to an uncomfortable silence until the iBlogger was turned off again.

"Remo," Chiun said, "I am sorry."

"For what?"

"For the incident in the city of the puppet President."

"What incident? You mean when I got knocked out?"

"Yes."

"No biggie."

Chiun turned his head and Remo glanced over, seeing a concerned expression. "What?"

"It was a biggie," Chiun said solemnly.

Remo and Chiun had been patrolling the White House grounds when the attack came, as expected. It was Ironhand, a mechanical man that was more than a hundred years old and now upgraded with the best military automation and stealth technology the U.S. had devised. Under the remote control of the German engineer Jacob Fastbinder, Ironhand had already stolen extensive military technology, worth millions on the open market.

His bold and successful operations caused panic among the research labs in the U.S. military infrastructure. The most highly prized research projects were moved to new locations—except for the highly autonomous, obscenely expensive miniature robotic defensive units deployed on the grounds of the White House.

The President had expected the FEMbots to use their own capabilities to not be stolen. CURE knew better. The FEMbots were just overpriced toys. They were no more dangerous than a radio-controlled poodle to the Masters of Sinanju.

Ironhand, when he came to take the FEMbots, was another story.

Hidden inside Ironhand and his companion, a ridiculous vintage-TV-show robot named Clockwork, were devices intended to spin up the robot's internal generator turbines. Unknown to Fastbinder, the proton emitters were deadly to the Masters of Sinanju. Remo had ripped the device out of Ironhand, and the act of actually touching the emitter had sucked his senses dry, leaving him in a state of deep unconsciousness for many long minutes as Chiun spirited him away from the White House grounds—also bringing the copper robot Clockwork. Chiun intended to present the spherical robot to Dr. Smith, to have it dismantled and analyzed, to identify how it affected the enhanced senses of a Sinanju Master while another human being felt nothing.

In a Washington, D.C., alley a few blocks from the White House, Remo regained consciousness, only to find himself in the presence of Clockwork, who fired up his generator turbines again and sent Remo into a deep sensory deprivation spiral—but not before Remo saved Chiun from the danger.

Afterward, Remo couldn't be revived.

"But I snapped out of it," Remo said as the Hyundai strained to keep going at highway speed on an shallow grade.

"You did not snap out of it, Remo. You were gone for many days."

Remo shrugged. What was Chiun getting so morbid about? "But I'm all better now. See? Eyes open, jaws flappin'."

Chiun looked more worried than ever. "Remo, you were beyond my ability to reach or to save. You were beyond the Void."

"Huh? How can anything be beyond the Void?"

"There is a place of nothingness…."

"That's what the Void is."

"In the Void there is darkness, and the voices of the Masters Who Came Before," Chiun said impatiently. "I believe that you went to where there was no sound. Nothing to see."

"Chiun—" Remo felt suddenly ill, physically ill.

"Nothingness beyond darkness and silence."

"Chiun!" Remo croaked, and he was there again.

13

The Hyundai sat next to the small corrugated metal office alongside the mine entrance.

"I'm okay."

"It was not my intention—"

"Let's not talk about it." Remo hastily got out of the car. He felt the sun on his flesh and allowed his skin to grow too hot, just to feel it.

Whatever had happened to him, it came on him fast. One second he was driving, talking to Chiun, and the next he was nowhere.

If there was a hell, a hell especially made for Remo Williams, Master of Sinanju, it was the place where all his senses sought input and found nothing.

It was over in seconds, and Remo found himself still behind the wheel of the car at the side of the road, shaking uncontrollably.

He had blocked it out after it happened, but talking about it brought it all crashing in on him. Remo had ignored Chiun's concern and started driving again, hoping the memory would stay in the little brain box where he put it. Now, at the mine facility, he was de-

termined to get down to business. He didn't want to
even think about it anymore, because thinking about
it—

"Can I help you?" There was a silver-haired woman
at one of the utility desks inside the metal building.
Remo was standing there daydreaming.

"I'm, uh." He got out his ID. "Sorry. Nuclear Regulatory Commissary."

"You mean the Nuclear Regulatory Commission?"

"He is feeling ill from the road," Chiun said, entering behind Remo. He snatched Remo's card and
shoved both their IDs at the woman. "We are here to
inspect the murder scene."

"There was no murder," the woman snapped. "I'm
going to phone these in."

"Do so."

Remo used the time to breathe and regain his com-
posure. Man, he never wanted to go through that again.

"All right. Let's go," the woman said, slipping on a
hooded sweatshirt, despite the summerlike heat outside. "You guys bring wraps?"

Remo shook his head.

"You're gonna be cold, but not for long. Then you
get real hot." She laughed. Remo felt like she was
laughing at them, not with them.

He didn't care if he felt cold or hot, so long as he
felt something.

THE WOMAN FROM THE OFFICE took them down to a
staging and machinery level in a natural cavern fifty
feet below the surface. The air was chilled and circu-

lated by a rack of blowers striving to drive the cool air
into some of the lower work levels, where the temperature was again elevated. It was an odd and un-
pleasant place, the once-living stalactites and
stalagmites now smothered and dead under the grime
that spewed and seeped from the groaning, clattering
diesel and electric machines.

The woman informed a supervisor that Chiun and
Remo were there about "the so-called murders."

"There were no murders," the man said, instead of
saying, "Nice to meet you," or "Nice weather we're
having, ain't it?"

"Let's go," Remo said, steering the man into the elevators that took them down again. "So what was it,
then, if it wasn't murder?"

"Oh, it's not murder," the man insisted. He was a
sallow-faced little man with unhealthy yellow eyes
and flesh that seemed too loose on his body. "There's
no way it could be murder. It's just that some employees quit. They left."

"Yeah. You run this, whatever it is?"

"I've been first shift supervisor here for three
years," the man said. "Hal Wools is the name. And you
should know what this place is. It is the answer to the
great problem of nuclear waste. The NCR has officially recognized it as such. As soon as we're running
at full capacity, we will be able to accept and permanently store all the nuclear waste that the U.S. ever has
or ever will produce." He tried to smile.

"Here?" Remo asked. "In this glorified root cellar?"

"Here," Supervisor Wools insisted, "in the world's

most secure and safe storage facility for nuclear wastes."

"Hmm," Remo said. The elevator was rattling downward, into the blackness, and the air lost its chill. By the time they left the elevator stopped on a dingy rock platform at five hundred feet, the air was getting warm.

"Because of the depth of the shaft, multiple elevator banks are used to reach the storage facility, which is one of the deepest points ever reached by man inside the earth." Wools tried to come across as confident.

"You sound like a tour guide being held at gunpoint," Remo said. "Come clean with us, Wools. What happened here?"

"Exactly what I said," Wools insisted. "They left. Quit. It's not pleasant working in the dark at eight thousand feet down, even though we pay well enough. Sometimes our people get fed up and scram."

"Twelve guys, all quit without telling anybody and flee a high-security facility without being seen?" Remo asked.

"Yes, uh-huh."

"At one point, leaving a puddle of blood behind?"

"Puddle? More like a smear. Some guy must have banged his arm or something."

"What do you mean when you say when this place gets up and running?" Chiun ventured.

Wools's eyes couldn't find anything to look at in the dim light of the elevator, so he tried to look at everything at once, except Chiun. "You know, when we are able to start accepting full-size shipments of waste. So far we've got no more than a few tons of low-grade nuclear waste."

"So you've been doing what for the past three years, just getting things ready?" Remo asked.

"Getting things ready? Try pulling off one of the great feats of mining engineering of all time. We enlarged a small, dry gem mine into a vast storage hub for the world's nuclear waste. The resources have been staggering. The cost—I can tell you nuke guys—the cost is gonna be over a billion."

Remo glared at Wools. "A billion invested dollars, right?"

"Yes. No government funds."

"So if there was a murder down there, it means there's another way in that you don't know about, right?"

"That's impossible!" Wools chuckled.

"That's the most insincere laugh I think I've ever heard, and I was talking to a used-car salesman just today so you know that's saying a lot. Bet you've got a financial stake here, huh?"

"Yes, and so do you!" Wools fished a roll of documents out of his pocket, peeling off a small stack each for Remo and Chiun.

"They're worth about three thousand bucks each today," Wools said somberly, "but if this place is even half as successful as the company projects—pow! You're looking at a tens or hundreds of thousands!"

"Thanks, but no." Remo handed his shares back to Wools.

Wools looked hopefully at Chiun. "No better than a check," Chiun declared, gesturing at the shares he had discarded on the floor of the elevator.

"You always carry printed shares around with you like this?" Remo asked.

"Yeah. All the time." Wools retrieved his documents while Chiun peered out the sides into the blackness below.

"Remo, it worries me," Chiun said in Korean. "I fear this place might make it happen to you again."

"Don't even talk about it, Chiun. Let's just leave it alone."

"Also, I did not have the opportunity to finish my apology. It was I who brought the sickness upon you."

"Chiun, just stop, okay? Save it for later. Like when we're sitting at home some night with nothing better to do, then maybe we'll talk." Remo could hear himself being defensive. Well, he had the right to be defensive. Whatever happened out on the highway had been just terrible.

He shut off the memory, hard, and concentrated on the here and now.

"I have a bad feeling about this little rat and his billion-dollar rodent den," Remo said, still in Korean.

"He has said almost nothing that is truthful," Chiun agreed. "We should be prepared to encounter dangerous radiation."

"We should be looking out for knives aiming at our backs," Remo added, nodding at Wools, who didn't notice. He was too busy plotting.

14

It took six elevator rides to get them all the way down to the bottom. As the final lift came to a noisy, clanging halt, Remo and Chiun gave each other a silent signal to be wary.

Because there were so many things wrong down here, Remo didn't know where to begin sorting them out. His senses were flaring from the overload, trying to come to terms with the alien environment. There was the smell of rock dust, so thick and so old it was beyond conception that it should have ever been stirred up. There was the smell of fuel and sweat, and the tinge of radioactivity poisoning the air.

Most subtle and yet most powerful was the combination of signals that told them they were somewhere foreign, where the pressure of the air was different than it had ever been, where the miles of rock above them blocked out the wisps of heat and electronic and pressure waves that had always been there.

And there was a smell unlike any smell Remo knew, and what made it so noticeable was that it was almost human.

But not quite.

Wools led the way. They went past corridors into vast, empty spaces for future waste storage, linked by a rail system for a waste transport car with a clicking electric motor.

"It's shielded for radiation and it moves slow to make any spillage impossible," Wools enthused, still trying to win them over.

"Where's it come from?" Remo asked. "You're not taking waste down the elevator on a furniture dolly."

"We have a transport system designed just for the waste containers," Wools said. "I'll show you."

"So why couldn't the guys have snuck out that way?" Remo asked. "Seems like the easy explanation for your little 'we quit' scenario."

"Believe me, I've tried to come up with a way to make that sound feasible," Wools admitted. "You'll see why I can't in a minute."

They found the shaft in a hermetically sealed chamber, where a series of mechanical cranes and claws were designed to lift the arriving cargo into the sealed transport car. There was no cargo arriving yet. The radiation level from within was elevated, but not deadly.

"Watch." Wools took the controls from a bored operator and pressed a button that opened a large pair of metal doors, revealing a transport car with a self-balancing cargo compartment, required to keep the waste level on the steep grade. The car was winched, front and rear, and as they watched it began to move, exiting the doorway and coming to a halt next to a waiting transport car.

"It comes down and gets off-loaded, then travels the second corridor back up," Wools said, and the car started again, heading through a second pair of metal doors that clanged shut behind it. "Now it's being superheated," Wools said. "This sterilizes it of any microorganisms that may be clinging to it. It will be heated seven more times on its trip to the surface, getting as hot as nine hundred degrees Fahrenheit. This way, when we go public we can assure the good folks of Oklahoma that no mutated bacteria and other lifeforms are being transported to the world above. As if. Anyway, it discourages stowaways."

"Couldn't the sterilizing be turned off?" Remo asked.

"It could, but the alarm system would start a cascading shutdown of all systems. We'd take weeks to get up and running again. Believe me, there's no way to make this sound like a plausible escape route."

"Okay," Remo said. "Show us the murder scene. I mean, show us where some disgruntled employee scraped his arm before sneaking out."

"Sure." Wools chuckled, giving Remo a friendly pat on the arm—or would have, if Remo hadn't somehow managed to be a lot farther away than Wools had thought.

Wools was not winning over the nonchuckling pair of Feds, he realized despondently. He moved on, taking them beyond the activity of the work zone until they followed a ramp down into a narrow, darkened tunnel lit by bare lightbulbs every fifty feet. Now that they were beyond most of the human works the scents of sweat and aftershave were reduced, so that the other smells stood out. Remo tried to place the smell that alarmed him. It was closer to human than he had first imagined, but still not quite a match.

There was another widening of the cavern where a huge air handler operated noisily, pulling in hot air from behind it, running it over a series of aluminum heat exchangers, and thrusting it back up the way they had come.

"See them pipes?" Wools pointed. "They're miles long. They got stuff like antifreeze in there but it's safer, in case of a spill. Goes all the way up to right near the surface, gets cooled down by the dirt, then comes through insulated pipes back down here for the coolness to get extracted and blown all over in the work zone. From here on it gets real hot."

Once beyond the air handler, the temperature rose quickly. When the sound of the giant fans dropped to a whisper, Wools stated, "Is 106 hot enough for you?" Chiun and Remo didn't answer, and Wools gave them the once-over when they were under the glare of the next lightbulb. "Hey, how come you folks ain't sweatin'?"

"We did a stint in Phoenix," Remo explained.

"Oh."

"This tunnel's man-made."

"Yeah?"

"You said it was an old gem mine?"

"Yeah, some good rubies came out of the Pit. That's what the hired hands call this place. The Pit."

"What kind of rubies?" Chiun asked.

"Red ones."

"Of what quality?"

"Not many gemstones, if that's what you're asking. The mine was played out fifty years back. Nobody with any brains would be breaking in down here to get at our gems, if that's what you were thinking."

"Have you checked thoroughly?" Chiun persisted.

"Heh-heh. Yeah. For a while some of the grunts had a sort of contest going as a way of passing the time, about who could find the biggest gem. Then the contest became who could find any gem. Know what? Three months later one guy finds a piece of rock with one little crumbly ruby in it, worth less than it would cost to extract."

Chiun pursed his lips in disappointment, but his eyes scanned the walls as he walked.

"This is the Intersection."

There was a small metal desk and a bored security guard who was watching them approach without much interest, an assault rifle over one shoulder.

"Here's the purported crime scene," Wools announced miserably.

"What, you mean the place with the yellow crime scene tape and the inch-deep puddle of dried blood?"

"Not a puddle so much—"

"It is like a catch basin at an abattoir," Chiun noted. "There is the blood of just one man here."

"He's not getting his severance pay, I guarantee you that. Left without any notice whatsoever."

"No man can survive after losing that quantity of blood. He is dead."

"You're exaggerating," Wools insisted.

"Who put up the tape?" Remo asked.

"Kerker County sheriff."

Remo turned on him. "Locals? You mean no other Feds have been notified?"

"Why would we bring in the Feds?" Wools asked, sweating even more than the heat called for. "This isn't federal land or a government project. Sure, the federal government will be our best customer when we open this place up—"

"If you open this place up," Remo said, walking away from the man.

"What's that mean?"

"Where does this go?" Remo was standing at the mismatched boards nailed in place over Shaft C. Chiun was peering into the blackness at the end of the tunnel, where the dangling lightbulb scarcely reached.

"That's an abandoned shaft," Wools said. "Dangerous down there. Nobody's been down there since a part of it collapsed in the 1930s."

"I see," Remo said. "So you don't know what's down there. You don't know if there's an access way to the surface, for example."

"There's not."

Remo raised his eyebrows at Wools, who flinched. Remo kept his eyes on the little man until Wools's skin was almost visibly crawling. "Okay, we don't know."

"And you didn't try to find out because it would ruin the site," Remo concluded.

"You got to understand, this is the deepest existing subterranean access on the continent! It was here or nowhere! And there can't be an access way that way. See for yourself—nobody's come through those boards since Teddy Roosevelt was in office!"

"Until recently," Remo said, snatching Wools by the collar and bringing his pasty face into close proximity of the wood planks. "Fresh damage to old rot. See it?"

"No, you can't prove—"

"See it?" Remo asked, mashing Wools's face against the plank.

"I thee it."

Remo dropped Wools to the floor, relieving him of his flashlight in the process. "Your man got any glow sticks?"

The security guard was standing around looking worried, but he had wisely refrained from unslinging his automatic rifle.

"Oh, it's okay," Remo said, shrugging off the collapsed Wools. "We're from the federal government. Got glow sticks?"

"In the emergency pack in the desk."

"Get them."

The guard handed Remo an emergency supply pack.

"You going in there?" Wools asked in astonishment.

"Yeah." Remo scrounged in the pack for other goodies and came up with a nonmilitary Meal Ready-To-Eat, featuring a menu of ham steak and au gratin potatoes. "MRE, Little Father?"

Chiun glared at him.

"Just trying to break the tension with humor."

They slithered through the wood planks and into the blackness.

Watching them disappear into the blackness, Wools wondered if those two were crazy. They hadn't even turned on the flashlights yet.

"They're dead meat," the guard said.

"That's okay," Wools said, feeling a rising tide of optimism. "They're with the federal government."

15

"That slimy little weasel hopes we never come back," Remo said. "Thinks that'll put an end to his problems."

"He is mistaken," Chiun said, and sniffed low among a jumble of rocks. "It is very close to being man, but it is not quite like a man."

"A lot of not-men," Remo said. "Lots of them, ripped to shreds by all the rotting little pieces." He was trying hard not to step in the decaying shreds of flesh. "What do you think did this, Little Father? Even if that guy had a machine gun, he wouldn't have made mincemeat out of them like this."

Chiun found a particularly large chunk of discarded abdominal flesh and shifted his body so that the glimmering light of the faraway bulb could reach it. Despite the near blackness, his eyes could see well enough. "Eaten."

"By what?" Remo asked.

"Each other. Look."

Remo got as close as he needed, and no closer, to the chunk. He saw human teeth marks.

"Christ," he muttered. "They turned on each other.

Some of them get wounded, probably shot by the guard, and they go into a feeding frenzy."

Chiun nodded grimly.

Remo sighed. "So what are they, why'd they come here and why are we the schmoes who have to go down there and find out?"

"We are not the schmoes," Chiun said sharply. "You must retreat now."

"No way."

"You know what I fear. In the blackness of the earth below—"

"Shh! Stop. We go together."

"I would keep you from relapsing."

"Then don't keep going on and on about it. Just pretend it's not an issue."

"But it is," Chiun said with stamp of his foot.

"Not unless you make it one."

Chiun and Remo faced each other, bathed in the hothouse of decay, and Chiun pursed his old lips. "You will go, regardless of my wishes."

"I will."

"You are a stubborn young goat, Remo Williams."

Remo had the perfect response almost coming out of his mouth before he swallowed it and nodded. "Let's go."

WHEN THEY WERE WELL around the next corridor, the light of the distant bulb failed to reach them at all.

Aboveground there was almost always at least some glimmer of light, no matter how dark the night, and a little light was all the Sinanju Masters needed to see by. They would expand their pupils, seeing in the darkness better than any great cat. Here, under the earth, it was different. There was no moon or stars or other light source. It was absolute blackness, and their eyes could not make use of light they did not have.

"Turn on your light," Chiun said.

"I'm starting with one of these deals to see how long they last." Remo withdrew a plastic glow stick and bent it, cracking the plastic vial inside and mixing the chemicals to create a lime-yellow glow. It was dim by human standards, but bright enough for Remo's eyes to see the extent of the tunnel. The mine shaft was a broken mess of fallen rock, and it soon petered out in a jumble of boulders. The blood trail led them through a narrow crevice, and they found themselves treading in a natural cavern in which Remo sometimes was forced to walk sideways and had to constantly stoop. They emerged a quarter mile later into a larger, descending cave, which was naturally stepped. A stream pooled on each level before cascading down.

Chiun sniffed distastefully at the water. "Poison."

"Radiation taint," Remo agreed. "Come on."

Chiun sighed and followed as Remo led the way, leaping down the large steps until they reached a foul, steaming pond where the water evaporated and condensed the pollution into a near-toxic swamp. Remo and Chiun bypassed it swiftly, slipping into the corridor that extended beyond, but not before their eyes fell on the familiar shapes cooking in the miasma.

"Human bones," Chiun said. "Or close to human."

"I don't care how much Smitty bitches, I'm not sticking my arm in to get him a sample," Remo said.

Down the tunnel they went, finding the waning blood trail easily enough. The temperature was reaching the extremes of the Sahara Desert, and the blood put out a potent stench as it rotted. There was no skill needed in finding the path. They went on for miles until, at the bottom of a sandy cavern, they found clear footprints.

"They look like people," Remo said with a shrug.

"Here are shoe prints of their captives."

"How long have we been down here, anyway?"

Chiun looked at him oddly, but realized even his sense of the passage of time felt blurry. "Three hours and twenty-seven minutes since we left the idiot miner."

"These things are good for shit," Remo said, displaying the glow stick, which was already losing its luminance.

"We should go back," Chiun said.

"Forget it. We've got three glow sticks left, plus the flashlight."

The corridors were descending only slightly for all their ups and downs, so Remo estimated they had covered just three more land miles before he and Chiun froze simultaneously, straining against the heavy silence, and heard sounds far ahead.

They were in a sort of grotto, with a forty-foot ceiling over an intersection of two narrow passageways. Remo tossed the glow stick far back up the passage the way they had come, then he and Chiun relied on their memory of the interior layout of the grotto, scaling the jagged walls and finding easy perches halfway up.

They waited in blackness as the sounds came nearer.

"They move slow. Let us speak to pass the time while these man-eaters approach," Chiun suggested.

"Okay," Remo said. "But not about you-know-what."

"Agreed."

"Tell me about your travel trailer."

"No."

"Fine."

So they didn't speak again as the distant rustling and scraping sounds became distinct, then they made out the panting and grunting. The steady airflow from below brought them the odor of the creatures, a nightmare stench that was almost human, mixed with the decay of human flesh. The smell was overpowering as the scrabble of their feet came just outside the grotto, and then creatures emerged.

Remo realized what had been bothering him: as the band of almost-humans closed in he should have picked up the faintest glow of their light source, but there was nothing. The band was now in the grotto with himself and Chiun and still no light. He could hear the slapping of their bare feet and the snorting and grunting. Seven of them, he judged by their noise, and all adults.

The band came to a nervous halt just outside the grotto, making rasping noises that might have been speech.

Remo turned on the flashlight and wedged it in a crack in the wall, filling the grotto with a dismal yellow light.

Chiun did not object. They had both ascertained that these creatures were blind. Otherwise, why would they travel in the black earth without a light of some kind?

So the glow stick Remo had tossed up the hall as a lure would be unseen, but if the creatures had enhanced sense of smell, which was almost a necessity, then they would return to the grotto soon enough.

They did, dropping their wordless jabbering to snakelike whispers. One of them ventured through the entrance into the grotto, sniffing with his head hung low, then following the scent, raising his head toward Remo and Chiun and growling hungrily.

Remo saw something that was almost a human being, with the bloodless white flesh of an albino. His hair was white where it wasn't matted with mud, and a few wisps of white beard showed where they were not sticky with filth.

"Yuck," Remo observed.

The albino dropped into a crouch, growling viciously, "Food!"

"What do you know, it talks," Remo observed.

"And climbs," Chiun added.

The albino's fingers spidered on the rocks and quickly found strong handholds, carrying the creature up the wall as the others streamed up after him, joining the attack. Remo waited until it was within reach, then snatched the first attacker by the hair. The albino clawed Remo's arms until Remo gave him a shake so hard his teeth chomped together and broke off in chips and shards. One of the other albinos came within arm's reach, and Remo used the body of his companion to pound him. The figure toppled off his perch and landed on the rocky floor twenty feet below, motionless.

"Who are you?" Remo asked his captive. The thing growled and hissed. "C'mon, I know you speak English."

Remo held his hand out experimentally, tantalizingly close to the attacker, whisking it away just before the jaws snapped down on his fingers. The clack of the teeth was tremendous. These were not warning bites; they were take-off-a-mouthful-and-eat bites. The attacker became angrier, like a terrier teased with a dangling hot dog.

"Come on, talk to me."

"How long will you toy with him?" Chiun asked. One of the attackers came near enough to lunge at the old Korean, and Chiun's hand sliced through the air, his scythelike fingernails passing without effort through the exposed throat of the animal creature.

Remo's attacker was startled when he sensed the sudden eruption of blood smell and the crunch of the severed head, then the toppling body reached the rocky floor below. Immediately there was a riot of noise as the albinos descended upon their slain companion.

"Where do you think you're going?" Remo grabbed his attacker by the wrist and held him out over the grotto, where the creature struggled in vain and slobbered.

"Look at him. All he cares about is getting in on the free lunch," Remo said. "I have a feeling these guys aren't going to be offering up a lot of good hard information."

"And I for one have no desire to witness their feeding orgy," Chiun added. He stepped off his perch and landed amid the frenzy of cannibalism, robe flapping and hands striking before his sandals were even in contact with the blood-spattered rock. Remo sighed and jumped down with him, lashing out with one hand here and there. In seconds the band of albinos was extinct, save for the sobbing, drooling survivor in Remo's other hand.

"Boy, he really wants his lunch."

"Like all whites, his behavior is dominated by his gluttony. Put this one inside a restaurant where fried cattle is served and he will arouse no special notice."

"Yeah, well, this one might serve some other purposes, too," Remo said. He released the albino's wrist and pointed at the rear entrance to the grotto.

"Home, boy!"

The albino went in the wrong direction, making a dive past Remo at the strewed and bloodied corpses, only to find himself somehow back on his feet exactly where he had started. Remo snatched for the creature's large earlobe and gave it a pinch.

The albino shrieked in pain.

"No din-din. Go home."

The albino lunged again.

"Who would have thought your eloquent argument would fail to persuade him?" Chiun asked.

"C'mon, dude, I don't have all day." Remo gave the albino increasingly painful lessons. The banshee wails became deafening.

Chiun yawned loudly.

"You think you can do better?" Remo demanded.

Chiun marched forward and snatched the creature by the neck, paralyzing him instantly. As the wide-eyed, O-mouthed albino toppled, Chiun snatched at its long and filthy mass of hair, twisted it into a rope and grabbed hold of it before the body cracked against the stone floor, then he marched off into the rear tunnel.

"What's going on?" Remo demanded, following.

Chiun tossed the twisted rope of hair into Remo's palm, then whisked his own hands together to fling off the detritus. "If there was a shark in a lagoon filled with chum, you would not get him to follow the inlet to the open sea, regardless of how many times you poked him with a stick."

"Huh?"

"But if you tie a rope to his tail and drag him away from the blood smell, he will be more cooperative."

"Cooperative how?"

"It does not matter how. What matters is that he will no longer be inflamed with blood lust."

"I don't see why I would ever want cooperation from a shark."

"Are you being deliberately dense?"

"Deliberately dense like a fox," Remo retorted. "Okay, I get it. Whitey's feeding drive is stronger than all his other instincts, even survival and the need to escape pain."

"Yes."

They followed the clear trail left by the band when they had come up, and when they were a mile from the grotto the smell of the blood was erased by the distance and the upwind airflow. Chiun released the albino from his paralysis with another pinch of the neck nerves, then pushed the groggy creature to its feet.

"Home, Whitey," Remo said.

The albino lunged with two hands and his chomping jaws, brought up short when Remo ghosted out of the way and flicked him in the ear.

The dismayed albino dropped into a crouch, cranked his head back and forth, then sprang wildly at Chiun, who stepped out of the target zone at the last possible instant. The albino's senses told him his prey was still where it should be until the moment he crashed into the rock floor. Then he was on his feet, howling in frustration.

Remo moved in and tapped him on the shoulder. "Here, Whitey."

The albino attacked, and grabbed empty air. Remo tapped him again and again until the albino was a frantic dervish lunging in all directions. The dismayed creature finally collapsed blubbering.

16

Interstate 10, passing south through New Mexico just before crossing into Texas near El Paso, was lined on either side with barbed wire and warning signs. Some were faded beyond legibility, but the newer signs read something along the lines of:

Danger
Unexploded Ordnance.
White Sands Missile Testing Range.
Do Not Leave Highway.

The message was then repeated in Spanish for the benefit of illegal aliens traveling from Ciudad Juarez.

Jesus Merienez had never actually seen any live ordnance during his fourteen trips on this route. This time it was no different.

In fact, at night, far from the interstate, with the sun down and the air cool, the missile testing grounds were delightfully secluded and peaceful.

Then, just as he was tossing away his last Tecate can and preparing to crawl into his bedroll, the earth started shaking under his feet. He screamed. He tried to run. Some American bomb was exploding right under his feet! Exploding very slowly!

No, it was a volcano. He'd never heard of a volcano in the southwestern deserts of the U.S., but what did he know?

All this speculation was immaterial as he clawed and scrambled for freedom from the bucking, roiling sands of the desert. Swimming in the flowing, vibrating soil was more difficult than swimming across the murky Rio Grande. His screams were snuffed out by soil, and his legs were smashed under an unbearable weight. The air filled with bolts of lightning that anchored in his eye sockets. For one hideous instant he felt the vitreous fluid inside his eyeballs come to a boil, then burst.

He knew he was dead. He should have given up, but something made him fight to survive. He clawed through the cover of moving sand, reaching for the sky, and his hand emerged from the soil. He could feel it out in the open air.

He didn't feel it for long. The weight that was pinning him down settled onto him, tons and tons of gleaming metal, and Jesus was mashed from his belly to his feet, like a scorpion killed by a cowboy boot.

The electricity died away and the hatch opened with a clang. The young man who emerged had a sandy-blond buzz cut and a freckled face. Jack Fast leaned out of the earth drill and spotted the hand protruding from the soil.

"I thought I ran over something," he remarked to himself.

Jack looked around the vast, empty desert, then back at the hand, which twitched slightly as the nerves went through their own death spasms.

"Man, you must be the unluckiest dude ever!" Jack said. "What're the odds I'd come up right underneath you like that? I'm speechless, too."

Jack ducked back inside, and an Army-surplus backpack sailed out a moment later, landing in the soft, freshly dug soil. Next came a plastic crate, dark blue, with a dire warning embossed in the plastic: Property of Oberhurley Dairies, Waukesha, Wisconsin. Unauthorized Use Is Prohibited and Will Be Punished to the Fullest Extent of the Law.

Jack emerged from the hatch himself, manhandling a rolled bundle of plastic bubble wrap, large enough to contain a cadaver. The roll of bubble wrap banged against the side of the earth drill, making Jack wince, but he got it to the desert floor without apparent damage.

He turned the tumbled backpack upright. "Would it have hurt ya to lend a hand?" he asked the protruding limb of Jesus Merienez.

Jack Fast unrolled the bubble wrap, revealing a pile of thin metal rods and carefully folded reams of aluminized nylon fabric. The rods were threaded at each end, and Jack began screwing them together.

"Okay, I know, it's titanium, but tungsten is just too darn brittle," he said to the hand. "Titanium bends. You gotta be flexible, you know?"

The pinkie quivered.

"'Course you know. Now, the connects are threaded

and they deform when you screw 'em, to lock 'em together. Once I put her together, this baby ain't coming apart unless you rip her apart."

In minutes he had the first slender pole assembled,
as thin as a soda straw and 114 feet long. He rested it
gently atop the yucca plants that peppered the desert
floor, then assembled another rod of similar length,
which attached to the first rod at one end. The third rod
was almost as long, and connected to the other two to
form a massive triangle that appeared fragile as ancient
parchment.

"Bet you're wondering what this dude Jack is up to,
huh?" he asked the hand. "Well, forget it, I'm not
telling. It's a surprise."

He reinforced the flimsy triangle with a series of
support bars, all of which met in the center of the
structure. That was where Jack put the generator. He
had a bad moment as he hoisted the generator and the
proton cell out of the backpack and he almost lost his
balance. Titanium or not, one of the thin rods would
deform under the weight of a human dude like him.
He managed to save himself from falling by dropping
the equipment into the sand and doing a lot of two-arm
windmilling.

When it was over, he leaned on his hands and
panted.

"What're you laughing at, Lefty?" he demanded.

The hand of Jesus Merienez wasn't even quivering
anymore.

Jack was more careful as he attached the equipment
in the middle of the titanium frame. He had person-

ally done the math on this device, so he knew what it was capable of, but even he had a hard time believing all those tiny little metal sticks were going to hoist the proton cell and the generator and the cargo....

Well, it would. He knew it would 'cause he was Jack Fast, and he was an engineering wizard and he had calculated it over and over. So what if he was in high school? Nobody could say he wasn't a genius.

"Chill. It'll work."

The cadaverous hand of Jesus Merienez was, in fact, chilling. Jesus had lost more than two degrees of body heat. He was cooling faster than a typical recently dead human adult male because of the tremendous deformation of the lower torso and extremities. Jesus was literally spread thin.

Now came the trickiest part of the operation, Jack explained. The fabric was a strong synthetic, like the material used in high-performance airfoils, and was reinforced for strength and durability with an ceramic-aluminum thread.

"Are you listening?" Jack asked the hand as he worked. "This is all going to be on the quiz Tuesday. Yes, ceramic-aluminum. Now shut up while I do the hard part. See, I've got enough material here to make a mosquito net for a used-car lot. Now, inch-per-inch, Charmin weighs more than this stuff, so one good breeze could mess me up really good. You sneeze, Lefty, and I swear I'll kill ya."

Jack was sweating as he attached the material using tiny clips, then, when it was in place, misted it with a chlorine mixture that turned the material liquid just long enough to adhere it. Once he got rolling, he could adhere a ten-foot strip of material every two minutes. When one side was done he began rolling the ten-foot rolls across the frame and adhered them to the opposite side. It took two hours for the entire frame to be covered in material.

By then, the corpse of Jesus Merienez was down to 90.3 degrees Fahrenheit. The fingers, which had been clenched in a animal-like claw, were drooping like fading blossoms.

"You look tired," Jack said to the hand. "Me, too." He jumped up on the earth drill, and his top half disappeared inside. He came out with a pair of Coronas. He grinned at the hand, then frowned.

"Don't give me that stuff. Dad says if I'm old enough to steal secret military hardware I'm old enough to have a brewski." Jack sucked down the first beer, tossed the bottle into the backpack and started on the second one as he inspected his handiwork.

"Oh, no! Look." He pointed into the middle of his construction. "I've got a run in my airship!"

There, amid the vast frame of dark gray fabric, a tiny cactus spine was protruding through the fabric, almost invisible in the starlight. The tear spread for two feet.

"Oh, well, bound to happen. Watch how I fix it. I learned this from my girlfriend's mom. She uses nail polish when she gets a run in her nylons. I use this stuff." Jack scrounged out a small spray bottle of thick liquid. "Works even better than Revlon." He crawled on all fours under the fabric and squirted the stuff over the run, creating a flexible mend.

"Now, we are ready to go." Jack told the hand, retrieving his beer and sucking it empty. He fished a remote control from his pocket. It had come with a ninety-nine-dollar Nishitsu DVD player that died years ago. It was easy enough to put a booster in the remote and use it to get the thing started. He pressed Power.

The tiny proton cell whizzed up the turbine. It was virtually silent, but a tiny amber LED told Jack it was working. The teenager stood silently, almost thoughtfully as the proton cell did its work.

"See, I didn't feel a thing, did you?" he asked the hand of Jesus. "There's something about that proton field, though. It sends those kung fu dudes into conniptions. At least I think it's the proton charge. Well, whatever." Jack heard the generator begin working, powered by the proton cell. He was using bursts of electricity to create electricity, but what the heck? It worked, didn't it? And man, did it give him a lot of power to work with.

"Hey, you ready? I swear you never saw anything like this before." Jack pressed the channel-up button. The huge framed triangle shuddered, crackled with electricity, then rose in a billow of desert dust. Jack hastily dragged on the plastic filtration mask he had clipped on his belt, and watched the airship rise. It blotted out the stars; it was acres big.

"Is that cool or is that cool?" Jack demanded. His eyes, as blue as the tropical ocean in a travel brochure, glinted with wild excitement. "Fetch, boy."

He pressed Play, and the airship drifted away in virtual silence.

When he turned back to the drill, Jack found the hand of Jesus was buried in dust up to the cuticles.

"Oh, man, you missed it? Sorry about that." He pushed off the sand until the hand was exposed again almost to the elbow, then Jack set up his laptop to monitor the progress of the Jack Fast's Amazing Invisible Airship. Not that he had to do anything. The airship was already programmed to do the work all by itself. Like everything Jack Fast engineered, it worked perfectly.

After an hour, Jack got out the cooler to make some baloney sandwiches.

17

The Object of Plausible Denial—OPD—lay under a rock.

It had fallen out of the sky when it shouldn't have and hadn't exploded when it should have. It bounced and skidded across the desert floor for 87.62 yards before becoming wedged under the big rock. The skid marks were erased by a brisk wind before they could be sighted from the air by the U.S. Air Force search planes. The Air Force devoted almost ten thousand man-hours to the search effort, but the device was never found.

There were two schools of thought on how to handle the loss of a device that dangerous.

One group wanted to warn the population, offer a reward for finding the device and create enhanced public safety through a high degree of awareness. The safety-first group was actually just one engineer with a defense contractor from Dallas, and before long he was persuaded to move to Iowa. He spent the remainder of his engineering career designing coin-operated laundry appliances—sophisticated laundry appliances, with lots of elaborate features.

The second group decided not to tell the public, not even tell that peanut farmer who was technically commander in chief at that time. Yeah, right, like *that* idiot peacenik could be expected to make a rational decision about a lost bomb. The best thing was to simply categorize the lost device as an OPD.

The device, once designated top secret, was now designated an Object of Plausible Denial, which meant its existence was creatively erased in all Air Force paperwork. The engineers and officers who had sweated and labored to create the device purged it from their memories. If you asked them what they were doing during that eighteen-month phase of their careers, they would tell you it had something to do with developing advanced, ultrastrong bungee cords for high-speed ground-to-air pickups. But the cords snapped a lot so the project was shelved.

Without evidence, it was easy to convince others and themselves that the device had never existed.

There was one man who was given the burden and responsibility of retaining the facts of the lost device, just in case this information would ever again be needed. Which it never would. Just a formality, really. The man was chosen for his security level and his youthfulness. He memorized all the data on the device, so when the data was destroyed the young officer was the only remaining source of data on the device. This was how the military did things. It was OPD SOP.

Decades later, the young officer was a retired old officer and even he had forgotten about the device. He had also forgotten about his wife, his dog and his ranch house in Houston—everything except the inside of the He's Not Here Tavern.

Amazingly enough, the forgotten OPD was found again. It took minutes for Jack Fast's airship, mounted with its stolen, top secret ordnance detector, to zero in on the OPD, where it had lain undiscovered under a rock since 1978.

This particular ordnance detector, ironically, had been stolen from the U.S. Department of Defense just a few months before and had just been reclassified as an OPD.

"Morons," Jack Fast thought as he watched his laptop display. He had no idea what the thing under the rock was, but he knew he wanted it. He deployed the pincers, lowering the high-tensile cable until it grasped the one small corner of a bent tail fin that protruded from under the rock. The pincer closed with magnetic force that had the proton-driven generator turbines humming constantly. The airship ascended and the OPD emerged from its shelter for the first time in decades.

Minutes later, the airship deposited the device gently on a flat, empty patch of desert a hundred yards from the drill, then it rose again and began looking for more OPDs.

Jack wondered how many lost objects the military had lying around out there. Lots? He hoped there were lots.

Pretty soon, he knew the answer.

There were lots.

18

Harold W. Smith knew many of the nation's dirtiest secrets, and he had no compunction about revealing them if it served his purpose.

His purpose was to protect the constitutional democracy of the United States of America. He knew full well that most of these secrets had become known to him by blatantly violating the golden rules of the Constitution. It was more than an irony; it was Smith's grim reality.

Sometimes, when he allowed himself to speculate on the possible alternatives, he shuddered to think what might have happened. Smith knew that almost any other man, put in his position, would have eventually been corrupted by it. It was too much power for a man to have.

So what would happen when Smith was gone? He was old, after all. Mark Smith was a dedicated young patriot who could surely handle the responsibility of directing CURE operations.

But Mark Howard was only human. Would he succumb? Would he be corrupted? It was almost un-

thinkable that he would. It was unrealistic to think
that he wouldn't.

Where did that leave Smith, when the time finally
came that he could no longer handle the daily grind of
running CURE? Would duty require him to erase
CURE, to wipe the slate clean, so that no one could
prove CURE had ever even existed?

Which brought Smith back to his current problem,
which pertained to the Experimental Low-Altitude
Organic Deactivation Device, Serial No. A002. It had
been test-fired in White Sands years ago and was lost
within seconds of its launch. Since it couldn't find the
device, the Air Force had decided to pretend it had
never existed. It wasn't the first time nor the last.

Smith had always monitored these devices when he
could. A002 had a radioactive signature that couldn't
be traced from a distance until new spy satellites were
orbited in the 1990s and new ground-based sensor
systems were positioned throughout the White Sands
Missile Test Range.

By then, nobody even remembered the lost A002,
or its predecessor the A001, and the radioactive signature was too small to register on the security systems.

Harold W. Smith had fed the signature of the A002,
and a thousand other ordnance specifications, into the
immense network-monitoring systems that resided in
the CURE mainframes, the Folcroft Four. You never
knew when one of them might pop up out of nowhere.

Like tonight. The White Sands Range monitors
sensed the signature, analyzed it and decided it was an-

other small radioactive material spill. The location was put on the list for cleanup by the radiation cleanup crew. They called themselves the Hot Janitors. The Hot Janitors had about three weeks of work to do before they'd get to the A002 site.

But the Folcroft Four saw the same bit of radioactivity and recognized it. Smith's quick probe of the White Sands duty roster showed no scheduled work that would have unearthed the A002. His analysis of the other security feeds at the missile test range found no sign of intrusion. Just a small dust storm.

As Smith watched the blurry thermal satellite feed, he saw the dust storm make a ninety-degree turn.

He grabbed the red phone.

19

General Tainey liked his command to run smoothly. "A well-oiled machine, son, that's what!" He had said these words recently to a lieutenant colonel who had been inefficient and sloppy. "Can't afford to have craziness and what-all—not when you're shooting off missiles! Every damned hand needs to know what every other damned hand is doing!"

The lieutenant colonel had tried to defend his actions. A substandard batch of amphetamines, issued by the Air Force to combat pilots, had been the real problem. The stay-awake pills were too strong. One pilot was experiencing cardiac arrhythmia. Another flopped on his back without any pulse whatsoever.

"That's two," the general pointed out acerbically.

"All six pilots took doses from the same batch, General. I felt it was best to get them medical attention before they had severe reactions."

"Which you didn't even know they would have, now, did you son?"

"It seemed likely—"

"It *seemed likely?* Them ain't the kind of words you

can depend on, dammit! Whatever seemed like was going to happen, I know what did happen! Exercises were shut down for eight straight hours! And it's likely I am gonna get my ass chewed out! And if I get my ass chewed, you will be emptying my wastebaskets!"

Somehow, the commanders up the ranks had bought the whole story about the dying pilots and hadn't even reprimanded the general, so he'd gone easy on the lieutenant colonel and hadn't ripped off all his stripes. Just some of them.

Now there was another debacle in the works. Two, in the same damned month? New assholes were gonna get chewed big-time.

"Yes, Mr. President," the general answered politely. He could out-protocol any President you threw his way. "You say I have an intruder, Mr. President?"

Okay, so that rattled the general a little.

A moment later, the general forgot his manners. "May I ask where you received this intelligence, Mr. President?"

The President answered. The general's face colored.

"Right away, Mr. President."

General Tainey slammed the phone and stomped out of his office, surrounded by yammering aides, and burst into the missile range command center, where more than thirty Air Force men and women busied themselves.

"What the hell is happening on my missile range?" the general exploded.

He got thirty blank looks in answer.

"We got intruders on my missile range, and you don't even know it? I just told the President of the United States of America that we were on it! Now get on it!"

One of his aides scurried up with a portable phone. "General Brown for you, General."

"General *Brown?* General Brown from where and why do I care?"

"From the Joint Chiefs, General. Calling with additional orders from the President, General."

Dammit all to hell! Worst thing about a crisis is when all them ninnies upstairs started adding their two cents' worth. Why couldn't they just let a man do his job? "Yes, General Brown?" he said politely.

"General Tainey, your standard security systems are unable to pinpoint your intruder. I suggest you deploy your low-altitude motion-detection drones."

Tainey chewed on that and responded, "General Brown, I don't think I follow you."

"Don't play games with me, General Tainey. You have four experimental drone aircraft sitting in Hangar GH457, all equipped with Ultra-High Resolution LADAR devices."

"Uh-Uh-Ultra-High Revolution what?"

The lemony voice of the strange general was like acid in the brain of the commander of the White Sands Missile Range. "General Tainey, I know the Air Force is terminating the UHR-LADARs. I know they are in the process of being redesignated Objects of Plausible Denial. I also have photographic and thermographic records of the crash sites of the two failed

UHR-LADAR drones. In my possession are complete financial records of the UHR-LADAR project. I am fully aware that the project is being scrapped and denied because of minor cost overruns and major financial bungling."

"I don't know any General Brown with the Joint Chiefs!" Tainey blurted, because it was the only response he could come up with.

"You decide how to deal with this, General Tainey. You can get those UHR-LADAR in the air right now and defend your missile range against this intruder, or face a court-martial for embezzlement and fraud."

"But I didn't!"

"You did, General."

"It's SOP!"

"Your choice, General Tainey."

General Brown hung up on him. General Tainey had a long moment of indecision. The phone bleeped in his hand and dragged him back to the here-and-now, which was the command center at White Sands Missile Range, which was where a bunch of folks were standing there waiting for him to give them some kind of orders.

"Well?" he thundered.

"No sign of any intruder yet, sir," a security officer reported.

The phone bleeped again.

"That's the President for you, General," an aide hissed.

Dammit! "Yes, Mr. President?"

"General Tainey, I understand you're deploying a sort of robotic aircraft that senses motion."

Dammit all to hell! "Yes, sir, doing it now."

"Keep the Joint Chiefs posted."

"Of course, Mr. President."

General Tainey hung up the phone and started shouting, and he didn't stop shouting for four solid hours. All the while he was thinking that this General Brown, whoever he was, sure had some connections.

20

The UHR-LADAR took motion detection images so sharp and clean they were like high-contrast, three-dimensional photographs. This required a high degree of interface with the drone control systems, and some penny-pinching in that department had resulted in an aircraft that was almost guaranteed to crash itself once in every one hundred hours of flying time.

The drones were airborne in minutes, and Dr. Smith tapped into their command data feeds, praying they would stay aloft at least a little while.

JACK FAST GOT a beep from his laptop.

"Oops. Time to go," he informed the hand of Jesus.

He tapped out a command and checked the coordinates of the airship. It was miles away, but at top speed it would be back in time to make an escape. Besides, the intercept aircraft were moving slow, like prop planes. Some sort of special surveillance craft. Yawn.

The aircraft's surface was practically sparking with voltage as it sailed across the desert, a black shadow growing bigger. It came to a stop over the long row of devices that had been collected from all over the missile range. Each one of them was a lost secret—an officially forgotten piece of technological history. Sure, some of them were old and probably useless, but every one of them was a technological mystery for Jack to explore.

Now all he had to do was get them home without blowing them to smithereens.

The airship sank to the ground atop the row of ordnance relics, and Jack cut its power. He walked up and down the framework, snapping the titanium crossbars with a pair of specialty metal snips, then folded the framework into a much narrower profile.

Six minutes gone. He had three minutes until the surveillance craft arrived.

"Could you give me a hand?" he asked the hand. "Ha! I kill me. You, too, I guess. Ha!"

Getting giddy, Jack, he told himself, and without any more screwing around he unleashed a spray of chlorine solution on the airship. The synthetic materials shriveled when it contacted the chlorine, while the ceramic-metallic threads were unaffected. The material shriveled and hardened and shriveled again, until it formed a smelly plastic mass that cocooned the ancient ordnance inside.

One minute left. Jack Fast snapped a high-tensile cable to the nose of the titanium-ribbed glob of plastic. The other end was hooked to the earth drill.

Jack jogged to the drill, tossed in the laptop and waved to the hand. "Bye, dude."

The hatch slammed and the drill became a small lightning storm that was swallowed quickly by the earth, dragging behind it the plastic-shrouded remnants of the U.S. military's greatest technological gaffes.

WHATEVER WAS on the screen, General Tainey couldn't figure it out. Neither could the operator. Neither could the Joint Chiefs.

The fallout over the drones and their highly illegal but unextraordinary obfuscation began even as the drones started falling into the desert. By daybreak, they were all as completely wrecked as the career of General Lawrence Tainey.

Only one man saw any meaning in the confused, holographic images transmitted by the dying drones, and even he had a hard time believing his eyes.

21

Mark Smith rolled in looking groggy. He was still on a light dose of pain pills, Dr. Smith knew. "Sorry for waking you, Mark. What do you make of this?"

Mark wheeled into position behind his desk and examined the rotating, three-dimensional image on his pop-up screen. It was the middle of the night and he felt muddled. "Holographic image. Flora looks like southwestern United States. By the rate of travel of the camera source I'd say it was taken by some sort of high-contrast photo recon system."

"LADAR," Smith explained, "mounted on a robot aircraft. It took these images from four to ten miles away."

"I didn't know we had anything that good."

"We don't. Not anymore," Smith said sourly. "But the real problem is what you see on the screen. I want you to tell me what you make of it. Watch."

Mark Howard was watching and trying to make sense of it, and not having luck. The scale seemed wrong. The amber thing looked like the tail section, including strange fins or motors, of a missile or rocket of some kind, but the plants were recognizable yuccas, even colored green by the software, and if the rocket section was that big compared to the yucca, it had to have come off some huge rocket....

Then he saw the human shape, digitally colored white to stand out against the amber shape. He opened the amber shape and disappeared inside. The shape started moving, which made the treads visible. Some new kind of tank? He had already assumed he was looking at one of the military testing grounds in the vicinity of El Paso and southeastern New Mexico, so a new tank would make sense there.

Shapes appeared in the air around it.

"What the hell?" Howard looked at Smith, who was determined to not give him any information. Howard was to make his own deductions, without Smith's influence, then they would compare their assessments.

Okay, so what were those jagged bars in the air around the tank, appearing instantly then fading in less than a second? If they were being electronically rendered by motion-detecting LADAR, they could only be sudden atmospheric disturbances. Their sudden appearance and dissolution meant static electricity, probably. What else could do that?

Then Howard saw the creeping, elongated mass and the cable. The test tank was towing something?

Then he saw the tank tilt and open up the earth, and go inside, dragging its cargo behind it.

"Oh, no." Mark looked up at Smith, but Smith nodded back to the screen, where Marked watched the gaping hole sit, and sit, then collapse in a plume of dust and vanish.

"What did you see?" Smith asked.

"I saw a manned earth drill towing something into the subsurface, then close the door behind it," Mark said. It was obvious, but hard to believe.

"At least we're in agreement," Smith stated. "But that means we have a big problem." He explained what had happened in the past few hours. Lost and officially forgotten military hardware had been stolen from White Sands.

"Fastbinder," Mark declared.

"The man we saw was not Fastbinder," Smith said.

"He was in an earth drill," Howard pointed out.

"But this earth drill bears no resemblance to the one disabled by Remo under the Fastbinder laboratory," Smith responded. "There are no exterior hydraulics. Remo said the back end of Fastbinder's drill was flat, but this is tapered on both ends."

"He was stealing secret military ordnance," Mark added. "That's what Fastbinder was all about. What makes you think that's not him in there?" He tapped his screen.

Smith snapped out a few commands and the image moved back several minutes and went into slow motion, then zoomed in tight on the moving man. The entire image was composed of digitally drawn triangles and polygons, but the man's face became infinitely more detailed as it filled the window, nearly to life-size.

"Just a kid. With a crew cut. This LADAR technology is amazing, Dr. Smith," Howard said.

"Yes." Smith was clearly irked by the loss of the

drones, which he explained had all fallen out of the sky during the reconnaissance flight. This amazing stealth spy technology had been trashed by corner-cutting.

"He's talking. He's happy about something."

"Yes."

"Who's he talking to? Maybe Fastbinder is inside the drill."

"That's unlikely. I had conventional spy aircraft perform a sweep of the area as soon as I knew something was happening. It's good enough to show there's no more than one human around the drill for quite some time."

"So who's he talking to?" Howard wondered.

"He's just talking to himself. Why not? The real question is, who is he? We must assume he was tied to Fastbinder in some way."

Mark Howard was trying to piece this all together and was niggled by something else. As he fiddled with the image he said, "Okay, but this is obviously a more advanced earth drill. We might assume this young man was out driving it around at the time Remo and Chiun buried Fastbinder. Why couldn't this kid have saved Fastbinder?"

Smith frowned. For some reason that hadn't occurred to him. "Of course he could have. Therefore, we must assume that is exactly what happened."

Mark Howard nodded and scanned the image along the length of the oddly shaped mass that enclosed the bulk of several odd-size bundles. Smith explained how the high-altitude spy plane showed a huge triangular black patch that maneuvered through the desert. The stealth ship had set off no security alerts at White Sands, which was another pointer to Fastbinder, who had developed a vast inventory of stolen stealth technology in his military laboratory raids. The airship had been deflated or somehow shrunken around the salvaged ordnance.

"You must admit it's ingenious," Mark said. "It's a very efficient way to take all the irregular shapes under tow. It cushions the ordnance from damage while transporting them belowground. Whatever material the airship was made of, it has to be extremely strong. It just might contain a blast if one of those bombs goes off."

"Ingenious," Smith agreed sourly.

"How many pieces of abandoned ordnance were you tracking, Dr. Smith?"

"Six," Smith said rely. "He salvaged all of them."

"But the thief took a lot more than six pieces—"

"I'm aware of that."

Mark Howard nodded and began shifting the image again. "What's this? Who's this?"

"Who is where?" Smith tapped in to the image Mark Howard was manipulating, and for a moment he experienced grave concern. Had Smith missed seeing another person in the image? That would have been a substantial lapse.

"Do you see it? Here." Howard zoomed in on the earth under the earth drill, before it had started to move.

"Fingers?" Mark posed.

"Perhaps," Smith said, sounding doubtful. They looked like a couple of exposed roots to him. But when

Mark advanced the image and rotated it, the thing protruding from the ground was undoubtedly a human hand.

"Maybe that's Fastbinder," Mark suggested.

"Maybe," Smith said, shaking his head. "There are a lot of unanswered questions here, Mark. Let's see what we can dig up."

"At least Remo and Chiun are already on the job."

Smith nodded. The irony of the situation hadn't escaped him. He hadn't believed Fastbinder could have been responsible for the killings in the depths of the nuclear waste dump, but now it seemed likely that he or his protégés were.

"Whiteslaw," Smith declared grimly. "He may be the one calling the shots if Fastbinder is out of the picture."

"I guess Remo was right. We should have been dedicating more CURE resources to tracking him down."

Smith chewed on that, and he didn't like the taste of it. He chewed on a few antacids, which didn't make the taste any better, and then told his assistant that Remo and Chiun had not yet returned from the depths of the Pit.

SARAH SLATE ASKED no questions. When the phone rang in the deep of the night and Mark Howard told her he needed to get to work, she helped him dress and wheeled him to the end of their hallway. Then she returned to Mark's room and tried to go back to sleep, distracted by the empty place beside her.

What was she getting herself into?

She was a very young woman, with more money

than she knew what to do with. The world was wide open to her, and yet she had holed up miserably in the family home, living without purpose, weighed down by her family history. It took the intrusion of not one but two Masters of Sinanju, and Mark Howard, to shake off some of the dust.

Ironic, wasn't it? She would never have known about the Sinanju if it had not been for the reckless adventuring of her family, which was exactly the irresponsible behavior she despised. If an ancestor had not once befriended a Master, and written about it in his diaries, she would never have allowed them to enter her home, expose her to danger and introduce her to Mark Howard. Even more ironic was that the danger had been of her family's construction. It had been Ironhand, the miracle of engineering created by family patriarch Archibald Slate a hundred years earlier, that had come to the Slate home just a few weeks ago to shake her down for more of Archibald's engineering developments.

So, if she had been a woman born to a normal family, she never would have been in that danger—and she never would have needed saving.

Funny thing. While the Masters had defeated Ironhand, it was Mark Howard who had sacrificed himself to protect Sarah Slate.

Was he in love with her? She didn't know. Maybe he simply had Florence Nightingale syndrome, falling in love with the woman who nursed him back to health.

Was she in love with him? Surely not. Probably not. She was attracted to him, and caring for him while he recovered from his wounds was the least she could do. But she wasn't in love. Was she?

And what if she was? Mark worked for some sort of a secret organization. The funding had to be substantial if they employed the Sinanju Masters. Mark had hinted that the organization was tiny and she would be in grave danger if she ever learned much about it. Mark was concerned that she already knew too much.

But Chiun would protect her from harm.

Chiun. She smiled in the darkness. Maybe it was Chiun she was in love with. "You're the Korean grandfather I never had," she had told him. He had been momentarily ecstatic until she explained she had been joking—she wasn't really Korean.

Chiun had her eating rice morning, noon and night. "It will keep you healthy," he told her.

"Is rice the secret to Sinanju?"

Chiun smiled, eyes shining. "Some secrets of Sinanju have been stolen, but they are never given away. Eating rice is simply common sense."

"So why do the Sinanju villagers roast pigs?" Remo had interrupted, just before Chiun dismissed him.

Then there was Remo. He didn't seem interested in her, and yet there were times when she would run into him and feel an almost overwhelming physical attraction to him, however brief.

"Oh, sorry," he said once when they met in the hall. "Still trying to figure that out."

What had he meant by that?

Sarah had heard conversations indicating that Remo

was the Reigning Master. A white American Reigning Master of Sinanju? She had sparse secondhand knowledge of Sinanju, but it still didn't seem likely. Maybe it was a joke. Chiun never behaved as if Remo was the one with the authority, that's for sure. The two bickered incessantly.

And yet there was such great love between them, like the strongest bond between any father and a son. Sarah would never forget the sorrow in the old man's eyes when he thought Remo was gone forever. Nor would she forget the joy she saw when Chiun knew Remo was on the road to recovery.

Just remembering it made her smile as she drifted off to sleep again, in Mark Howard's private suite, deep in an isolated wing of Folcroft Sanitarium. Her last thought was of Chiun. When would he return?

22

"Cheer up," Remo told the albino. "A little crushed dignity never hurt anyone."

The albino flinched and squatted, groveling with pitiful mews and grunts. "Oh no, you don't. Get up. Come on. Go home. Go."

The albino whimpered.

"Don't make me bring out my finger again, Whitey," Remo warned, holding out his hand as if to flick the albino's ear. The creature squeaked and fled down the corridor. Remo and Chiun followed.

"He thinks he still has ears." Remo grinned. "Wonder what he thought he was eating for dinner."

"Enough," Chiun said. "I prefer not to remember it, thank you." Remo had subdued the murderous albino by snapping his ears repeatedly until the confused creature was too terrified and exhausted to fight anymore. By then his ears had been flicked away in tiny chunks of flesh. The albino wasn't so beaten that he didn't sniff them out and pop them in his mouth as he was herded away from the grotto. Hours later, the albino was nearly dead, and Remo knew he'd pass out on his feet from exhaustion before long.

"Might as well sleep," Remo decided. "Who knows how much farther we'll have to go."

They found an ideal spot soon enough, with a wide, shallow lake being fed by cool and thermal springs. The albino fell panting on the warm stone floor. Remo waded into the water up to his waist, waited a minute, then snatched up a couple of eyeless fish.

"Cousins of yours, Whitey?" Remo asked. The fish were albinos, too, just as colorless as their captive, who sniffed at the fish smell and began salivating.

"This must be a rare delicacy among you No-Seeing Friend-Eaters," Remo said, tossing the first gasping fish into the air and snicking at it with economical hand movements. His one extended fingernail made quick work of the fish, severing the head and tail, slicing it up the middle, scooping out the insides, and depositing a neatly butterflied pair of fillets in his hand.

The cast-off parts landed inches from the albino's face and he devoured them in seconds.

"I may be fast, but you, my friend, are *fast*," Remo said, as he performed the operation again on the second fish.

"You failed to remove the skin," Chiun sniffed.

"I failed on purpose." Remo walked on the slippery boulders to the steaming hole that fed hot spring water into the lake. It was amazingly clean, with just a touch of sulfur smell. He quickly stuck the folded fillets inside on a natural rock shelf, waited a few minutes and snatched them out again.

"Steamed and clean," he announced. "Now the skin comes off and you've a nice fish with only a trace of stinky stuff in it." He deposited a cooked fish on a boulder near Chiun, who sniffed it, shrugged and ate the steaming morsels with his neat fingers.

"Not bad, eh?"

"It is acceptable," Chiun admitted.

"It's a trash fish pulled out of a cave pond and cooked in a hot spring. I say, all things considered, it's not bad."

"Palatable," Chiun allowed.

"Whatever."

Chiun awoke three hours later, when the smell reached him. Remo sat up soon afterward.

"More Whiteys are coming."

"Many more this time," Chiun said.

Remo considered it. Whitey was still sleeping, but soon the smell of his own people would doubtless wake him, too. Remo looked down the lake cavern, where a single corridor continued. That's where the albinos would come from.

"Hey, Little Father, come on."

Chiun looked at him suspiciously.

"Come on, Chiun, I have an idea."

"Never a good thing."

"Fine." Remo slipped away on his own to the opposite side of the cavern, and he took the flashlight with him. His feet found the natural pressure of the lake surface, and he ran over the top of the lake. He was halfway across when he heard the near-silent slapping of Chiun's sandaled feet alongside him.

They perched on the tumble of boulders against the far wall and waited. The flashlight's jaundiced glow began sputtering, then faded to darkness.

"Time for more glow sticks," Remo said, withdrawing one and cracking it carefully. The chemicals didn't mix completely and the glow it gave was dim. "Maybe it will last longer this way."

Chiun looked uneasy.

The glow was enough for them to watch the scene on the rocky ledge that was the far shore of the lake. First Whitey was aroused by the smell of his people approaching, then he sniffed around for his captors. When he couldn't find them he began crowing.

"He's a happy rooster."

"Not for long," Chiun said.

The albino, his head filthy with dried blood, looked as if he'd come to the same conclusion and scampered into a high rockfall, wedging himself in an alcove. Minutes later the albinos started pouring from the corridor and gathered at the base of the rockfall, yelping like dogs. They were stamped from the same filthy mold as Whitey: albinos with pasty flesh and eyes that had fused shut from disuse. Their hair and beards were all white beneath a lifetime of mud and slime. There were women in this group, with breasts and no beards, but still plenty hairy.

Remo listened for words in the racket, and he was finally rewarded.

"Come down," someone growled.

Whitely barked a response that was wordless, but plain enough to understand. "No way."

The mob became angry and agitated, until the one who spoke said sternly, "Shut up."

The mob shut up.

"Where are your others?" grunted the speaker. He stood straighter, which made him look taller.

Whitey whined and growled.

"Killed by Bright Light men?"

Whitey confirmed that with a mutter.

"We will go and eat them." The talker grunted an order, and the entire naked army marched out of the cavern.

"Well, we didn't learn a heck of a lot," Remo said when the albinos were gone. "So much for Operation Sit on a Rock and See What Happens."

"We learned that some of them have more developed language," Chiun said.

Remo shrugged. They already knew that. But the leader of the albino pack seemed to have a lot more to say than Whitey did.

Whitey crept out of his hole and descended cautiously, senses tuned for the return of his hungry fellow albinos. What he heard was a sound so alien he didn't recognize it, but he could tell the staccato splashes were coming at him fast.

"It's just us, Whitey," Remo said, catching the albino by his greasy hair before he could bolt back into the rocks.

"You do not intend for him to lead us farther down?" Chiun said. "We have light enough for the return trip only."

"We haven't learned anything, Chiun. We gotta find out what the deal is with these cave people."

"And what if we are still many days' journey from the dwelling place of these cave people?"

"We won't know that until we get there."

"Meanwhile, you will allow the army of cave people to enter the mines and kill the nuclear wasters?"

Remo considered that. "They did say something about a big lunch. I guess we ought to stop it from happening. You're off the hook, Whitey." Remo released the albino, who immediately crept back into the rocks. "Let's go."

Chiun said nothing as they started back the way they had come, their eyes finding more than adequate light in the green glow of the stick. Remo thought he knew the real reason Chiun was insisting on their return. Chiun was fearful that running out of light, being in utter blackness, would send Remo into a relapse of his episode in the car.

"Hey, Chiun, I think we'd do pretty well down here without lights. Better than the cavemen."

"Undoubtedly."

"Wanna try it?"

"The cavemen are not completely blind, Remo."

"Yeah, I noticed the talkative one said something about the Bright Light men. I bet their eyelids just grew over from lack of use. But shine a bright light on them and they'll see it through that pasty skin of theirs."

"I believe so."

"But who are these people, anyway? They must have been down here for generations, right? So where'd they come from? Why do they speak English? What's got them all ticked off at us surface dwellers all of a sudden?"

"I have none of these answers. Perhaps the talker in the group will be persuaded to answer your questions when we overtake them."

Remo didn't think so. The albino had barely used complete sentences and he talked as though he had gravel in his cheeks.

23

"Nice to see ya again," Remo said to the guard at the desk at the Intersection.

The guard had his feet on the desk and was leaning back on the back legs of the chair, but Remo's appearance sent him tumbling to the floor, shouting out a profanity that was cut off with the heavy clonk of his skull hitting the rock floor.

"You have a way with people," Chiun observed.

They walked into the outer perimeter of the work areas at the Pit. The control operator at the silent shipping dock was almost as surprised at the guard, but jumped to his feet instead of landing on his head.

"Is Wools around?"

"I'll call him. Stay right here."

"No, thank you. You'd better call the medic, too. Your guard at the Intersection just gave himself a concussion."

"Wait, where are you going? You can't just walk around down here!"

They walked, and weren't surprised when the red lights began flashing in their wall fixtures and the alarm started blurting raucously.

HAL WOOLS COULDN'T BELIEVE how his luck was flip-flopping. First the NRC weirdoes show up, getting nosy, then they go for a little exploring into the Pit of No Return. Then, more than a day later, just when he's starting to breathe easily, the sons of bitches return.

Well, they were still in *his* mine shaft. Wools was the king of the Pit, and nobody left the Pit without Wools's say-so, especially if they threatened the future of this facility. Everybody down here agreed with him on the need to protect the facility, as scared as they might be of whatever was making people vanish. After all, they were all going to be millionaires when this thing became fully operational.

"They're heading for the elevators," reported one of his staff on the walkie-talkie.

"Get security there in force. Do not let them board the elevator. Repeat, *do not let them board.*"

Wools ran for the elevators himself.

"OH GOOD, it's here already. I hate waiting for the elevator." Remo nodded to the point man of the ranks who had taken up a position between the Masters of Sinanju and the elevator. "Nice of you all to see us off."

"We can't let you board the elevator, sir."

"Sure, you can."

"I ordered them not to," Wools panted as he arrived, winded from jogging.

"Hiya, Hal. I'd come with us if I were you. You're

not safe down here. The same folks that killed the guards and took the other MIAs are coming back soon."

"What are you talking about?" Hal didn't sound as if he really wanted to know.

"Listen, Hal, and all of Hal's friends within the sound of my voice. The truth is that there is an access way through Shaft C. Some very bad people are lurking around down there, killing some of you, taking others." Remo had decided against revealing that the killers actually lived inside the earth.

"Liar!" Wools growled.

"In the last day we saw no less than two teams of attackers on their way to the Pit. The first team was just six guys, but the second team was almost thirty. We disabled both the teams, but there could be more right behind them."

"Preposterous!" Wools tried to laugh as if Remo were telling a grand joke. "You're spreading lies!"

"I'm giving these people the chance to save themselves," Remo responded. "I'm taking that elevator to the surface right now—I'd advise the rest of you to follow me."

Wools's face darkened. "I can't let you go." He turned to his forces. "Arrest them."

The security forces moved in on Remo and Chiun, only to find Remo and Chiun everywhere else but where they had been. The pair moved through the ranks like slippery shadows, grabbing guns. In seconds the armed guards were no longer armed.

"We'll just take these with us," Remo said, dropping the pile of automatic rifles on the floor of the elevator. "Wouldn't want you shooting at us when we're on our way up."

"Stop them!" Wools shouted, and his men descended on the elevator as the gate shut. Two of them blocked the gate bodily. Remo spun them like tops, their arms flying out uncontrollably and slapping the other armed men before they collapsed, dazed. The gate on the elevator slammed shut.

"Bye, now."

"Get them," Wools shouted.

Probing fingers reached through the gate and attempted to reach the emergency stop button, but Chiun snicked at them with his razor-sharp Nails of Eternity. The fingers plopped to the floor of the elevator and their former owners retreated, trying to hold their blood in.

"We'll send back the guns and the fingers when we get off," Remo said. "You'll need them both when the cavemen get here."

"Please. Come back. We can talk." Wools could still be heard pleading with them when they reached the elevator's upper platform and switched to the next lift.

"What a drag it is just getting in and out of here," Remo complained on the fourth elevator. "Little Father, you don't have any desire to live in a cave, do you?"

"Of course not. I desire to live in a splendid vintage caravan."

"Oh. Still on that kick, huh?"

"It is not a 'kick.'"

"'Course not."

Chiun pulled his iBlogger out of his sleeve.

"Holy crap, you've been carrying that thing all this time? It can't get a signal down here, can it?"

"Alas, it does not," Chiun admitted, fiddling with the thing briefly. "I had hoped, however."

Chiun tried the device repeatedly as they came closer to the surface, but he didn't get reception until they were aboveground and inside the metal building. He gave a cry of delight and let Remo handle the security staff that was waiting for them. Wools had phoned ahead.

Remo thought it was just as well that Chiun was preoccupied. These guys were just hired muscle and didn't necessarily deserve death because they worked for the wrong company and got in the way of the wrong elderly Korean. Remo simply snatched the rifles from the three men, bent the barrels into horseshoes and handed the weapons back to their owners.

"You're welcome," he said.

A pair of state troopers loitered around their rental Hyundai in the parking lot. "Is there an Embassy Suites in the area?" Remo asked.

"You're not going anywhere, son, until you have a talk with our friend Mr. Wools," the veteran trooper said, withdrawing his handgun from its holster. "Assume the position."

"Jeez, Dad, that's a tempting offer, but no thanks." He stepped up close and put the barrel of the gun into the trooper's mouth, then forced the man's finger onto the trigger.

"Back off, scumbag!" shouted the second trooper, a rookie who was fumbling for his own weapon. Chiun, never taking his eyes off his iBlogger, elbowed the rookie, who was destined to spend the next fifteen minutes writhing on the gravel, hacking up breakfast and holding on to his bruised abdomen.

"You shareholders in Mr. Wools's little projects?" Remo asked the trooper who gagged on his own handgun. The trooper nodded, teeth clacking against the barrel.

"Now, I asked you another question…" He extracted the gun.

"No Embassy Suites for a hundred miles," the trooper blurted.

"Hmm. Courtyards? Hiltons? Sheratons? Hyatts? You got a Holiday Inn around here, even?"

"There's a Motel 6, nine miles up the road."

Remo tossed the handgun over his shoulder. The trooper watched, dismayed, as his weapon became a tiny black speck that plunged out of sight on the far side of the metal mine building.

"When we have the caravan, finding a hotel will no longer be a problem," Chiun lectured as they drove off in the Hyundai.

"We'll have to find campgrounds instead."

"We'll need only a Wal-Mart, the store that allows campers to park overnight on their lots free of charge."

"That'll be convenient if you run low on kimonos."

"REMO, THANK GOODNESS. Where have you been for the past twenty-six hours?" Smith's voice was extra lemony this afternoon.

"Don't even start, Smitty. We were spelunking with albino cannibals. Chiun will back me up on that. Won't you, Little Father?"

Chiun waved over his shoulder dismissively. He was sitting on the floor in front of the television—which was dark. The Korean master was intently poring over the latest entries on his iBlogger.

Mark Howard was also on the line and it was he who provided the obligatory echo. "Albino cannibals?"

"Yes."

"Any sign of Fastbinder?" Smith asked.

"No. You were right about him."

"I was wrong. Fastbinder almost certainly has something to do with the attacks at the waste site."

"What? He survived?"

"Fastbinder or one of his comrades." Smith briefed Remo on the activities of the earth drill at the White Sands test range.

"I guess the odds of somebody totally unrelated to Fastbinder showing up with an earth drill a few weeks later is pretty slim," Remo said. "You sure it was a new earth drill?"

"Absolutely," Mark Howard said. "Totally different profile. It used some sort of electrical discharge to tunnel into the earth. The earth drill you saw operated mechanically."

Remo was relieved. When he broke something, he liked it to stay broken. It was a self-confidence thing. "So where'd they come from?"

"Unknown," Smith said. "We can assume they were based outside the Fastbinder home adjacent to his Museum of Mechanical Marvels, or were simply absent when you and Chiun paid your call."

"Coleslaw's behind it," Remo declared.

Smith made a sour *humph* sound. "Senator Whiteslaw is likely involved in some way with the new Fastbinder threat, although not active in the field. Remo, I'll be the first to say your instincts were on target about Whiteslaw. CURE should have given him a higher priority."

"CURE *did* give him higher priority. I'm a part of CURE, remember? It was you who downplayed it, Smitty."

"Very gracious, dimwit," said a quiet, high-pitched voice from the direction of the television.

"Please give me a full report on your activities at the waste site," Smith said.

Remo complied, keeping his smart remarks to a minimum and feeling like a jerk. When he was done, Smith and Howard could be heard snapping at their keyboards like dueling pianists. Remo wondered if they had touch-typing races on slow days.

"You gave us a lot to chew on," Howard remarked. "Do you have any idea where these albinos originated? Who they are, how long they've been down, anything?"

"I've told you everything."

"Remo, were their eyelids actually grown together, or were they simply naturally closed?" Smith asked.

"Uh, grown together. Why?"

"That indicates these people have spent more than a generation belowground. That, and their lack of oratory skills. It's as if they're reverting to an animal state."

"You have an idea why they'd go subterranean in the first place?"

Mark Howard spoke up. "Centuries ago, people with extreme photosensitivity would live in caves—those with extreme cases can be burned even by UV radiation from diffused sunlight. A family group sharing the condition might have sought the safety of an underground existence, especially in the Southwest, with intense sunlight and vast cavern systems."

Dr. Smith, the man with so little imagination he had amazed CIA psychiatrists, cleared his throat thoughtfully. Remo knew he disliked stepping into the realm of the unknown, but he also hated to leave any mystery unclassified.

"It sounds plausible, Smitty. Go with it. Junior's theory also accounts for their drained brains. If it was a family of pioneers that went belowground in the good old Wild West days and started interbreeding, you'll end up with lots of stupid people today."

"It would also account for the irregular state of their degeneration," Howard added. "Some folks have more bad chromosomes than others—there hasn't been enough time for the badness to become consistent throughout the population. That gives you Talkers and Grunters."

Smith ahemed. "Mark, please research this. Maybe we can estimate the size of a family group likely to share this photosensitivity, and from there the size of the group that originally went belowground. We'll then extrapolate an expected range of chromosomal degradation through incestual reproduction."

"I love it when you talk dirty, Smitty," Remo said. "But why do you care about all this stuff?"

"It may tell us the size of the albino population, even point us to historic records. We need to know what to expect if and when they attack again."

"You are going to close the waste site, right?" Remo bristled. "It's bad news."

"Nobody is going to be happy about closing that waste site, including the federal government, but it will obviously need to be shut down. That will take time. We'll order an evacuation at once."

"Chiun and I should go back in there with lots of batteries so we can ferret out Caveman City."

"They're only a part of the real problem—and the real problem is Fastbinder or whoever is using his technology. Our next step is to identify the young man who was responsible for stealing the abandoned ordnance from White Sands," Smith said. "This might not be possible if the boy is as young as he looks. He may not have any digital photographic record. We'd like you and Chiun to investigate the spot where the earth drill surfaced. We think there's an undiscovered body at the scene."

"Why undiscovered? Bodies usually make themselves known."

"It was partially buried when the earth drill emerged—that's when we spotted it—and after the earth drill made its escape there was no sign of it. The cadaver may have been obliterated."

"And now what's left has been ripening in the sun for a day. Sounds like pleasant work." Remo had to agree that Fastbinder was more important than the albino army, however they figured in. "And Whiteslaw?"

"He's now at the top of our priority list," Smith declared. "He'll be able to provide us with intelligence on all of this. Who's behind it, how many of them, what they're actually trying to accomplish."

Remo laughed grimly. "What they want is the same thing as always. To corner the market on secret military technology."

Remo felt a dark cloud hanging over him when he hung up. Chiun was watching him, the iBlogger now sitting dark on the table.

"What?"

"Remo, you will now listen to what the Master Emeritus says to you."

"I always do. Okay, go ahead."

"No."

"Okay. Shoot."

"I would go to White Sands alone. This is the work of Fastbinder, or those who possess Fastbinder's machinations. Those machinations could be deadly to you."

"To both of us," Remo insisted. "Remember Barkely, California? I lasted longer than you did when those nutcases hit us with those proton death rays."

"My son, you are now in an unstable state. I fear the memory of your time beyond the Void—"

"Stop, Chiun. I don't want to go there."

"Remo, listen to yourself if not to your father in spirit. You fear even to summon the memory lest it bring on a relapse. What would happen if you were to experience the actual thing yet again?"

The veins were standing out on Remo's freakishly thick wrists. He was pacing now, clenching his fists and grinding his teeth. Chiun's eyes grew hollow as he watched his protégé fight the inevitable memory. He heard Remo's pulse race, then plummet, then race again. The skin of the Reigning Master flooded with hot blood, then the circulation sank deep into the extremities and he became cold.

Remo did all this consciously, engaged in hard battle with his own mind, and Chiun didn't dare distract him further. Or should he? Would it be better for Remo to face this memory now? Surely he would have to do so eventually.

For good or evil, Chiun couldn't be the one to do it. He carried his own fresh scars of guilt for bringing that harm upon the one he loved best in all the world. If the Slate child had not been there to insinuate herself, Remo might never have returned to the world of consciousness.

Remo's internal discord finally waned, and he came to sit on his own mat on the floor, facing Chiun.

"You're right about one thing. I am afraid, Little Father."

Chiun nodded.

"Being afraid means I can't allow you to face this alone, because then you'd be at greater risk of facing what I'm afraid of." Remo's explanation puzzled himself. He tried again. "A mother jaguar who is traumatized of the water will still go with her cubs into the river, to protect them from drowning."

"Now I am an infant cat?" Chiun asked, trying to sound indignant, but his heart wasn't in it.

"You see what I mean." Remo insisted.

"I see," Chiun admitted.

24

The airfield was dark except for the tiny jet waiting for them. Remo thought the thing looked like a steel mosquito, but it got them into Alamogordo in a big hurry. Another rental car took them to a BP truck stop near the missile test range, and from there they went on foot. Almost exactly twenty-four hours after the earth drill left the scene, Remo and Chiun arrived at the place. They bypassed the five-point guard perimeter. The final protective barrier was a web of pressure-sensitive wires buried to form an electronic moat almost twenty feet wide. The wires would trigger an alarm if any creature heavier than a desert hare crossed it, so Remo and Chiun thought like desert hares and skimmed over the sand. The alarm never noticed them.

They found the place littered with fluorescent yellow tape and tags. The Air Force forensic team had found out nothing from their investigation of the site, but they sure were making a good show of it.

"I didn't know you actually wrote your own blogs, Chiun."

"I do not, and now seems an odd time to bring it up."

"I thought you were sending a message before. Just before we parked the car."

"I was just reading the latest entry from a lascivious woman in Montana."

"Oh." Remo sniffed. "Smith was right about a body. Let's see if it's anybody we know."

SARAH SLATE WOKE UP early and was surprised to find a blog appearing on the laptop Mark had provided her. It had been directed to her from Chiun, but she had never known him to record his own entries, only to read others'. Then she realized it had secure status— it was for her eyes only.

She smiled. Maybe a love poem?

But there was just one word, meaningless, but somehow it disturbed her.

The entry was simply "Song."

"I DON'T KNOW HIM. Do you know him?" Remo asked.

"Of course not," Chiun said nasally. They had both ceased to breathe near the stench of the corpse, that of a middle-aged, underfed man with a dark complexion. His head and one reaching arm were all that had survived mutilation.

"You know this guy, Junior?" Remo asked. He was holding a phone with a built-in camera, which he had reluctantly agreed to carry to the scene.

"Yeah, he's this guy I work with," Mark Howard replied sarcastically. "Look at the display."

Remo glanced at the three-inch screen and found his own face on it.

"This thing's broken, Junior."

"Is it possible you were simply pointing the wrong part?"

Remo had to admit it was possible. He turned over the phone and clicked the green button until the face of the dead man showed up on the screen.

"How's that?"

"Great, Remo."

"What's wrong now?"

"Nothing. I wasn't being sarcastic. It's a perfect image."

"Oh."

"I've already got an ID. Jesus Merienez. He's got a INS record twelve feet long. He's an alien smuggler, dope smuggler, you name it. He's made a career of illegally entering the U.S. from Mexico."

"So he's camping here to stay off I-10 and gets squished by the earth drill?"

"Looks like it. We'll get better results after a more thorough search, but so far he's strictly minor-league compared to Fastbinder."

They combed the site, looking for clues the Air Force team might have missed, but found nothing until they approached the crater of loose earth where the earth drill submerged. The crater was surrounded with yellow plastic tape, and there were no footprints on the sands. Remo walked away from it over the path the earth drill might have taken. At twenty paces he stamped his foot hard and felt the vibrations. He walked another twenty paces and stamped again. It felt different.

"Only the entrance to the tunnel was sealed off," Remo observed. "There's still hollow space down there."

"What did you just do?" Mark Howard demanded on the telephone.

Remo knew he shouldn't have agreed to bring the camera. He hated being micromanaged, but his curiosity was piqued. "I dunno. What did I do?"

"The security on the site was just triggered by the seismographic monitors. Did you push over something big?"

Remo explained his foot stamping. "If you want us to go exploring down there, you had better acquisition a bunch of convicts with shovels. I guarantee you Chiun won't help dig out a hundred feet of loose dirt."

"Remo, forget it and get out of there. The Air Force guard detail is moving in on you."

They slipped past the converging guards, who saw nothing and no one until they crossed the perimeter of the dig site and found the swollen corpse of Jesus Merienez. It was quite obvious that the dead man had exhumed himself. What other possible explanation was there?

25

If you're visiting Topeka and have a craving for sauerbraten, you're in luck. Alten Haus on Piedmont Avenue is world-famous for serving the best sauerbraten outside of Germany, and the chef responsible is—was—Heinrich von Essen, who began learning to cook when he was just tall enough to reach his mother's plump knees. When he emigrated to the United States he brought her recipes with him and became the famous Sultan of Sauerbraten. He was credited with single-handedly jump-starting the first American sauerbraten craze of the twenty-first century.

Von Essen's salary climbed with every new restaurant he defected to, until he found himself in the unlikely metropolis of Topeka, where a wealthy restaurateur was determined to establish the premier German eatery in Kansas. He succeeded.

Alten Haus was booked months in advance. Heinrich von Essen was getting a salary plus a percentage, and he never dreamed he could be so rich. He was on top of the world.

But not for long.

The rear doors flew open and slammed into a garbage can and the cleanup staff started shouting. A sleepy Heinrich von Essen looked up from the legal pad, on which he was jotting down needed supplies. Another five minutes and he would have been on his way home to bed.

His desk was in a private end of the kitchen, and he couldn't see the cause of the commotion, but he could hear the terror in the voices of his staffers. Then, to his horror, he saw blood splatter across the far end of the kitchen.

Somebody had just been murdered.

Von Essen got to his feet and ran, but someone stomped after him. He didn't get halfway through the dining room before a tremendous blow cracked the back of his head. He was semiconscious when he saw his attacker.

The deathly pale creature had no eyes. Its face was smeared with blood, which came from the joint of flesh it was feeding on. The joint was a human shin and foot, with a bloody black sock still on it. It was one of von Essen's kitchen staff.

He thankfully passed out before he saw any more.

When he awoke, he was being dragged across wet grass by his collar. There were hordes of pale humans converging and bringing other captives. Von Essen saw a sign for Paradise Caverns, which rang a bell as a local tourist attraction.

None of it made sense. What was happening?

The blind captors dragged von Essen and the other prisoners through the shattered doors of the ticket building and entrance to the caverns. They crowded into the cave entrance, at the back of the building, and von Essen glimpsed the starry sky one last time through the distant doors before the earth swallowed him up.

They plodded along the paved tour walkways and reached a splashing waterfall. The dim security lights showed von Essen his horrible fate. One after another the blind men plunged into the water, dragging their prisoners behind them. Von Essen didn't have the strength to struggle.

He was dragged under the water, and the light showed him that the crowd of blind men were pushing and shoving one another as they forced their way through a tiny gash under a rock ledge. One by one the blind men and their prisoners wriggled through it. Von Essen's lungs were already exploding, and he became lost in the chaos as he was shoved and kicked through the small hole. Just when he thought his life was over, his head broke the surface. He choked and heaved and breathed, and was dragged under the water again.

It seemed like hours before they were out of the water, then he was set on his feet and commanded, with a push, to walk. His leather Oxfords didn't work out well on the slippery rocks. His impatient captors dragged them off his feet.

His body was an ocean of pain and exhaustion. He no longer cared what was happening or why; he simply prayed that it would be over soon. He didn't know that his journey had only just begun.

NOBODY SERVICED Nishitsus like McGarrity Nishitsu in
Apache Flats, Missouri. Mr. McGarrity had commercials made especially for airing overnights. "It's
2:00 a.m. and your Nishitsu needs a tune-up—where
do you go? McGarrity Nishitsu! I'm Mike McGarrity,
and I'm here to give you my solemn promise—nobody services Nishitsus like McGarrity, twenty-four
hours a day!"

For a chronic insomniac like Jon Usumi, working
overnights wasn't so bad. Sometimes it was a drag
when the second shift left him their unfinished work,
but mostly you got easy jobs from other insomniacs.
Oil changes, tune-ups, fix a belt, test an electrical system. But every once in a while some oddball would roll
in with a really strange job, and wouldn't you know it
always happened when Jon was on the shift all alone.

Some sort of a sound caught his attention, and he
dragged his head out from under the hood of the 2003
Nishitsu Grasshopper. The Grasshopper was the latest attempt by the Japanese home office to cash in on the
economy SUV market. The Grasshopper's fuel pump
was so flawed it could cause a fire when the vehicle
wasn't even running, and Jon could replace one without
looking. He squinted at the open garage entrance as he
worked.

There were people out there, but they were staying
in the darkness of the lot. The inside of the repair
garage was ablaze with bright light.

"Hello?" Jon called.

He heard growling.

"Who's there?"

A man came out of the darkness wearing sunglasses—and nothing else. He was a hairy, filthy creature with flesh as white as death. He had an armful of rocks, which he dumped on the spotless floor of a repair bay. Then he started throwing them at the lights.

"Hey! Stop that."

His aim was good. The second rock shattered an overhead lamp.

"Hey, asshole, what do you think you're doing?" Jon grabbed his cell phone, which elicited excited grunts from the group still outside in the darkness. The one with the sunglasses sent his next rock flying at Jon. It slammed into his rib cage with bone-crushing force, and the phone clattered across the floor.

Jon crawled for the phone as he heard more lights being taken out by the rock thrower. The garage grew darker. The people outside became more excited. How many were there? Who were they? *What* were they?

Another rock sailed out of nowhere and knocked the phone away just as Jon reached for it again. The pain from the broken ribs was blinding, but it would be a lot worse after he'd been forced to march for forty-eight hours.

As the repair bays grew darker, the creatures outside entered and helped with the rock throwing until every bulb was shattered and only the Exit signs illuminated the place. Jon never did reach the phone.

They were albinos, all of them, just like the one in the sunglasses, and they were all as filthy. Jon might not have been so quick to judge them if he'd known he'd be just as dirty soon enough.

The albinos started grabbing toolboxes and equipment, and Jon noticed they were looking at their hands. As he struggled to sit up, he glimpsed one of the hands and saw a permanent marker drawing of a ratchet wrench toolbox. The albino grunted over the hand and searched until he found the toolbox, which he poked experimentally, then grabbed. Other albinos took tools of every description, and several went behind the parts counter, stuffing auto parts into sacks.

They'll take what they want, then leave, Jon thought optimistically. But one of the albinos had to have had Jon's picture on his hand. The albino grinned and reached for him.

"Don't! Please!" Jon Usumi tried to run and found himself locked in the arms of the ugliest, biggest brute in the entire group. Jon shouted and struggled. The brute growled at him. Jon kept shouting until he found himself hanging by his ankles. The brute pounded Jon's head on the once immaculate garage floor.

He had to pound Jon three times to make him shut up.

DEPARTMENT OF HOMELAND Security Special Agent Charlie Roca didn't trust what the system was telling him.

"Can't fucking be."

"You want me to play it again?" cried the system operator.

"Yes."

"Fine." The operator played the video, which was now forty-five seconds old.

The monitor showed the main compartment of Emergency Federal Command Authority Station #5. The nuke-proof bunker was deep underground, right below Roca's feet and protected by eighteen layers of structural and radiation shielding. There was just one way in or out, and that door was bolted shut.

But somebody had just made another entrance. The video clearly showed the wall of the command authority station blasting open. The figures on the bunks— eighteen of the finest bureaucrats in the U.S. government—scrambled out of bed as something big penetrated the interior of the station, filling the room with flashing light that fried the camera and turned the screen black.

"Jesus." Roca snapped at the communications officer, "did you reach them?"

"No answer!"

"Dammit!" He grabbed the phone that put him in direct contact with the director of homeland security, and at that moment the power went out.

"How could this happen?" he demanded. The station was equipped with more redundant systems than he could keep track of.

"They must have cut the umbilical to the station!" the operator gasped.

"What? How?"

The ground started shaking.

"Now what?" Roca demanded.

"Oh, shit!" The operator stared at the floor of the

control and command center, horrified, and then he ran for the door. Of course he couldn't open it. They were sealed in—for their own protection.

When the ground yawned open and fried the command center with dust and scythes of static electricity, they had nowhere to run.

FOUR MAINFRAME COMPUTERS were nestled deep in the basement of Folcroft Sanitarium.

Other hospitals possessed mainframe computers—mostly relics of the 1970s, when a big organization needed big hardware to organize itself electronically. Mainframes such as that had since been replaced with smaller boxes that could do much more—sometimes the central boxes disappeared entirely in favor of a network of computing power.

Supercomputers continued being built, and they were used to crunch data points by the trillions. The military used computers like that to electronically organize and stage its resources—every soldier, every tank, every roll of toilet paper—and to create scenarios that used those resources. Meteorological research around the world used these computers to look for patterns in weather based on millions of concurrent measurements of temperature, wind speed, air pressure and geographical factors.

The supercomputers below the sanitarium, the Folcroft Four, were not in the service of Folcroft Sanitarium. They served CURE. They routinely, automatically hacked into government systems around the world. Harold Smith's programming skills had made them into a data-gathering powerhouse that the Pentagon could only dream of. Mark Howard had come in with some knowledge of evolutionary programming—he was teaching the Four how to identify patterns, however disconnected the data making up the patterns, and to initiate searches based on these digitally identified hunches. New chips and new storage drives were being added routinely to the system, to keep them current with the best technology.

The Folcroft Four identified a curious pattern at fourteen minutes and nine seconds after two in the morning and, thanks to Mark Howard's programming, wasted three seconds looking for a match between the name "Jacob Fastbinder" and various name databases in North Carolina. There was no significant match. Another curious pattern was identified, and the name search expanded across the United States and around the world. Other Jacob Fastbinders were found, analyzed and discarded as being unrelated to the Jacob Fastbinder in question.

With the odds calculated against success as being borderline, the next identified pattern was almost too far-fetched for the Four to pursue, but their latest upgrade had nearly doubled their processing power and the Four calculated they had 0.156 unallocated seconds of processing time to spare during this quarter minute, so they went on a wild-goose chase. They hit pay dirt.

The Folcroft Four were not pleased or proud of their accomplishment. They were only machines, after all. They just sent the results Upstairs and kept looking for more patterns, however oddball.

THE PRESIDENT PICKED UP on the first ring. "Smith, do you have any idea what's going on here? I've got people disappearing across the country! Mass kidnappings in Topeka, Tucumcari and Jefferson City! I never even heard of Jefferson City!"

"Yes, Mr. President. And Fort Worth."

"I didn't know anything about Fort Worth!" the President exploded.

"One of the new emergency federal command authority stations belonging to the Department of Homeland Security."

"Mother of God, they're supposed to be impenetrable. The director's going to get his butt bounced out of the District of Columbia if he doesn't have a good explanation."

"I'm sure he's still trying to get information himself. The station went off-line abruptly."

"That's not supposed to happen—"

"Mr. President, I believe this is the work of people who were once in league with Jacob Fastbinder. A subterranean transport is being used, one that is far more capable than the one CURE disabled in New Mexico. That would explain the penetration of the DOHS station."

"I thought Fastbinder was dead," the President said. "You told me you killed him."

"Fastbinder may be dead, unless he was rescued by the new earth drill. We never suspected its existence. Senator Herbert Whiteslaw is probably involved."

"Who else?" the President demanded. "Whiteslaw's a talker, not a doer. There has to be somebody else behind all this madness."

"There is, sir," Dr. Harold Smith said, gazing at the photograph blown up on his computer screen. It was a pilot's license photo of a blond young man with an easy grin.

"We learned a moment ago, Mr. President, that Jacob Fastbinder had a son."

26

"Fastbinder was somebody's *dad?*" Remo demanded.

"Even he didn't know about it until a couple years ago," Howard explained. "The Folcroft Four had a hell of a time making a match on the face from the White Sands video, then a couple of minutes ago, bingo. His name is Jack Fast, born seventeen years ago to a real estate agent whose name appears on a lot of the title transfer documents from the startup of the Fastbinder U.S. division. The kid never had contact with his father until Fastbinder moved to New Mexico permanently. Looks like the kid showed up on his doorstep. Fastbinder had a DNA test done the same week, and the lab results show the kid is his. The mom named the kid Jack Fast."

"Why do we care about a snot-nosed teenager, even if he is Fastbinder's snot-nosed teenager?" Remo asked. "What harm could he do?"

"This kid could do plenty," Howard said. "His profile is almost unbelievable. He's some sort of child prodigy. He was in the local papers for building his own mainframe when he was eight years old. He staged all kinds of elaborate practical jokes on the locals. He flew a flying saucer over the town, he put a fake sea monster in a local retention pond. He had a pilot's license when he was eleven, hacked into the New Mexico secretary of state's office when he was twelve. When he got his driver's license he built systems for hacking into his hometown's traffic signal system in real time and adjusted traffic patterns to suit himself."

"You mean, so he always got the green? Man, he could market that thing and be richer than Ron Popiel," Remo said. "So Fast is a chip off the old block."

"He's more than a chip. Jacob Fastbinder didn't accomplish in his whole lifetime what this kid's done since puberty," Mark Howard said. "You want to know who could build an earth drill that's better and faster than Jacob Fastbinder's? The answer is Jack Fast."

"Okay, so what's this smart-assed pizza face up to? Stealing the weapons from White Sands I understand. The whole thing with the albino cavemen doesn't make sense."

"Well, that's the real reason we called you. The situation with Fast and the Cavemen has exploded since we last talked."

Remo and Chiun, sitting in the rental in the BP truck stop, exchanged looks. "Junior, we last talked ten minutes ago. How much could happen in ten minutes?"

"Just wait'll you hear how much. Dr. Smith is getting off the line with the President now."

A moment later, Smith added his especially somber

voice to the call. "The albinos and the earth drill have staged vicious and violent attacks in the past half hour. So far we know they have committed murder, thievery and mass kidnappings. They occurred in Topeka, Kansas, Apache Flats, Missouri, and Tucumcari, New Mexico."

Remo was stunned. "How?"

"In at least two of the cases, their trail has been traced to previously unknown access caverns into well-known mines and natural caverns. My own rough estimates say that upward of three hundred albino assailants surfaced for these attacks." He sounded tired. "Clearly, the albinos' population and geographic coverage is more vast than any of us imagined."

"How'd they exist down there for so long without the surface world knowing about them?" Remo muttered, but before anyone could answer, Remo's gears shifted. "Did you say the earth drill was involved in one of the attacks?"

"Seven minutes ago the earth drill burrowed into a the subterranean bunker that was home to a new emergency federal command authority station, one of seven recently installed by the Department of Homeland Security."

"Which is for what purpose?"

"The AFCA stations are tools of authority for use in case of nationwide catastrophe," Smith said. "If there was a nuclear exchange or some sort of terrorist attack that shuts down communications and infrastructure nationwide, the AFCA stations should survive. They're equipped with the best-shielded equipment and logistical experts. Even if EMC blasts destroyed every electronic chip on the continent, the AFCA stations would supposedly survive. They would get messages via shortwave from whatever the top surviving federal authority was and pass on those messages to the their geographical district."

Remo was on information overload until he put some of the pieces together. "If I'm an electronics whiz like Jack Fast, then I'm drooling to get my hands on that stuff."

"Exactly," Smith said.

The phone disappeared from Remo's hands. "Emperor," Chiun asked, "when you say all electronic devices would stop working, would this include iBloggers?"

"I'm afraid I don't understand."

"Yes, Master Chiun, all iBloggers," Mark Howard explained.

"Could one take steps to have his iBlogger shielded in special ways to protect it?"

"Perhaps, but we can discuss it later," Howard said. "What we don't understand yet is the reason for the kidnappings."

"When is this EMC blast scheduled?" Chiun demanded. "Will it be tonight?"

"Give me that," Remo said, removing the phone from Chiun's hand.

"Remo!"

"Listen, Chiun, there's not going to be an EMC blast tonight, probably never, and even if there was and even if you managed to get some special shielding so your iBlogger would still work, it wouldn't matter."

"Why not?"

"Because every other iBlogger would be fried! Computers and toasters and every other damn thing with a computer chip inside of it, which is everything, would be dead. *Reader's Digest* had a blurb about it."

"So there would be no more blogs for me to read," Chiun said with somber understanding.

"Yeah. But like I said, it's probably not going to happen."

"What of television?"

"Televisions would all stop working, too," Remo said. "Right?" he asked into the phone.

"Well, if you happened to have one without microchips in it, then it would still work," Mark Howard explained. "You know, the old tube sets?"

"Where does one purchase old tube sets?" Chiun demanded.

"It doesn't matter, Chiun," Remo said, getting exasperated. "You'd have the same problem. Even if you had a TV that worked, there'd be nothing to watch because every TV station would have technical difficulties for eternity."

Chiun sat back in his car seat, eyes full of dread.

"Can we get on with this?" Dr. Smith asked.

"Get on with it," Remo said. "What's with the kidnappings?"

"The staff of the AFCA station was taken, but that's just the start," Smith said. "Ninety-three human beings were taken."

"And I know why, Smitty," Remo said morosely. "They're food. The cave guys are rounding up cattle."

"I think not," Smith said. "The albinos came to the surface with very specific targets. In Topeka they raided the offices of a dentist who happened to live in rooms above his practice. They took every piece of equipment they could carry and they took the dentist, as well. In Apache Flats, Missouri, they targeted a car dealership with twenty-four-hour service. They stripped it of portable tools and took the mechanic who was on duty."

"Just like in the bunker," Remo observed. "The hardware and the people to work the hardware. What are they trying to do, set up their own full-service civilization down there?"

"Remo," Smith said, "I think you've hit the nail on the head."

27

Gerhard's Grunts were the meanest bastards you were ever gonna meet. It wasn't a boast. It was just reality, and you might as well deal with it because you never wanted to call one of Gerhard's Grunts a liar.

The grunts were in Afghanistan. They were in the second Iraq war, too, but as Gerhard himself would tell you, "That was a tea party compared to fucking Afghanistan."

Afghanistan was deadly. Afghanistan was fucking hell. Maybe not for those pretty-boy Marines. They never saw any serious combat. Not for the Rangers or the SEALs. They spent that fucking war with their pinkies up their noses to the second knuckle. You wanna know about Afghanistan, you talk to the grunts.

When the spooks thought Osama was running around the lawless mountains, they sent in the grunts. When the Pentagon was certain Osama was hiding in the no-man's-land on the untouchable side of the Pakistani border, they sent in the grunts. When the bombing was called off and they needed somebody to penetrate the unstable, miserable catacombs of the mountains, filled with decaying bodies and survivors who had fed on nothing more than their hatred of Americans for weeks, they sent in the grunts.

It was the catacombs where Gerhard's Grunts made their reputation. They went into those rat holes and met with some of the fiercest resistance of the war. There were Taliban freaks who would leap onto them from ceiling perches and attempt to chew the grunts' throats open. There were al-Qaeda toads who would sneak up on them and try to blow themselves up close to the grunts. Even if they couldn't kill a grunt, they saw it as a success if they gave their life simply to blind or maim one of the hated Americans.

The grunts started coming out of the Afghan caves on stretchers. The wounded man would be latched on to an ambulance chopper basket, then the rest of his buddies would go back into the caves. The grunts began to refer to their cave, whatever cave they happened to be in, by one of the cruder four-letter words for a woman's private parts. "And we're the pricks you've been waiting for, so like it or not, it's time to fuck."

Everybody knew the grunts were in Afghanistan and suffered heavy casualties but didn't lose a man. In fact, every wounded commando eventually returned to the grunts. When Gerhard himself was targeted by a BBC news correspondent after the war, she asked him what his men had actually done in Afghanistan to sustain so much injury.

Gerhard sneered at her and said, "We fucked it."

"So," asked the stammering correspondent, "how was it, fucking Afghanistan?"

"Dry," Gerhard said. "Painful. But we were the right pricks for the job."

That interview never aired.

When word came down from the commander in chief that an insertion team was needed in Topeka soon, the military's sharpest minds immediately thought of Gerhard's Grunts.

By the time their transport was descending on Kansas, they had seen the video footage of attacks that had happened throughout the middle part of the nation. The footage showed swarms of freaky albinos committing theft, violence, murder, kidnapping and cannibalism.

As the transport plane touched down in Kansas, Topeka was just waking itself up. It was a cool, blue-sky morning, full of promise. The people were oblivious to the overnight violence. If the federal government had its way, they would never know. This was going to stop here and now.

A U.S. Army cordon surrounded the Paradise Caverns, with tanks and jeep-mounted machine guns, enough firepower to reduce the building to rubble.

Outside the Army cordon was a ragtag jumble of local police. A Topeka police official stormed up to the first of the grunts' vehicles as it stopped for the Army checkpoint. He had a speech all ready—he had delivered it several times that morning. He started delivering the speech to Gerhard. It had something to do with the Feds not respecting the authority of the chief of police of a major metropolitan city. What was Gerhard going to do about it?

"Fuck you, Chief," Gerhard answered, and they rolled into the protected realm where the local law was not allowed.

The grunts exited the vehicles, fully armed and fully prepared to move in. The Army officer in charge of the scene told him that there hadn't been any sign of the albinos since the overnight attack. "If you're lucky they're long gone."

"If I'm lucky," Gerhard said disdainfully, "they're inside waiting to engage. Battle is my job. What the hell is yours, soldier?"

The grunts went into Paradise Caverns, followed the route of the albinos to the cavern's subterranean waterfall and started blowing up the rock. In minutes they revealed a hidden passage, then belayed over the cascade and marched into the earth, leaving behind the glorious Kansas dawn without a backward glance.

Their base communications operator kept in constant radio contact to insure their retransmitters were situated to maintain a signal. They fed back continuous data streams, including infrared video images.

The on-site CO was in a command truck in the parking lot outside the cavern, and he couldn't see anything in the images except for an occasional rock and a grunt's foot. After an hour the CO called in personally.

"What's the terrain like?"

"It's like a sidewalk in Central Park," Gerhard explained. "If I didn't know better, I'd guess we were on a part of the paved walkway for the regular cavern tours."

"Blasted?" the CO asked.

"Worn," Gerhard radioed back.

"You mean eroded, like by water?" the lieutenant commander said.

"No, sir, I mean worn. By foot traffic."

"Oh."

"Our worst problem is the litter. Shoes. Personal effects such as wallets and keys. Soon as the air started getting hot we started seeing a lot of clothes. Sweaters and jackets, then shirts and bras and torn pant legs. Now short pants, socks, everything. The victims must be just about naked. Hold on."

There was a pause as the team went into silent running and the CO went into tense sweating in his command truck. Naked victims? Foot-worn pathways? How much foot traffic did it take to wear a path into the rock floor of cave? He didn't know, but he knew it was no small amount.

Gerhard spoke from miles away below the surface of the green earth. "Sir, we have a body."

"Show it!"

Gerhard pointed his helmet-mounted lipstick video pickup. The body was revealed in the imperfect infrared signal.

"Holy mother of Jesus, what is it?"

"This ain't one of the victims, sir. This ain't even a human."

The CO couldn't take his eyes off the naked, gaunt creature sprawled in a crevice off the side of the trail, his upper torso and his hips twisted unnaturally away from each other.

"There's another up the trail. Watch it, grunts!"

They advanced barely a foot at a time, and the lieutenant colonel could almost feel what it was like to be down there, nerves in a razor edge, adrenaline pumping, senses tuned to every real and imagined movement. The cavern opened and many bodies came into view, sprawled in the jagged crevices, facedown in a deep trench with its trickle of water.

Gerhard halted the grunts and called for silence, then ordered an audio sweep of the cavern. The CO heard the amplified whimpers on the open communications feed.

"We got voices, sir," the grunt told Gerhard. "Can't tell if it's our civilians."

"This smells like an ambush," Gerhard declared. "Yeep, give me some death certificates."

Grunt Yeepod switched his lipstick video pickup to thermal, and the image became a green sea of warm stone. He advanced into the open cavern, sweeping the roof's hidden recesses, and finding nothing but rock. He lingered on a pool of cool air in a corner of the cavern, and the CO topside was fascinated by the liquid-like signature of the cool air seeping from a hidden vent behind a pile of toppled boulders. He even stepped closer to glance into the shallow pool of stone where the cool air collected like water in a pool. It was a perfect hiding place, but empty.

Yeep moved across to the strewed corpses and gave them the once-over with the thermal video pickup.

"Dead," he reported in a whisper.

"Check again, Yeep," Gerhard snapped. "They

ain't people. They might be colder'n us, even when they're alive."

"They're close enough, Ger. They might be a little colder but they ain't that much colder."

Yeep checked again. Sure enough, the thermal images showed piles of cool semihuman creatures. "Definitely dead," Yeep reported.

The CO, observing all of it, had a strange sense of suspicion. Something was bothering him, but he couldn't put a label on it. Should he tell Gerhard?

Hell, Gerhard was a professional and the lieutenant colonel had never actually spent any time in, er, the field.

Gerhard moved the grunts into the cavern, rechecking the crevices and every possible hiding place.

The CO felt itchy all over. "Did the other grunts see Yeep's thermal video feed?" he asked the operator.

"'Course not, sir." The operator never looked up from his signal booster adjustments.

"Even Gerhard?"

"No way he could, sir. They don't have displays, just pickups."

So only Yeep and the colonel had actually seen the thermal images, and only Yeep and the colonel knew about the cool airstream that filled the pool alongside the footpath, and Yeep hadn't found anything to fear in it. It was empty, right? The natural ventilation shaft was blocked by boulders, so what danger could it possibly pose?

The whimpering on the grunts' audio pickups became clearer when they were about to enter the confines of a tight corridor.

The lieutenant colonel knew he'd be a laughing-stock if he did this, but he just had to do it.

"Gerhard!"

"Sir?" he whispered, bringing the grunts to a halt.

"Captain, I think something's wrong. I have a bad feeling about all this."

"You have a *bad feeling,* sir?" Gerhard could barely contain his scorn. Gerhard and the grunts had heard the rumors about the lieutenant colonel's so-called field experience.

"Call it instinct," the CO said.

"Maybe call it intuition," one of the grunts said.

Oh, great, now he was going to be known as the special forces commander who had women's intuition instead of battlefield instinct. "Listen, Gerhard, I have a feeling this is some kind of an ambush."

"I'll take your feelings under advisement, sir," Gerhard replied.

Gerhard started to say something else just as every telephone inside the truck started ringing and then the grunts' signal died. Audio, video, data, it all stopped coming into the command center in the parking lot. Only then did the lieutenant commander figure out what was bothering him.

"They're dead," he declared hollowly.

The operator was cursing his equipment as he tried to restore communications. "Could you get that, sir?"

The lieutenant colonel absently picked up the closest of the ringing phones, but they all stopped ringing.

There was nobody there.

MARK HOWARD AND Harold W. Smith didn't speak. Smith laid the phone in its cradle. He had been calling to tell the idiot in charge to pull his men back, but then the signal died. It was too late. Gerhard and his grunts were beyond saving.

GERHARD NEVER KNEW fear until he saw the dead men crawling out of the gash in the rock and coming for him.

This was not war—it was monstrous, and it was an unclean way to die. The grunts began firing and attempted to push back into the cavern, but the dead things were coming too fast. The grunts were bottled in tight. Only two of them could fire at once, and the dead things were shielding themselves with big slabs of shale they found sitting around. The rounds from the grunts' rifles started ricocheting noisily.

"More from the rear!" one of the grunts shouted, and gunfire filled the cavern in the rear.

Trapped. Like rats. Gerhard gave the order for a full-throttle retreat, and he triggered his rifle into the approaching horde of dead things. His rounds smashed their shields and tore into their bodies, killing them again, but there were too many, and soon they mobbed the tunnel entrance, ignoring the brutal barrage and their wounded companions. The shale shields were brought together in a V-shape that...

"Shit!" Gerhard tried to pull back on his trigger but he wasn't fast enough, and a half-dozen rounds bounced off the shale slabs and came back at the grunts, bouncing crazily inside the tight corridor. Two of the deformed bullets chopped through Gerhard and another grunt.

The lucky grunt fell dead. Gerhard's back had been sliced open, and both shoulder blades were fractured. Despite all that, he couldn't help but wonder: where had these naked dirtballs learn a trick like that?

"Get in close and shoot those fuckers!" he exploded, and staggered at the mouth of the corridor, pushing his rifle around the stone shields and unleashing a burst that ended prematurely when the gun was yanked out of his hands.

The shale shields crashed into Gerhard's face, shattering his night-vision goggles. He lived for another minute or so in darkness punctuated by an occasional muzzle blast.

He swung his arms at the attackers, but they swarmed him and bored him to the ground, their savage fingers stripping him bare of his clothes and gear.

The gunfire died soon, then the last of the scuffles ended with the crack of somebody's skull against a rock floor. There was a lot of eager snuffling, and the sound of activity moving back to the open cavern.

"Grunts?"

"Here, Ger," said a muffled voice. It was Yeep!

"They pinned me, then they left with all my stuff." That was Lay!

"Are you people the Marines?" asked a stranger's voice, far back in the utter blackness.

"Who are you?" Gerhard demanded.

"One of the prisoners. I'm supposed to translate their orders. The cavemen don't talk very well."

"Fuck their orders," Lay groaned.

"Are any of you bleeding?"

The two grunts said they were only bruised. "My back ripped wide open," Gerhard said. "You got a kit?"

"Stay where you are. You other men come with me right now."

"Hey, buddy, we don't take orders from anybody but Ger. Not from you, and sure as shittin' not from them cavemen."

"Do it for your own good," the faceless man pleaded.

"Go to hell!" Yeep growled. "We're staying with Ger."

Gerhard heard the hasty clatter of their soldier gear getting dumped in the cavern, and he knew what was next. The cavemen wouldn't want a wounded prisoner slowing them down. "Grunts, go with him," he said, struggling to get to his feet. His shoulders had frozen up, and he couldn't even turn onto his stomach.

"No way we're leaving you, Ger."

"Go now and that's an order!"

Gerhard knew the cavemen would kill him. Very soon. That was okay. He was resigned to death. They gathered around him, snuffling. The rock would bash his brains out any second now.

What he felt next wasn't a rock at all. It was teeth. Gerhard was lunch.

THE CO HEARD the gunshots.

"Coming from a half klick upstream," the shell-shocked communications operator blurted. "There's a shotgun mike on the retransmitter there."

"So we'll hear them when they retreat!" the lieutenant colonel cried optimistically.

"I suppose so."

The special forces commander was reporting to one of the many officers who were demanding an explanation. "When they start the retreat we'll be able to hear them, General, even if all their radios are inoperable."

The CO listened and his voice grew pale. He covered the mouthpiece. "Can you patch the audio feed into the phone line for the general?" he asked the communications operator.

"Give me an hour," the operator said over his shoulder disdainfully.

"It will take some time, General," the CO said. He was at his smarmiest. Smarminess was what got him the high-profile special forces assignment.

"Hold the phone up to the speaker if he really wants to hear it," the frantic operator said with a sneer.

"I have an idea! I'll hold the phone up to the speaker. Okay. Here you go, General. We should hear the grunts any second now."

He was correct. Almost as soon as the phone was against the speaker, it vibrated with the sound of Gerhard himself, screaming. And screaming.

28

The billboards were still there: You're Getting Close to Total Amazement; You're Only a Mile from the Marvels—And Ice Cold Refreshments; Pull off Now To See the Most Incredible Attraction on Route 66!

Somebody with a can of red spray paint had defaced the last billboard with the message, Closed 4 Good.

The sign out front was still and was mounted with a harsh security floodlight, making Fastbinder's Museum of Mechanical Marvels look even more desolate.

Remo pulled into the gravel parking lot, where a few scrubby weeds had already grown up to give the place a deserted look. The yellow crime-scene tape had turned to tatters in the weeks since the buildings were gutted. The investigation by local and state police was at a standstill. The eyewitness accounts of the vandalism weren't reliable. The former manager of the museum claimed it was two men who caused all the damage, without tools, and one of them was at least eighty years old. Yeah, right.

The local cops would have forgotten the crime, too, if they could, but there was the matter of the missing millionaire. Obviously he'd been murdered, and the prime suspects were the directors of the company Fastbinder's grandfather founded—the company that was warring with Jacob Fastbinder III until the day he disappeared.

"You'd think somebody would clean up this place," Remo said as they strolled among the shadowy piles of wreckage. Once the museum was a showcase for unique mechanical antiques, lovingly restored by Fastbinder himself. Some of the first commercially produced radios were there, and mechanical calculators from the early 1800s. There was a huge restored cotton gin, one of the original machines responsible for the industrial revolution. A shelf of typewriters displayed a Remington Model No. 2 from 1876 and a 2003 AlphaSmart electronic—both of which retailed in their time for less than two hundred dollars.

And there had been robots, large and small, some pointless, some actually useful. The most versatile robots had not been put on display, though. Fastbinder used them instead to steal secrets from the U.S. Military.

None of the mechanical marvels remained after Remo and Chiun worked them over, and the scraps that were left could never be salvaged and rebuilt. The museum would have to be cleaned with shovels.

They left the museum and headed for the house. Fastbinder had made a home out of an old distribution facility, large but low ceilinged. The cinder-block walls were covered to the eaves with sand drifts.

The lazy breeze stalled and reversed course just

long enough to carry to them the smell of rotting human flesh. The smell was stronger when they stepped inside.

"Three weeks, maximum," Remo declared. "Whoever it is, they died after our visit."

Chiun nodded and picked his way through the remnants of Jacob Fastbinder's home and workshop. If anything, he and Remo had been even more thorough in their destruction of the machines here, including an army of robots that ineffectively fought against them to buy Fastbinder escape time.

Chiun descended into the crater that was left when Fastbinder's earth drill tunnel collapsed. That's where the smell was.

A bizarre picture materialized in Remo's head: Jacob Fastbinder surviving, somehow, for weeks and weeks, and digging his way up from the dead earth drill, only to succumb and die after all these weeks—and within a few feet of the surface.

"Naw. Couldn't be him. Could it?"

"No," Chiun declared, waving his hand at the ground at super speed to fan away an accumulation of dust blown in through the shattered windows.

Remo felt better when he saw a shallow oblong impression appear in the surface. "Somebody dug down, not up."

"Of course. Now you dig down, too."

"Your turn. I dug up Jesus in the desert, remember?"

Chiun stepped out of the crater and stood stoically watching, his hands tucked in his sleeves.

Remo started scooping handfuls of sand out of the

crater, flinging it so fast that it scoured a pile of rusted metal scraps, which shone like chrome before the sand covered them.

"So I have to do everything. I *always* have to do everything. When I was training I did everything. When I was a Master I did everything. Now I'm Reigning Master and I'm still doing everything!"

"When you finally accept a pupil of your own, you may order him about willy nilly. For my information, do you plan on doing this any time soon?"

"Why, you looking forward to retirement?" Remo asked as he unearthed a body.

"Perhaps?"

"Yes or no?"

"Yes."

"Then I'm gonna wait twenty years before I get a pupil."

"Thank goodness. I dread living in that dank and drafty cave."

"I'm getting a pupil right away. First kid I see, I'm drafting him on the spot." Remo gingerly lifted out the corpse and peeled off the blanket that was wrapping it. "Okay," Remo corrected himself. "Not that kid."

She was sixteen, maybe seventeen, and had once been exquisite. Death transformed her into a horror of bulging, sightless eyes and a gaping white mouth. She was nude, with a pair of jeans and a T-shirt wadded at her feet. Remo took her slim pink wallet.

Chiun stepped into the empty grave, testing the consistency of the soil between his fingers. "The ground was not dug deeper than this," he declared.

"So Fastbinder wasn't dug up this way," Remo said.

"I guess that doesn't mean anything, if the new-model earth drill could have tunneled in from anywhere."

Chiun nodded, but he didn't say anything. Chiun had perfected the art of the silent treatment, and Remo had been the artist's canvas. He knew when Chiun had a real reason for keeping his mouth shut.

"This place gives me the creeps," Remo announced. "I don't know why. You know why?"

"No, and yet I have likewise acquired these creeps."

Remo turned slowly in a circle, looking for something. He didn't know what. Chiun was doing the same thing, but standing perfectly still, allowing his senses to probe the environment.

"There's nothing here," Remo argued. "Just all the same junk as before, right?" His eyes searched the rubble he and Chiun had created, and he found nothing new except assorted vermin. There was no hum of power in the wiring, no visual security system watching them.

"Is there some sort of an electrical gizmo still fritzing around in the wreckage or something?"

"Let us leave this place."

"No way, Chiun. If there's something here, then we need to know what it is. I know what you're thinking and it's not that. If one of those Proton Annihilation Rays was activating in here, then there'd be all kinds of electrical stuff."

"Unless it is disguised, or unless it is another trap prepared especially for us. Remo, these people may have our measure."

"No way."

A heartbeat later his words became a mockery.

THE BLOND KID SKIDDED into his workshop in blue jeans and bare feet and landed on the chair, rolling eight feet to a perfect stop under his primary workstation. A window had sprung up with a digital video loop of a smiling, vivacious Nancy Fielding repeating, "There's somebody here!"

Boy, what a hot-looking babe! He had taken plenty of video to remember her by, some of it X-rated. Nancy hadn't known about all the hidden cameras, of course. She was as smart as a tack, but gullible, too, it turned out.

Nancy had helped Jack Fast hide out after the destruction of his father's museum and workshop, but she began getting suspicious when Jack told her that he was building a new mechanical mole so he could rescue his father. Nancy knew Jack was a genius, and she'd seen him engineer amazing devices, but a manned earth drill was beyond her ability to believe. Nancy had gently suggested that Jack was in severe denial over the death of his father. This scenario in which Jacob Fastbinder III escaped into the earth in a mechanical earth drill and was now waiting for Jack's rescue was nothing but fantasy.

So much for Nancy Fielding. Jack thought it was a real drag when people he liked didn't have faith in him anymore. Jack had to break up with her.

But Nancy was still useful. He rigged her up with the most benign and undetectable sensor he could think of—because the guys he was after seemed to carry around the best field equipment ever. His sensor was a simple thread of woven glass fibers—a silicon trip wire buried in the silicon-based sand of the soil. Even ground-penetrating ultrasound wouldn't find that! He buried the lead in the soil inches below Nancy—boy, had she been surprised!—and used a telescoping rod to extend the lead forty yards down. Later he burrowed in under the lab, found the silicon thread and attached it to mechanical amplifiers, all made from glass. There wasn't a trace of metal in the whole system until the wire reached the alarm electronics a half mile from the place.

"This is overkill," his father had said.

"Hey, Pops, you and I both know these guys have got some serious human amplification going on," Jack had said emphatically. "I don't want to take any chances of warning them off before they're right in the middle of my trap."

Time and again the alarm had sounded, the result of the weight changes occurring to the decomposing body of Nancy Fielding. "Hey, doll," he said in discouragement as he monitored another alarm, "you're just right. You don't need to lose an ounce."

"Who does not need to lose weight?" Fastbinder had said, popping into Jack's workshop.

Jack grinned oafishly. He hadn't exactly told his dad about Nancy Fielding's role in the experiment, but he was a first-class obfuscator. "The soil's compacting under the old lab and setting the thing off."

But there hadn't been a false alarm in four days.

"I got a good feeling about this one, Pops!" Jack exclaimed as Fastbinder entered the lab. A rearview mirror, originally from a 1956 Harley-Davidson, was now mounted on his monitor. He didn't like people surprising him.

"So? Let's see if this is zee real thing," Fastbinder challenged.

Jack bit his lower lip excitedly while turning on his monitoring cameras. They were mounted on the museum billboard and tapped into the security light power, thoughtfully provided by the State of New Mexico. The wide-angle focus showed them a parked car.

"All right, Pops, we got a bite!" The sandy-haired teenager was practically jumping up and down in his seat. "I'm zooming in."

The image adjusted smoothly as it zoomed in on the dark blotch in the distance—the laboratory and former home of Fastbinder and his son was set back almost a quarter mile from the museum and the famous Route 66.

"This is a good zoom, eh?" Fastbinder asked. "Not a digital?"

"Naw, it's a Zoom-Nikkor 200-400 mm. Cost me seven grand for all that glass. Don't worry, I had Nancy order it for me."

"Do you trust this girl to keep your secrets, Jack?" Fastbinder said. He was looking at the video loop still playing, muted in a background window on the monitor.

"She's not gonna be talking to anybody, Pops." Jack chuckled.

Jacob Fastbinder almost said something, then was distracted by the image on the screen. "Stop zee zooming a moment, Jack."

"Huh? What for?"

"Just stop it. Now move pan down to zee ground."

Jack was sitting up straight. "You see something I don't, Pops?"

"I don't see footprints."

Jack screwed up his freckled nose and zoomed in close onto the dirt, then swept the camera left and right. "What the hell? That drift sand's looser than my mom on a Friday. Where's their prints?"

"Maybe they brushed them away behind them," Jacob Fastbinder said.

"Naw, Pops, those are drifts. Smooth as a baby's butt. You see anything that looks swept?"

"Maybe they air-dropped onto the roof."

"Pops, come on, think about it! There's a car in the lot!" The grin was gone from Jack Fast's face. He did not like being stymied. He opened another window and brought up a thermal image.

"You have a night-vision camera up there, as well?" Fastbinder asked.

"Look! The car's hot, see? Just got there."

"But they are not in the laboratory, Jack, unless they move by levitation."

The teenager was thinking furiously as the video camera moved in on the laboratory again as tight as it could go. The lens picked up a vivid image of the front door, wedged open as it had been for weeks, but there was no sign of movement inside.

"I'm going to deploy," he declared.

"If you are wrong, you will need to travel all the

way back there to reset all that equipment," Fastbinder warned.

"These guys are slippery as snakes, Pops. If there is a chance they're inside, I gotta give it to 'em now."

Jack clicked back onto the alarm window and the sound returned. "There's somebody here!" Nancy Fielding teased.

"Okay, doll," Jack Fast said, "go get 'em!" He clicked Nancy, right on her pretty little mouth.

29

Remo Williams felt a hot surge of radiation over his head, outside the building, then he was assaulted from every side. Power coursed through the building, and electric devices blinked to life in every corner. Explosive puffs opened holes all over the ceiling, enabling electronic devices to drop into position on scissors brackets. There were cameras, microphones, who knows what. But worst of all were the thirteen simultaneous proton discharge events, which spun up various miniature generators like tiny ramjets and speared Remo with pinpricks of horror. His senses felt deadened, and the darkness of sensory erasure ate swift holes in his consciousness.

In a heartbeat the charges were done and Remo felt blessed normalcy. He had taken another proton discharge without succumbing to the blackness. Chiun shook off the unpleasantness and looked sharply at him.

"Everything's okay," Remo assured him.

"There's somebody here!" the dead girl said, proving Remo wrong. She lifted her head.

"Remo, let us go!" Chiun hissed.

"Yeah." But he couldn't take his eyes off her. She sat up suddenly, her neck distended, then stood with her arms and legs dangling and flopping lifelessly underneath her.

"There's somebody here!" Her gaping mouth never moved, and the sound seemed to come from the back of her head. She swayed abruptly toward Remo and Chiun with her dangling toes dragging on the floor and crashing into debris.

Remo and Chiun were on the move, and Remo was already cursing himself for falling for the distraction when the air filled with flying metal.

Remo snatched at the bullet-fast chunks flying at his body and threw them back the way they had come. They didn't go far before whipping back at him. At the same moment he felt the curious sensation of his shoes trying to levitate.

"Magnets." Chiun cursed as his hands plucked away at the litter of jagged metal that could have torn them to pieces.

"Electromagnets," Remo added as the hand-hammered shoelace eyelets tore off and flew across the room.

A HUNDRED MILES AWAY and 3.6 miles below the surface of the earth, Jacob Fastbinder watched in awe. The corpse of Nancy Fielding was jumping and dancing, limbs flopping everywhere.

One of the displays tracked how the powerful electromagnets were being manipulated by the light-sensitive motion detector. Every two seconds, the electromagnets were pulsed to the opposing side. The two figures were being bombarded with ferrous metal scraps, then bombarded again, while the scarecrow cadaver flew around the room trying to keep up.

"I suppose that is your girlfriend."

"We broke up," his son said, then grinned and winced as Nancy Fielding's skull was magnetically pulled into the cinder-block wall. "She can't last too much longer," Jack added.

She hung there, then flew again at the two men, who allowed her to sail past as they maneuvered for the entrance. Every scrap of alloy that should have sliced into them was pushed away, or sidestepped, or just ignored.

"How are they doing that?" Jack demanded.

Jacob Fastbinder swallowed thickly when he was unfortunate enough to witness Nancy Fielding's head become separated from the tangle of welded steel barbs that had been inserted in her skull. It was the steel that had been responding to the electromagnets. Without it, the cadaver flopped down and didn't get up again.

"That's what gives her get up and go," Jack explained offhandedly. "Good grief, these dudes move fast—oh no, you don't."

Jacob Fastbinder knew the intruders were going to escape—he didn't know how, but the shrapnel storm wasn't stopping them. They were at the door.

"Charge!" Jack Fast exclaimed with manic delight, thrusting one fist in the air and slamming the other on a large opaque button.

Charging, read a tiny window on every one of Jack Fast's displays, and all the metal plopped to the ground. The two intruders should have walked away, but they fell hard, just as lifeless as the mutilated corpse of Nancy Fielding.

30

Remo Williams heard something ugly come out of his own throat when the Nothingness swarmed over him.

The Nothingness hurt. It was the worst agony of all. He didn't know if he could take it, not this strong, not again.

The senses of a Master of Sinanju are heightened beyond what most humans would believe possible, and a Master is constantly aware of the hundreds of signals in his environment: sound and pressure and temperature and smell; the shifting pull of the earth and the moon; the weight of the atmosphere and the incalculably small deviations in pressure that come from a flying bullet or a speck of dust.

In the Nothingness, Remo had awareness but all his senses became useless, and if he could have screamed or prayed for mercy…

Then it was over. He picked himself off the ground cautiously, unable to believe that he had not plunged into a Nothingness again permanently.

"Remo." Chiun was coming to his feet, and relief showed on his ancient face—until the Nothingness came again. Remo was yanked back into his own special hell.

Then it was gone. He forced himself to his feet, grabbed Chiun and heaved them both toward the entrance. Chiun collapsed on the ground outside and fought to get onto his hands and knees.

It came again, sucked them into Nothingness, and Remo's last thought was that he could not take it. He would rather die....

To his surprise, pain came a moment later. He was draped over the steel frame of the doorway where he had collapsed. He drew his legs up under him and pushed away. He didn't care if he looked like a crippled frog, as long as it put distance between himself and the source of their suffering.

Chiun came to his feet but couldn't stand straight. He and Remo propped each other up like a pair of drunks. They went a few paces before the Nothingness sucked at them again. It was behind them, weakened, and the Masters of Sinanju swayed blindly, then staggered on.

When they reach the car they could no longer feel the pulses. They stood breathing, looking at each other.

"Chiun?" Remo gasped when he could talk again.

"I am enfeebled, but improving. How has it affected you, Remo?"

Remo allowed his breath to fill his body and send back signals of damage. "When it comes, Little Father, I wish I was dead. Dying would be better than that, whatever it is."

"You are too strong to succumb to such flights of

fancy," Chiun declared. "How are you now? Do you feel strong enough to throw rocks?"

"Definitely."

"WHAT ARE THEY DOING now?" Jack Fast whined.

He was sure those two would get their circuits fried by the proton discharges, but the discharge couldn't be sustained, and every time it stopped the two intruders managed to put distance between themselves and the discharge unit. Now they were in front of the museum, where they didn't seem bothered by the discharge anymore.

"I think they are picking up gravel," Fastbinder said.

"Oh no, don't do that you son of a guns!" Jack stood and grabbed the monitor as if he could shout at them. The pair tossed one rock each directly at the top of the museum sign and the stones became massive in the screen, like looming comets. It was so vivid that Jack Fast ducked and threw his arms over his head, but it was over in an instant. The computer window went black.

Jack Fast shrugged sheepishly.

"You found their Achilles tendon after all, Jack," Fastbinder said. "Zee proton drive did something to them. I saw it myself. You were right about that."

"Well, yeah, I knew that, Pops. But what I didn't count on was how quick they got over it. See, the proton discharge happens in a burst, it's over quick, but these guys get over it quick, too, looks like."

Fastbinder said nothing.

"Give me a break, Pops. I'm still experimenting with this."

"There is no time for experimenting. How long will it take to construct a proton drive capable of sustained output?"

Jack looked sheepish and irritated.

"You have everything you need to make more of zees proton output devices," Fastbinder said.

"Yeah."

"So? How long?"

"I don't know how to do it." Jack slumped in his folding chair.

Fastbinder stood straighter. "This has never stopped you before. Learn what you don't know. Make it happen."

"But that's just it. I know enough about it to be pretty sure I can't create a continual burn like that. A low-yield continuous output, yes. A momentary burst of high output, yes. A device with continuous high output—not doable, far as I know."

"You'll do it. You must. It is zee only weapon we have found to use against zees men of strange powers."

Jack Fast glared at the floor, then glared at the black screen. He played with the keyboard absently, bringing up the recorded video of the pair in the parking lot. Their faces were a blur, as if the focus had failed on them. Jack Fast knew they did this somehow, sensing they were being watched and creating the disturbance that fouled the image capture. He looked back even farther, pulling up the images from the cameras that were deployed inside the Fastbinders' old workshop. Jack rigged them to stay silent, using less electricity than a watch, until he gave the signal. Then the electricity surged, explosive charges opened the roof under the cameras, and they descended on telescoping mounts into the interior. He had figured that maybe, just maybe, when the proton charges went off and there was a lot of confusion, he'd be able to get a good mug shot.

He was right. After his software digitally combined details from several frames of video, he got the pictures he wanted.

They looked just the way Senator Whiteslaw had described them. One man with dark hair, an inscrutable expression and eyes that looked dead. The other man was an old Asian, and the image made every wrinkle in his parchment skin visible. He looked frail, this ancient man. Both of them were stricken with the force of—whatever it was, this assault that the proton discharge created against them.

"Herbie's gonna be happy anyway," Jack said.

"How can he use them? His life is in danger—as is ours. They will come for us, Jack. They may even come down here."

"This is our turf now, Pops," Jack said. "They're not welcome."

"You think we can find a way to defeat them, here, under zee earth?"

Jack Fast glared at the faces on the screen. "They're only human. I'll find a way."

31

"Give it a rest, dear," the first lady said, rolling over to escape the TV glare.

"Did you see this? Some Democrat marketing sleazeball has trotted out my DUI again."

"That's old news, dear."

"It's twenty years old! And I wasn't convicted! But the media's still making hay out of it! Why can't they leave it alone already?"

"It's an election year, dear."

"Then why don't they talk abut the election, for heaven's sakes," he muttered.

The first lady was just starting to breathe deeply when the President swore loudly. He had landed on a late-night talk-show monologue. The gap-toothed host wondered if the President was DUI when he'd dreamed up the WMDs.

"You son of a Hoosier! You think that's funny?"

"Go to sleep, dear," the first lady grumbled.

The phone buzzed and the President grabbed it.

"Mr. President, you're not going to believe this," said his chief of staff. "Whiteslaw is here."

THE PRESIDENT PUT ON his best game face when Senator Herbert Whiteslaw was ushered into the office after an extensive security check.

"Herbert, my God, it's good to see you. When I didn't hear from you—well, I feared the worst."

Herbert Whiteslaw shook the Man's hand and said curtly, "Mr. President, I must speak with you alone." Whiteslaw nodded at the Secret Service foursome and the chief of staff.

"My chief of staff is fully briefed on your activities, Senator," the President assured him.

Whiteslaw's eyes narrowed. "Mr. President, I'm here to discuss a new matter. I am sure you'll want it to stay between you and me."

The chief of staff wore a hangdog look when ordered to leave the office. The agents promised they would be waiting right outside the door should the President need anything.

"I guess the game is up," Whiteslaw said as the door shut. "All the games."

"That's right, Whiteslaw," the President said. "You'll face charges of treason. We've got a hundred men putting the indictment together."

"Not worried about it, and that's not the game we're talking about. I'm here to discuss assassins."

"Have you hired some to erase the pool of witnesses?"

"I mean your assassins, Mr. President. Two men, sanctioned by the President of the United States, to commit murder on U.S. soil."

The President raised an eyebrow and sat back in the chair. "I think you're mistaken."

"I've met them. They were my bodyguards when your press secretary went into the politics-and-murder business."

The President set his jaw. Orville Flicker had been a good man and an excellent spin doctor when the President had been just a state governor, but the PR man lost his head when the team moved into the White House. Flicker began getting crazy ideas, and after the President fired him, he got even crazier.

Whiteslaw sneered. "No more games, Mr. President. I'm here to talk about the election."

The President gave him a hard look. "What about it?"

"I want it."

32

Mark Howard tried to sound polite when he picked up the red phone, but it couldn't have been polite enough.

"Who is this?" the President demanded.

"Mark Howard, sir."

"Oh. Of course. You people know what's going on around here? About Whiteslaw and all?"

"We haven't yet located him, Mr. President."

"You could have located him right here in the White House, son, about ten minutes ago. You mean you don't have me video monitored these days? Don't bother answering, Howard. I wouldn't believe you either way."

"I don't follow—"

"Whiteslaw was just here, Howard. In the Oval Office. And you wouldn't believe what that SOB's got cooking."

Smith came through the door, dark splotches under his eyes. The CURE director had been sleeping in an unused room of the hospital, unwilling to make the drive home in case something developed overnight. He had responded in amazingly quick time to the buzzer that was tied into the President's red phone.

Smith took the phone and jabbed at the speaker button. "I'm here, Mr. President."

"Whiteslaw was just here, Smith. He's got the goods on your enforcement boys."

Smith's brow furrowed. "Have Remo and Chiun called in?"

Mark shook his head.

"That lowlife Whiteslaw has photos of the boys, taken today. Showed them to me on the Internet. Said he'll distribute them around the world, along with all the other evidence he's got on CURE. He's threatening to expose the shebang. Says he's got a whole package just ready to transmit to the media. We'll look like idiots if we bring up the treason charges after he goes public like that."

Smith's gray complexion became deathly pale. "Photographs are only circumstantial evidence," he pointed out. "Whiteslaw has nothing more except conjecture and assumption."

"He's got video, too, Smith. Real HDTV stuff. It's short, but it gets the point across."

"Video from where?" Smith demanded.

"I have no idea. Looks like some sort of old factory. Swear to God I thought I was looking at some sort of Jackie Chan versus *The Matrix* kind of movie, but there's your boys, as clear as crystal. I recognized them right off the bat. He e-mailed me the damn video if you want to see it yourself."

Mark Howard was already on it, bringing the most powerful CURE network software into play. In seconds he had opened the White House servers and culled the contents of every mail account that might conceivably reach the President. He found the video, snatched it up and erased every electronic copy he could locate. He overwrote the erased video hundreds of times, just in case.

"Got it," he announced.

"You boys are fast on your feet," the President said. "Listen, Smith, I know a movie could be made with special effects, and everything could be just flights of fancy, too. That's how we'll spin it for the press if we have to. But coming from a U.S. senator, and one who's been the target of an assassination attempt recently, that packs a whole wallop of credibility with the public."

"What are his demands, Mr. President?"

"Hold on to your hats, Smith. He wants me to drop out of the election. That's not all. He's going after his own party candidate, too. He's going to the party leadership to show them what he's got and let them know that the last President was in the know, too. You get it, Smith? He's trying to extort himself right into the White House."

"We'll make sure that doesn't happen, Mr. President."

"Wait up, Smith, I'm not done. Before you go sending your boys after Whiteslaw, you better know about the other ace he had up his sleeve. The man's in contact with the underground folks."

"The albinos?"

"And their leader. Get this—the cavemen have a king. He sent me a letter of introduction. He wants to start diplomatic relations! And you know who it is? It's that kooky German guy!"

"Fastbinder," Smith said.

"*King* Fastbinder. You believe it?" asked the President of the United States of America. "Sounds like the name of a bad guy in a Rankin-Bass Christmas special. So what am I supposed to do, Smith?"

"I'm not sure if there's anything that can be done," Smith said morosely. "If Fastbinder and his son truly have a media blitz prepared for distribution, there's not much chance we'll be able to stop it. That essentially means an end to CURE. What is more disturbing is the potential for mass casualties. The underground dwellers have inflicted an unexpectedly high number of deaths in the past twenty-four hours."

"Like a war. The good people and CURE aren't the only victims. My administration will go down in flames, don't forget."

"I'm not forgetting, Mr. President, but the problem is bigger than a single administration. If Fastbinder distributes his evidence, and if the public swallows the story, it will seriously scandalize several recent administrations. Both political parties could suffer a loss of credibility and the election may become another free-for-all."

"Worse than the last one?"

"Much worse. There would be no candidate getting enough of the popular vote to qualify to receive the votes of the electoral college in some states. If the disruption is substantial, the members of the electoral college could change their votes."

"Dammit, Smith, I'm already going to go down in history as the President who lost the popular vote. You know what that means? Every history book from now until forever's gonna have my name with a big asterisk next to it. 'Won the election but lost the popular vote.' So next term, you're telling me, even if I do win the thing, it might be even worse? Like, elected by the House or whoever does the electioning if the electoral college can't make a decision?"

"That's about right—"

"You know how much respect that's gonna buy me?"

"Mr. President, I have much work to do if I am to attempt to salvage this situation," Smith said.

"Keep me posted, for once?"

Harold W. Smith hung up the phone.

Mark Howard shook his head. "What a mess. No word from Remo and Chiun."

"Once again, we face a crisis and our enforcement arm is incommunicado," Smith said sourly.

"I'm worried about them, to be honest. You should see this video." Smith stood and moved behind the temporary desk, where Mark Howard was working for the time being as he healed from his recent injuries.

Mark played the video he had taken from the White House mail servers, and Smith was startled at first by the incredible definition of the image. "It's a military video standard," Mark explained, pointing to a serial number in the lower left-hand corner. "They use it for filming and analyzing missile impacts. Fastbinder must have taken some million-dollar video cameras at some point. It's been reformatted but the image is still crystal clear."

"What are we looking at?" Smith asked.

"The roof of the museum. This is the opening frame. Keep your eyes peeled." Mark clicked the window's play button and the video screen became a riot of activity that was over in just five seconds.

"Now, watch it at one-fifth speed," Mark said, and played it again, slow.

Smith was now able to make more sense of the images. There was a burst of fire and dust, and before the time marker reached one second the camera had dropped through the roof and stopped cold in its mounts, showing Remo and Chiun inside the desert warehouse that had recently been the workshop of Jacob Fastbinder and his son, the enigmatic Jack Fast. The images had the clarity of a studio portrait, but the Masters of Sinanju appeared stricken. Remo looked like a man who had been unexpectedly shot through in the chest, but who stood there, unable to come to terms with his shock and horror as he felt his heart come to an abrupt halt.

But it was Chiun who took Smith's attention, because the Master Emeritus was transformed into something ordinary by the force that was striking them. It was as if the proton discharge—surely that was what was hitting them in this moment of video—had made Chiun into any other elderly man, with sagging jowls, hurting eyes and a body as crooked as a jagged tree branch.

As the video advanced, both the Masters collapsed

hard, then seemed to regain consciousness in a matter of seconds, just as everything else in the room began to shudder and fly across the room and cascade down upon them. Smith was amazed that both men found the strength of will to react so quickly. Remo snapped at the debris and cleared the air of massive scraps that could have crushed him or gashed him in two.

Chiun was a wonder. He was on his feet and looked regal somehow, despite all the chaos. An airborne slab of torn steel plating, half a ton at least, ripped off a wrecked fabrication machine and caromed at Chiun, only to be deflected as if it were an inflated toy. His eyes, all the while, were on Remo. Smith knew he was trying to determine if his protégé was wounded.

At the end of the few seconds of tape, both the Masters looked directly into the screen and redirected pieces of flying metal into it, putting an end to their brief television appearance.

"Fast hit them with everything, all at once," Mark guessed. "The proton charge took them off guard so he could get a few good seconds of video, and he retransmitted it in real time."

"Go back to the first frame," Smith said. The still image of a rocky, sandy rooftop came back, with various discarded junk around it. Smith tapped the far right-hand corner. "Enlarge this corner."

The image enlarged but the details were still sharp. They began getting fuzzy when the image enlarged to sixteen times normal, but that was enough.

"What is that thing?" Mark asked. They were seeing what looked like a circular stepped device that was mounted on a framework of aluminum rails. "It's gotta be more than two yards around."

"Electromagnet," Smith decided. "These aluminum shafts are arms of a positioning device. I'm betting there are some big generators, big electric motors and a very powerful proton field generator. At the moment the camera breaks through, the proton device channels all the electricity it can generate into the motors."

"Yeah," Mark agreed. "They'd have to move as fast as hell. Wouldn't matter if they were burned out fast. Their useful life's gotta be less than a minute. Dr. Smith, when the second proton charge happened, Remo and Chiun wouldn't have been able to defend themselves."

Smith found himself thinking of the two Chiuns—the frail, crippled old man and the powerful Sinanju Master who swept steel slabs out of his way. Would he ever see the Sinanju Master again?

33

Dr. Harold Smith couldn't divest himself of the image of the crippled, weak Chiun. Years ago, when the two men met for the first time, Chiun was already elderly. Now both of them qualified as senior citizens. Smith had caught up and surpassed Chiun.

It occurred to him why he was so bothered by the image of Chiun he had seen in the video. For just a couple of seconds, Chiun had become the old man that Smith was—arthritic and frail.

As the hours of the long night passed, he found himself distracted more by the idea that if it had been him in that room, he would have succumbed instantly under the meteor shower of scrap metal. If Chiun had been weakened to such a state during the barrage, even for a second, he would have been pummeled into oblivion.

"Hey, Smitty."

Smith started violently out of his reverie to find Remo standing at his desk, disheveled but unhurt. Chiun stood nearby, hands in his sleeves and just as composed as he ever was. He was still wearing the kimono from the video, but it looked unblemished.

"Remo! Chiun!" Mark Howard exclaimed as he rolled through the doors in his wheelchair.

"Mark," Remo said. "Harold." He tipped an invisible hat to Dr. Smith. "What's everybody all excited about?"

"Remo, why didn't you report in?" Smith asked, his shock becoming a slow-boiling anger.

"Why should I? You said come right back, remember? Quick jaunt to New Mexico, back in time for breakfast? Well, it's not quite 7:00 a.m." Remo looked at the invisible watch on his freakishly thick wrist, gave an exaggerated nod and showed the wrist to Smith. "See? Besides, there was nothing you could have done anything about."

"That's not exactly true, is it?" Smith asked sourly.

"I insisted that we call before boarding the aircraft," Chiun sang out.

"You did not," Remo said.

"My wisdom was spurned, Emperor."

"What's going on, Smitty?"

Smith found himself physically fighting to contain an outburst. It seemed he was always fighting it now—the urge to lay into Remo for his long list of indiscretions and lack of professional behavior. But now was not the time. Right now CURE needed to work as a team. In fact, CURE needed to fight for its survival.

"We're in crisis. You, both of you, figure into it," Smith said. "Show them the video, please, Mark."

Smith munched antacids while Remo and Chiun watched the New Mexican video. Smith expected Chiun to be livid at this invasion of his privacy, and

Remo would likely make some remarks about having movie-star qualities—but they let an uncomfortable silence hang in the air when the video was done.

"We've been worried," Mark said. "We didn't know if there was a second proton discharge and what had happened if there was."

"What else? What's the President got in mind?" Remo looked to Smith, who was clearly fatigued and allowed Mark Howard to bring them up to speed on the reappearance of Senator Herbert Whiteslaw.

"Wait. I don't get it. He wants the President to withdraw from the race? What good will it do Whiteslaw?"

"The President's party will have to field an alternative candidate, but they'll be sure losers if the President retires under the shadow of some unspecified scandal," Mark said. "If Whiteslaw convinces his own party to withdraw its candidate for supposed health reasons and run Whiteslaw, the heroic recent assassination-attempt survivor, they'll have a strong chance of winning the election."

"What? How? How does that make them qualified for the presidency?" Remo asked. "Don't answer that. It was a stupid question. Everybody knows you don't need qualifications when you've got some good tricks up your sleeve."

"Exactly," Chiun trilled. "The tides of popularity ebb and flow and affections of the ignorant masses may be twisted around the fingers of a clever man. Is that not so, Emperor?"

"I suppose so," Smith said.

"The last election of a puppet president was a circus of fools, was it not?"

"That's not a fair example of how our democracy works, Little Father," Remo said.

"Do you have a better example in mind, such as the election of the Terminator Who Took California?"

"That's not a good example either."

"The truth, my son, is that this country does not even have the courage to behave like a true democracy, as the last farcical presidential election proves," Chiun lectured. "In a democracy the citizens cast their votes for a leader, and the man with the most votes is the winner. In this country, the one who leads the people was the popular loser! That is not democracy as the Greek idiots defined it, Remo Williams."

"Even the Greeks didn't do it exactly right, Chiun," Remo protested. "You had to be a citizen to vote, and you weren't a citizen unless you were a pure-blood male Greek landowner with a minimum of fourteen goats. Something like that, right?" He looked to Smith for confirmation. Smith looked weary, but he nodded. "Besides, we don't claim to be a pure democracy. We're a democratic republicancy. Or something."

"It is a fraud," Chiun said, shrugging.

"We elected a president, didn't we? We're doing it again, aren't we? Better than letting the local warlord take over."

"Have you noticed the billboards and the radio snippets and the television commercials? Chopped bovine sandwiches are sold in the same way as the presidential contenders. They call this an advertising blitz."

"It gets somebody elected, doesn't it?" Remo demanded.

"Somebody like the senator who sells secrets to the Arabian despots."

Remo fumed and turned on Smith. "Where is Whiteslaw?"

"Disappeared."

"Find him."

"We tried." Before Remo could complain, Smith added, "We tried hard and we're still trying. Whiteslaw evaded his Secret Service tail after leaving the White House. We assume he's undercover."

"He's got to poke his nose out again sometime."

"May we still be around to see it."

Remo glared at Smitty. "Giving up awfully easy, aren't you, Smitty?"

Smith looked glum. "Not at all. The publicity will kill CURE, as well as send the nation into a crisis of leadership."

Remo was exasperated. "Because of this video and some other circumstantial evidence? Smitty, nobody will believe it."

"Enough people will believe it for long enough to create chaos," Smith said. "CURE will be ordered to shut down, just in case an investigation happens. But what worries me most is the country. Whether Whiteslaw's blackmail succeeds or not, the outcome could be disastrous."

"But he won't succeed, will he?" Mark Howard asked. "The President is not seriously thinking of giving Whiteslaw what he wants?"

"Giving Whiteslaw the presidency will be far less disastrous for the nation than most of the possible alternatives." Smith sighed. "I wouldn't have thought he stands a chance if not for his connection to Fastbinder. Fastbinder has his own long list of demands, and he's promising to make war on the United States if we don't give in. We're between a rock and a hard place."

Remo was on his feet. "Not for long."

"Remo, you're not going to touch Whiteslaw. Let me handle it."

"Don't try to think, Remo, right?" Remo sniped. "Forget it. I'm gonna go get him. Right now."

"Remo, listen to your emperor," Chiun ordered.

"You don't even know where Whiteslaw is," Howard protested.

"I've got nothing better to do than look for him."

"Remo," Chiun and Smith barked in unison.

"Forget it. You know how many times I've been told to not go solve the Senator Coleslaw problem? Never again."

Smith's eyes were bloodshot. "Remo, I'm giving you an order."

"Harold, don't give me any more orders. I'm full."

The door slammed behind him.

The room reverberated with the sound, and Chiun's tight mouth seemed to vibrate with it. His face was hot, and he wouldn't meet the eyes of Harold Smith or Mark Howard.

"Master Chiun?" Smith asked expectantly.

"Yes." Chiun stood quickly and was gone.

34

Secret Service Special Agent Martina Vespana feared for her life. Her kidnapper was a madman, with a killer's eyes, and his behavior made a mockery of her fear.

"Who are you?" she demanded.

"Remo."

"Remo who?"

"I can't think of a last name at the moment. Call me Remo. Relax, will you?"

"Relax. Very funny." She fisted her hands a few times, and they felt fine. Just a moment ago she had been carried out of her ground-floor apartment in a state of complete paralysis, but now all her body parts felt functional again.

Agent Vespana yanked at the door handle and pushed, but the door closed again. Remo was holding it with one hand as he drove, but how had he grabbed it so fast? Remo's finger penetrated the door handle as if it were made of gelatin. Things broke inside the door, locking it for good.

"No, can't do that. I need you, Martina."

"What for?"

"Listen, I'm one of the good guys and I'm trying to stop a bad guy. I need to know what went down when you tailed him from the White House last night. Where he went, what happened when he disappeared, all that kind of thing."

"Why?"

"'Cause he's the bad guy, remember? He's doing bad things and he's going to do some extremely bad things if somebody doesn't stop him first. Apparently, I'm the only one who's got the brass cojones to do something about it."

"What is Whiteslaw doing that's so bad?" She was stalling for time, but she was also trying to get the truth out of this thick-wristed, undeniably attractive wacko.

"Did you see the Orville Flicker video? That was really Whiteslaw."

Weirder and weirder. Vespana had seen the tape, of course. Flicker had staged a bizarre campaign to launch his own political party, which had flourished for about two weeks, then vanished when the airwaves were saturated with the videotape of Orville Flicker selling military secrets to a well-known, now deposed Mideast despot.

"Sounds kind of paranoid, buddy," she said scornfully. "You under a doctor's care or something?"

"He fled the sanitarium this morning," someone squeaked in the empty back seat, making Agent Vespana squeak, too.

"Where did you come from?" she demanded.

"Korea." The withered old man, adorned in peacock colors, was so small that he could easily have been hidden in the back seat when they got it in, but Vespana knew she'd looked. It was part of her training to look. Did she remember hearing a tiny bump like very quiet car doors a few seconds ago?

"Whoever you are, help me! I'm a federal agent and I have been kidnapped."

"I know. This one received your name from another agent, named Stuart."

"Ohmigod, did you kill Agent Stuart?" Vespana demanded of Remo.

"I didn't kill him. Did you kill him?" Remo asked sarcastically in the rearview mirror. "He's been following my trail. That's how he caught me."

Chiun sniffed. Vespana didn't know what to think.

"Well, now you've got me, what are you gonna do? Drag me back?"

Chiun admired the scenery.

"Good," Remo said. "Let's go find us a son of bitch senator."

Agent Vespana was trained to lie under questioning, and she thought she was pretty good at it until she found herself paralyzed as punishment for her fibs.

"Look," Remo said in a reasonable tone, "I'm not going to try to explain to you that I'm a good guy and I'm on your side because you just won't believe me, so what's the use? But just so you can sleep better when this is all over, I'm a good guy and I am on your side. I'm doing a good thing, which is trying to catch this SOB Coleslaw who's turned his loyalty oath into a big unfunny joke. In fact, I'm doing it against orders, because it's the right thing and my boss has got his lemon-shaped head up his lemon-shaped butt. Have you ever been in that situation? Where you just know your boss is messing things up? Of course you have—you're with the Secret Service. Anyway, we're going to sit here all day if that's what it takes for you to tell me the truth about Humbert Coleslaw."

"His name is Herbert Whiteslaw, jerk." Vespana didn't know what sort of weirdo kung-fu grip had put her into this state of paralysis, but she could handle it. She wasn't even uncomfortable. If Remo wanted to wait all day, then he could damn well do it.

She lasted only ten minutes, however. That was when the lightning bolt of pain shot down from her shoulder into her stomach and forced a strangled grunt from her.

"Hey, cut it out, Chiun!"

"I have no wish to wait here all day."

"You weren't even invited."

"Sorry," Remo said to Vespana. "He's in his eleven-teens and more crotchety than ever."

"Don't let him do that again," she gasped. The agony was gone, but it had been unlike any pain she could imagine, and suddenly her paralysis was a smothering cocoon.

"Sweetheart, I can't make him not do anything."

Vespana felt the sweat break on her brow and trickled, stinging, into her eyes. Remo was whistling, and the sound cut like scissors into her brain. It was "25 or 6 to 4."

"Stop it!" she hissed.

"Well said," said the old man behind her.

Remo puckered and began whistling, "Color My World." Vespana used to love that song, but now it was the last straw as she descended into blind panic. "I'll talk if you just stop that infernal whistling!"

Her paralysis was removed with a quick touch, and she was too relieved to worry about the consequences of her betrayal as she led them to the scene of Senator Whiteslaw's mysterious escape.

THE JUBER CLUB WAS a Washington, D.C., institution, and its members were, too. No first-generation politicians or millionaires were invited to join, and the club had stopped taking new members anyway in the 1970s. There were more than enough members and their sons to sustain the Juber Club, and these days—as in the past forty years—even the private clubs were pressured to desegregate. Closed membership made that a nonissue.

Blacks? Jews? In the Juber Club? No, thank you very much.

Asians? Women? Never. That was the message the concierge communicated as he strode into the reception foyer.

"Don't even start, Jeeves." The one member of the trio who was at least acceptable in terms of race and gender was dressed like a truck driver.

"I must ask you to—" The concierge found himself walking with the man in the T-shirt. No, not walking. His feet weren't touching the ground.

"We lost him here," said the woman, who looked worried, but the concierge knew her now. Secret Service. She had been here yesterday. "While we were coughing up ID for Mr. Stick up the Butt, Whiteslaw slipped around this corner and into the library—we thought," Vespana explained. "When we finally got inside, no Whiteslaw."

Remo considered that, examining the short hall, then he idly bounced the concierge up and down.

"Does that help you think?" Chiun asked.

"Pay attention." Remo loved it when he had the chance to say such things to Chiun. As the wide-eyed concierge was bobbled, his shoes clattered on the marble floor. Remo was greatly satisfied to see Chiun nod in understanding.

"Female, did you hear the despicable senator's shoes clop down this hallway? Are you not trained to notice such things?"

Vespana had a smart-mouthed response ready, then it occurred to her that she hadn't heard the sound of receding footsteps.

"Proves nothing," she declared.

"Except that he probably did go into the library after all." Remo entered the library and locked the door behind them. "I bet there's a secret passage in this place. What do you say, Chiun? Sign out front says it was built in the 1850s, and even I know everybody would have been getting edgy about the slavery thing, so there had to be a lot of paranoid spies and politicos hanging around."

"Wherever there are politicians, you can be assured there will be a means of escape," Chiun agreed.

Remo tapped on the bookshelves until he found the section without a wall behind it, then tapped again until the tactile response led him to the instrument used to open the door. That took all of fifteen seconds, but for another minute he pushed it, lifted it, prodded it and yanked it. The wall wouldn't open.

"Little help?" he asked Chiun.

"I was not even invited."

"Okay, you, then," Remo said to the concierge. "Open it."

"Never, sir." The concierge, even dangling helplessly, felt he had bested his attackers. They would never learn the secret code that activated the door's mechanics.

"It's your library." Remo shrugged and tapped again, disintegrating the handcrafted bookshelves. The splintered cherry wood still smelled fresh, even 150 years after the bookshelves' construction.

The concierge was too shocked to notice he was being carried into the passage at amazing speed, down and then east under Front Street and then up again.

The building across the street from the Juber Club looked like just another federal office building, but when they ascended again to ground level they were in a windowless secret section, just wide enough for the elevator. When the elevator opened, there was just one button inside.

35

Alarms were ringing all over the system. Jack Fast knew the rats were finally in his trap. The old man was going to eat his words.

It was a real bummer when people stopped thinking you were the greatest. The old man gave Jack some serious attitude when Jack claimed the proton-beam chisel couldn't be adapted for a sustained firefight. Why not, Jack? Losing your touch, Jack? As if Jack hadn't already engineered the proton-beam chisel way beyond what those doctoral types at Singapore City U ever dreamed of.

Now Jack was going to hit the assassins with souped-up proton-beam chisels that worked in series. This was the most outrageously hostile hotel room on the planet—at least, as far as these assassins were concerned.

They were in the elevator now. Jack was monitoring the normal electronic controllers for the elevator, so there wouldn't be any extra sensors to alert the assassins. There were no cameras in the elevator because the assassins hated cameras—but there would be cameras in the hotel room. By then the assassins would be helpless and begging for mercy, and Jack was going to love watching that.

The 476 Hotel was a luxurious establishment that took pains to stay low-key. This included a number of highly exclusive suites for politicians and VIPs. The penthouse was a retreat for politicians, mostly Juber Club members, who needed to lay low for a while. Happened all the time. Whiteslaw rented it for a week, with Fastbinder footing the six-figure bill.

Which he let Jack know about in no uncertain terms.

"I certainly hope this works, Jack," Fastbinder said frostily when he arrived to monitor the ambush.

"Don't sweat it, Pops." What Jack had really wanted to say was—

The elevator reached the penthouse suite. The controls opened the doors, then closed them again, and Jack mouse-clicked the start button. The doors to the elevator burst into brilliant flame that raced along the seam. The phosphorous hidden in the rubber seals burned hot enough to weld the steel doors together in seconds.

The suite filled with the clanking of the chain as the elevator plummeted, its dismantled emergency brakes rattling noisily, until the building shook with the inevitable crunch when it hit bottom eight floors below.

By then, the proton beams began blasting the interior with wave after wave.

"Hey! Hey!" Somebody was pounding on the walls.

A thousand miles away, and three miles down, Jack didn't hear it because he hadn't turned on the audio pickups yet. They wouldn't have survived what was about to come. He clicked the button called Light & Noise just as the proton beams powered down.

The hotel suite became a sickening miasma of strobing yellow light and noise that was guaranteed to create instant nausea, dizziness and lack of coordination in anybody who wandered into it.

Jack chuckled and clicked the baked-potato button on his screen.

The magnetron in the walls of the hotel turned the suite into a house-sized microwave oven. The magnetrons rotated behind the metal deflectors that spread the microwaves thoroughly. You didn't want to have cold spots. Jack hated it when his mac 'n' cheese dinner came out of the microwave with steaming edges and a frozen middle.

The computer made a happy *ding!* and Jack grinned up at Fastbinder. "I coulda roasted a bison herd."

Fastbinder didn't share his enthusiasm.

Jack powered down, brought up the recharged proton chisels and added a crowd-dispersing pain beam for good measure, and finally powered up the cameras, which emerged from behind their protective metallic shields in the walls of the penthouse suite.

Jack saw human remains and whooped happily.

But Fastbinder frowned. Jack's pleasure was dampened instantly.

"It is just one man—and not one of zee assassins," Fastbinder said.

Jack stared at the screen and zoomed in on the smoldering corpse—it was the Juber Club concierge.

The microphones picked up the sound of his sizzling flesh.

"Missed again," Fastbinder said disapprovingly, even mockingly.

Jack wouldn't look at the old man, his face hot with shame.

"Something warned them that there was danger in zee room," Fastbinder pointed out.

Jack knew what the old man was really saying. "You screwed up. You tipped your hand."

Then the screwup became even worse as the image on the screen grew brighter, as if somebody had just opened the drapes. Panning up, Jack saw a new hole in the wall—right where one of his proton-beam dispersers was installed. Nearby another hole came into being, and briefly his camera picked up the flying remains of the proton chisel that had been there. A face appeared in the hole.

"Jack, I'm home!"

It was the stalker, the young one, grinning like a moron. He disappeared, and Jack adjusted the camera with growing dread. His worst fear was realized when his third and last proton-beam chisel popped out of the wall, propelled by a clenched first.

"It's like popping big nasty zits!" said the assassin through the hole. "You oughta know all about zits, Jack."

"How is he doing that?" Jack demanded. "It's fifty feet up! I put the chisels in the exterior wall just so's he couldn't get at them!"

"He is standing on zee ledge," Fastbinder said with a shrug.

Jack tried to picture the ledge wrapping around every floor of the 476 Hotel—just a shallow brick protrusion. "It's three inches wide."

"Yes, these men are very resourceful," Fastbinder said morosely.

"How'd they get up there so fast—it's impossible!"

"It is not impossible, because they did it."

Jack would have laid the old man flat, right then and there, just to shut him up, but the assassin on the computer screen caught his attention.

"I've had about enough of you and your weird science experiments, Jack." The man bashed his way inside, through brick and plaster. Jack could swear he used his bare hands.

"You're not very good, Fast," said the dark-haired man. "Not too bright, know what I mean? Kind of a dim bulb, huh?"

"Shut up!" Jack Fast exploded at the screen.

Of course, the man in the hotel room couldn't hear him, but the man kept goading him. "Henry Mulligan you're not." The dark-haired man reached into the wall with one clawed hand—penetrated the plaster as if it were paper—and yanked out the pain beam. "Alvin Fernald? He had way better inventions than you." He lifted the decorative table that contained the speakers, crashing them into the lamps containing the strobe lights, and left wreckage when he was done.

"He is using only his hands," Fastbinder murmured.

"Jack, these men are more than we thought they were. Every time we feel we have their measure…"

"Anyway," the assassin said, "let's face it, Jack, everybody is better than you. Even I could come up with contraptions that worked better than you do. I mean this? What is this supposed to be?"

The stalker's image flickered, and when the flicker was done his empty hands were holding a metal hunk of wriggling mechanical arms.

"What is that doing there?" Fastbinder demanded.

"I thought it would help," Jack whined.

"Come on, a robot spider? You think this is going to stop anybody?" the assassin asked.

"It cost a million dollars!" Fastbinder exclaimed. "It was not for this purpose!"

"I mean, who came up with this lamebrained contraption?"

In a fury, Jack stabbed at the buttons controlling the Israeli-made assassination spider. On the screen, projectiles spit from below its alloy mandibles—and the stalker caught all three between his fingers.

"I see. It's a poisonous spider. Real effective." The stalker flicked the projectiles away, then plucked the eight legs off the spider like petals off a daisy. "Jack's not a loser…Jack's a big fat loser… Jack's not a loser…Jack's a big fat loser." When he took off the last wriggling leg he showed it to the camera and said, nodding, "Jack is definitely a big fat loser."

"I am not!"

"I guess even your mom knew that, huh, Jack?"

"Shut up!"

"See you soon, loser." The remains of the spider flew into the screen and the video feed went black.

36

"Well, am I a good goader?" Remo asked Chiun, who stood waiting on the building ledge with his hands in his robe sleeves, as relaxed as if he were standing among the gardens of deadly briars near the Sinanju cave of hermitage.

"Yes, it was adequately done."

"I don't know why you wouldn't do the taunting."

"The objective was to make the cretin angry," Chiun said reasonably, "and this is one of your best skills, Remo. To irritate. To infuriate."

"I see." Remo nodded. "Skills you do not posses."

"My demeanor is far too pleasant," Chiun explained.

"Uh-huh."

"But in this regard, you shine, my son."

"So, maybe I'll be recorded in the scrolls as the Master Who Rubs People the Wrong Way."

"It would not be as uncomplimentary as it sounds."

"Remo the Goader would be easier."

"But uglier."

Remo sighed and gazed out over the roofs of the nation's capital. They were in one of the few upscale districts of the city. For the most part, Washington, D.C., wasn't a safe place. Remo could feel the specter of the recent badness that had happened to him in this city. The funny thing was that, as awful as it was at the time, it hadn't seemed so awful when he started recovering from it. If only Chiun hadn't reminded him of it.

Well, that wasn't fair. It would have come back to haunt him regardless, eventually.

"I am thankful that the mad pubescent scientist's devices did not discharge as effectively as they did before," Chiun commented as they strolled around the building to descend via the more conventional fire escape.

"Yeah. Jack's losing his touch."

"Maybe."

"Also, they were pointed in, so I just got the leakage from the blast."

"Perhaps so, but the emanations still felt as strong. Just not as debilitating."

"You think we're acclimating to the proton death beam?"

"I think so."

"Wishful thinking, Little Father," Remo said as they took the stairs to the sidewalk. "Fine, thanks," he said offhandedly to a worried throng of women, which had been gathering ever since one of them spotted the two men walking around the high building ledge.

"Fine? Why were you gonna end it all if you're fine?" demanded a muscle-bound woman in a ponytail.

"I wasn't gonna jump—he was." Remo jerked a thumb at Chiun. "I goaded him into coming down."

"In truth, he is the one who sought to end it all. I would never take the cowardly path of escape, however grim my life might become," Chiun explained to the women. "Fear not. I am taking him back to the hospital."

The bodybuilder didn't look as if she believed either of them. "Stay put. Here comes the doctor."

Remo realized that the gathering of women stretched as far back as he could see and most wore T-shirts promoting a three-day breast cancer charity walk.

"Here, Doc!" The bodybuilder waved at a car emblazoned with signs for the walk and its sponsor. The words Safety Patrol were soaped onto the rear windows. The woman who rushed out was in a white sweatshirt with a large red cross, and she carried a bag of bandages, joint braces and water—most of the injuries on the walk were from stressed knees and dehydration.

"Where are they?" she asked.

"Right…" The bodybuilder looked all over the place. The general confusion spread through the crowd. A throng of women had witnessed the near suicide and had gathered around the two men. So how had they slipped off unseen?

"We all saw them!" the bodybuilder protested, and many women raised their voices in agreement.

"Somebody get hurt?" asked a eager young woman in a windbreaker that was zippered to her throat.

"Don't talk to her. She's a reporter, and she's bad news," the doctor announced.

"OH, NO," Remo groaned. They were watching from their car, parked up the street. The doctor's warnings were unheeded and the eager women began telling the tale of their strange interlude with the two men who had been walking on the high building ledges.

"The emperor shall be most irritated with you, Remo."

"Why with me? You were a part of this, and, incidentally, it was the right thing to do." But he knew Chiun was right. Smitty was going to be pissed, and that ticked him off big-time.

37

"Jacob Fastbinder has come up with a name for the cave people—he is calling them Albinoid," Smith said, ignoring the media circus brewing in Washington, D.C., over the disappearing human flies. "It's a part of this propaganda package he is prepared to release to the world media." Smith picked up a printed report that was so heavy it thumped when he dropped it again.

"He's going to try to convince the world that his cave people are a genetically distinct race of human beings, which is actually a savvy move," Mark Howard said. "Think about all the mileage he'll get from that."

"He'll get sued is what he'll get," Remo said. "Isn't an Albinoid a freakishly strong mint?"

"He's angling for pseudo-scientific credibility," Mark said. "He wants his cave people to have the same genetic distinction as the Caucasoid geographic race, the Negroid geographic race, the Australoids, the Mongoloids, the Indic and so on."

"Please don't explain what you're talking about," Remo said. "I'd rather listen to Smitty bitch than you lecture."

"This is important," Smith snapped. "It may seem obtuse, but it's actually a stroke of deviant genius. If Fastbinder makes good on his threat and unleashes this on the world—" Smith tapped the press kit "—then the trouble really starts."

Remo turned to Chiun, who didn't meet his gaze. "You don't understand this either, huh?"

"Here's the two-minute version," Mark Howard said. "For decades the scientific community divided the global races in a handful of major groups. You have the Caucasoid, or European geographic race, which we call Caucasian. You have the Indic or Hindu geographic race, which lumps together a lot of the people on and around the Indian subcontinent. Australoids are dark-skinned peoples indigenous to Australia. Negroid are dark-skinned peoples indigenous to Africa. These groupings are so generalized that the scientific community has moved away from them."

"What of Koreans?" Chiun demanded. "If the Hindus rate a geographic race, then the Koreans deserve one, as well."

"Part of the Mongoloid geographic race," Mark said offhandedly.

"What?" Chiun squeaked. "I am no Mongol!"

"Not Mongol, Mongoloid," Howard said. "It's just a scientific classification—"

"Mongols are nursed by camels and keep fleas as pets."

"It's just another name for the Asian geographic race, Master Chiun," Smith said reassuringly. "It's simply the name of the race that encompasses all the Asian peoples."

"All Asian peoples are not Korean and no Koreans are Mongols!"

"This is all beside the point."

"What is the point of this insult, Emperor?" Chiun squeaked.

"No insult was intended, Master Chiun," Howard interjected, an air of desperation in his voice. "Remo?"

Remo was counting ceiling tiles. "Not my can of worms."

"I refuse to be labeled a Mongol!" Chiun declared.

"We didn't make up the label, Master Chiun," Smith said reasonably. "As Mark said, the scientific community is abandoning these groupings. They are now considered misleading."

"They certainly are!" Chiun squeaked.

"It's Fastbinder who is resurrecting them," Mark Howard added, following Smith's thread and steering the conversation back on track. "He want to make use of these labels to stir up fears of racism. If he calls his cave people Albinoid and puts them on par with the Negroid classification, he'll garner sympathy. Fighting the Albinoid people will seem racist. Invading the subsurface will be called colonialism."

"Even if the subsurface is America's subsurface?" Remo growled. "Even if the cave folks are nothing but inbred hillbillies who wandered into a cave during Civil War days and were too dumb to find their way out again?"

Mark shrugged.

"Can't somebody do a test to prove they are inbred

hillbillies, and not their own race?" Remo demanded irritably.

"Of course they can," Smith said reasonably. "Their tests will include evidence that the Albinoids have no blood-grouping distinctions that signify racial uniqueness. What will it prove? Once Fastbinder riles the extremist antiracist, no scientific data will turn the tide."

Remo glowered at the floor. "Yeah. If Jesse Jackson decides to throw his weight behind the Albinoid cause, no amount of facts or common sense is gonna shake him loose."

Smith sighed. "What we need to keep in mind is that, if we reach the stage where Fastbinder goes public, it's already too late. The U.S. would have an intransigent foe literally underfoot and no way of fighting him. It may be necessary to wipe out the subsurface dwellers before their existence becomes known."

"You mean Fastbinder and his evil henchmen?" Remo demanded warily.

"I mean all of them. The entire subsurface population."

"You're talking genocide, Smitty."

"A last resort, of course."

"It is not a resort at all. Forget about it."

Smith looked squarely at the Reigning Master. "Remo, Albinoids have attacked and killed innocent human beings indiscriminately. I know it was Fastbinder who goaded them into it—"

"So we get Fastbinder."

"Then what?"

Remo looked at Smith. "I finally get time off?"

"Then the cave people are unguided. They are without a controlling influence. They'll be a continuing threat."

"Maybe we'll never hear from them again."

"They have discovered treasures and endless food supplies aboveground," Smith asked. "Quite frankly, the humans they've encountered haven't put up much of a fight. What would keep them belowground when Fastbinder and his son are removed? Remember how difficult a time we had tracking al-Qaeda in the tunnels of Afghanistan? The Albinoids have a thousand times as much territory, maybe a hundred thousand. Tracking them will be impossible. No one who lives in the vicinity of their exits to the surface will be safe from their raids." Smith allowed those words to settle. "We've made projections."

Mark Howard brought out a printout of a United States map. He sketch a ragged border in pencil that included the entire southwestern states, up to the San Andreas fault, then east to the Mississippi River. "The subsurface system extends as far as this, roughly, from what we've ascertained from the raid patterns."

"There's not caves under all that," Remo scoffed.

"We don't know where they are for sure," Mark said. "If we had attacks on the same scale as the recent attacks, if they continued at only half the current frequency, then we're looking at about two or three thousand dead every year. Our estimates, based on the suspected subterranean population, and the mounting savagery of their attacks show the average dead doubling by year's end. We also believe our population count is low. We might be seeing much higher victim counts, on the level of five to ten thousand per year. The resulting panic would send populations fleeing toward the coasts and the major metropolitan areas."

"Come on," Remo said.

"Some states would likely be vacated. Kansas, Texas, New Mexico. Those who remained would be picked off or create autonomous military communities."

"Like in *Road Warrior?*" Remo asked. "I think you're stretching the what-ifs a little thin, don't you?"

"It's happening already," Dr. Smith said. "Kansas. A whole town emptied out in ten hours, but a local militia moved in and took over the buildings. White supremacists. They claimed to have formed the independent Nation of God Almighty. That was at noon today. This was taken from the NOGA Webcam at 3:00 p.m."

Mark Howard's next picture showed a lot of dead people, and one live albino, who was eating a cat. Well, after nothing but human for breakfast, lunch and dinner, day in and day out, who wouldn't want a little variety in their victuals?

"They were gone before the National Guard arrived, but the NOGA militiamen were wiped out or missing. I think this illustrates that my projection of the future is not at all outlandish."

Remo nodded. "Guess not."

"If this continues, if the death toll rises, if they continue to pose an ongoing threat to the very existence of the United States," Smith said, "then extermination is not out of the question."

Remo stared at the photo. "You're right. Let's just pull a Final Solution on 'em. Makes perfect sense."

"It might make sense, eventually," Smith said somberly.

38

The President didn't ask for war. Not for this one, anyway. It came and got him.

The second invasion came at one o'clock in the morning, and it came silently, with the darkness, starting in Wichita.

"Not again," muttered Paul Pirie, who wasn't supposed to be working the overnight shift anyway. He had seniority, and that meant he got the day shift. It was in the labor contract. But it was also in the labor contract that he had to cover for other foremen of comparable seniority and responsibilities. That was fine when the other foremen properly scheduled their absences. Vacation time required a minimum lead time of three months. Major illness required a package of medical records proving the illness was legitimate and required a lead time of one month. If the illness was suspect, as determined by the elected captain of the local, then you better get sick on your vacation and you better schedule it, like the book says, three months in advance.

Moller, the overnight foreman, had given no notice,

the inconsiderate son of a bitch. Just went and died without letting anybody know about it ahead of time, and who suffered because of it? Who had to work extra hours because that A-1 asshole Moller had to eat bacon and doughnuts every day for breakfast? Who paid the price?

Paul Pirie, that's who. And he wasn't going to take it. He had grievances filed against the company and against the estate of the late Mortimer Moller. When the claims analysts told him he didn't have the basis for grievance, Pirie filed a grievance against the claims analysts.

"I fought for this union, and for once this union is gonna fight for me!" Pirie pounded on the desk of the head of the local, spilling beer. Tom Berry, head of the local, wiped it up without complaining and strolled into the break room to pour another. He returned to his seat and sipped the foamy head off the beer.

"In fact, we've fought for you nineteen times since 1999," Berry said, pushing a frosty mug over to Pirie.

Pirie drained his glass halfway. "This is different!"

The claims analyst looked expectant and took a sip. Pirie took a long, slow draft to stall for time. "There should be somebody else to cover in case of absences," he argued.

Berry nodded into his mug. "That's you."

"Somebody hired only to cover unexpected absences," Pirie insisted, and took an angry swig.

"Somebody union, of course," Berry said, suddenly taking Pirie more seriously.

"Of course." Pirie clomped his beer glass on the desk.

"Get you another?" Berry took the empty mugs into the break room and emerged with them full. He also had a paper plate of Krunchy Kreme doughnuts. "Just got the two o'clock delivery—still warm," Berry explained.

Pirie chomped half a doughnut in one bite. "Very nice," he said. Not just the fresh doughnuts—the whole setup was nice. Free beer, free doughnuts. Pirie wondered if he ought to try to get the job as head of the union local next time they had an election.

"Now, I hear what you're saying, Paul. We need a designated employee who has seniority enough to take a foreman's role, but who isn't a full-time employee. Maybe a retired foreman, who can be on call to fill in when an unexpected absence occurs."

"Yeah," Pirie said, chewing thoughtfully. "But he's hired to be the fill-in guy, see. He expects to be inconvenienced. See, it ain't fair that I got to cover the late shift for that fat ass Moller. I didn't plan on it, and I ain't being compensated for it. Well, not adequately compensated." In truth, Pirie got double time and a half for every minute of the late-night shift. He and Berry estimated that it would take at least quadruple time and a half to adequately compensate somebody for covering a shift if he had not expected to cover it.

"I'll present it to the company first thing in the morning," Berry said. "They'll go along."

"You think? Won't they say it's too much money?"

"They always say that. But if we get an agreement out of them now, then we don't ram it through at next year's contract negotiations. It'll cost them a hell of a lot less to play ball now."

That guy Berry was the smartest union politico that Pirie had ever known, and he'd known several. Berry kept the local branch of the union working like a well-oiled machine. Damn, the U.S. of A. needed more guys of such caliber, then maybe all the damn unions wouldn't be withering away, and taking workers' rights into the toilet with them.

Despite making double time and a half, he was still surly about working the night shift. It was a smaller work crew and he, the foreman, was required to even work the assembly line from time to time. That's what he was doing when the lights went out—trying to get imperfect plastic doggie heads onto plastic doggie bodies.

There was no plastic head, no matter how messed up, that could be made to go onto its dog body. Sometimes, when you were done, it didn't look as good as it was supposed to look. But who cared about some fool cartoon dog from some fool cartoon movie? And the kids got the fool doggie for free anyway when they bought their Hamburger Hooray Meal—so what if the dog had a scorched plastic welt where his mouth should be.

As the sounds of the machinery died away, Pirie was still absentmindedly forcing the plastic parts together. He waited. This might be just another flicker in the power grid, or it might be a full-scale blackout. That meant...

"Time to party!" whooped a nearby line assembler as the emergency lights came on and directed employees through the vast, dark maze of the manufacturing floor of Cut-Above Plastic Components. They were laughing and whooping—what could be better than getting time and a half for doing nothing? Their labor contract guaranteed they got paid no matter what closed the plant, including act of God, act of war, or act of the President.

"It's not that big," announced a woman with a battery-powered boom box who was listening to talk radio. "Just a twenty-mile radius."

"They got power in the city?" Paul Pirie asked. The city of Wichita was nearby. "They know what made us go black?"

The woman grinned. "They got no clue. They just said it's major."

Pirie liked the sound of that. If he was real lucky, the power would stay off for the rest of the shift. It was time to sit back, relax and have some grub. He wandered over to the buffet, where the cafeteria staff was serving up midnight lunch over little fire pots to keep it hot. The labor contract stipulated that, regardless of the catastrophe, there had to be food for the idled personnel.

Pirie filled his plate with mashed potatoes, stew and gravy, and only noticed the heavy silence as he took a seat at a cafeteria table. There had to have been thirty, forty employees sitting around, and none of them said a word.

"What's going on?" he asked a woman at his table.

The woman, by way of answer, started screaming. She flung her arms up, spattering Pirie's face with blazing-hot beef stew. He ran around the cafeteria shouting in pain while she ran around saying, "They're coming! It's the apocalypse! I don't want to be left behind!"

More people panicked, and when Paul Pirie got the beef stew out of his eyes he saw what all the excitement was about.

It was about albinos who killed people. Gaunt, naked, filthy rat-people with pink eyes, who swatted at the plant workers with casual ferocity. Pirie saw heads smashed and chests caved in.

The killing died down abruptly when the albinos discovered the beef stew, which they ate with…enthusiasm.

Amazingly, if Pirie's stewed eyeballs could be trusted, the albinos were interested in factory equipment, as well as people.

One of the albinos spoke to him. It took him a while to figure out that the grunts and hacking coming out of the creature's mouth were actually words, but a few fists in the gut improved his hearing. The albino was ordering him to dismantle some of the machines on the assembly line.

The albino gave him a sheet of paper printed with a list of equipment—mostly it was small, specialty stuff used in the engineering lab. Pirie didn't ask questions, just got his shift personnel to work tearing down the machines. The albinos opened up expandable, bullet-shaped sleds with heavy-gauge wire sacks suspended inside the framework. The parts had to fit into the sleds.

"We don't know how to take these things apart," hissed Alma, one of the senior assemblers.

"They don't know that," Pirie whispered. "Just keep taking apart until they're small enough to fit in their sacks. The sooner we're done, the sooner they leave."

The dismantled components were stuffed into the suspended sacks and wired closed. Other sleds were filled with high-grade steel sheets and plastic blocks used for prototyping.

"What are they gonna do with all that stuff?" Alma demanded.

"I couldn't care less," Pirie said. "I just want them to go away."

The albinos did go, but they took the entire night shift with them.

"WHY?" PIRIE CRIED. He was hitched to an equipment sled and had marched for an hour in the blackness of the cavern.

Everybody in town knew about the cavern. The Boy Scouts explored it every summer. You couldn't get lost because it was only a hundred feet deep. Who'd have thought it contained an access crack that led into a cave that was miles and miles long?

"You to put this back together," grunted the albino who did all the talking, and he waved at the sled full of components.

Alma, who was tied up alongside Paul, cackled joylessly. "You want to tell them or should I?"

"Shh!"

"Hey, you, what if we can't put them back together?" Alma asked. She clearly felt she had nothing more to lose.

The albino shrugged. "If you got no use, then you get eated."

Alma laughed again. She'd lost her mind. Pirie envied her.

"WHAT ARE YOU planning?" Chiun demanded over the noise of the rotors.

"I'm not planning anything."

"Do not use that tone of voice with me, Remo Williams," Chiun snapped. "I see your brain working."

"My brain works?"

"Infrequently and poorly, so it is like a poorly kept automobile that functions loudly and with much gear grinding."

"I'll try to hold it down. Yippee, we're back in Kansas."

Smith had called in an Air Force helicopter to transport the Masters of Sinanju to the nearest of the incursions from below. It was a measure of his concern that he had allocated military resources even as the U.S. Military secretly mobilized itself to carry out the largest domestic defense operation in the history of the country. To further speed up their deployment, Smith had Remo and Chiun take a chartered jet from the Rye airstrip. That was far too close for security in Smith's eyes. The jet put them in Wichita, then the helicopter took them at top speed over the suburbs. They would be at the entrance site in minutes, and Remo still wasn't telling Chiun what he had up his sleeve.

Green County State Forest passed by under the chopper. The overnight campers who survived the attack were gone, and the park rangers had been escorted firmly away. Now it was a staging ground for military operations, with vehicles and troops swarming around the entrance to a rocky hole in the ground.

Their Air Force pilot, as ordered, landed long enough to have his priority shipment of supplies off-loaded and he kept his eyes facing forward at all times.

He didn't know who his passengers were and he didn't care. All he knew was that when he was on his way back to Wichita and he glanced in the back, the passengers were gone.

THE CORDON AROUND THE CAVE entrance was fifty men strong. Somehow, they never saw the two new arrivals. The heat sensors missed them. The motion detectors decided the readings it got were far too fast to be animal, too slow to be airborne munitions.

"Why have they not come inside?" Chiun demanded after he and Remo had entered the small cave. "They wait outside like frightened villagers sitting in ambush around a wolverine den."

"They don't know how to come inside," Remo said. "Junior says they've never simulated this kind of military operation on this scale. They're waiting for the official plans, I guess."

"Plans made by men who weren't forward thinking enough to anticipate this? They are doomed."

"You got that right. No matter how many men they send in, they'll be able to attack two or three at a time at best. Those poor schmucks try coming down here and they'll be dead ducks."

Remo felt the weight of his responsibility on his shoulders and increased his pace, coming to the freshly chopped gap in the rocks where the Green Cavern had once dead-ended. Beyond it was an endless variation of rocky rooms, halls and pits. The narrowest passages had been widened with hammers. By the light of a glow stick, Remo and Chiun descended with the speed and smooth motion of slippery cave salamanders.

The trail was unmistakable. There was blood and worse on the cave floor. There was discarded clothing and wallets and keys. There were bodies, some with big mouthfuls of flesh missing.

They found one of the bodies alive, and she lived long enough to babble about a forced march, about being chained like a beast of burden to help haul the invaders' booty. "I wasn't fast enough. They had a bus to catch."

She had been abandoned—but not before a few of them chewed open her stomach. A quick snack before they moved on. "They wanted to keep eating." She chuckled, blood coming from her mouth.

Remo inspected the wound and inventoried her missing entrails. Nothing could save the woman. He ended her suffering with a touch to the neck.

"A bus to catch?" Chiun asked.

"Transportation, back to wherever King Fastbinder has his court. I bet it's the new earth drill."

They ran on, bounding over boulders, dancing through jagged, water-carved canyons and slipping down endless jumbles of rock. They were on their third three-hour glow stick when the clink of metal and the cry of human voices came from far below them.

Without a word Remo shot ahead, and Chiun raced
to keep up. Faster than any man could move on the
earth above, Chiun moved among the rocks and run-
nels of the earth below, and still it wasn't fast enough.
Remo flowed like quicksilver, with all the skills and
speed of a Master of Sinanju.

Chiun heard the sound of running water soon
enough.

REMO FELT THE SPACE open up in front of him as he
homed in on the river, and came to a sudden stop at
the end of the tunnel. He had an instant to take in the
river that moved fast and deep close by, and along the
riverbank was a collection of transport watercraft.
They consisted of long, tapered frames of steel bars,
and inside each was a mass of polystyrene foam. People and the stolen booty were chained inside hollows
chopped out of the foam. The rear of each watercraft
was cross-braced with steel rods that were latched in
place, and a braided steel winch line connected all the
watercraft together in a train. The fourth pod carried
no prisoners and no gear, only a small army of albinos, using chains as seat belts inside the contraption.

The last detail to catch his attention was the series of
steel rungs driven into the rock on the shore, and the long
steel chain that was slithering out of the rungs. The albinos had just cast off, and the powerful current was already muscling the transport pods away from the shore.

"Not without me you don't." Remo called for Chiun
over his shoulder, then slipped into the water in a dive
that didn't ripple the surface.

The river was a monster, and its gigantic muscles propelled Remo out of the cavern and into the tight tunnel beyond close behind the pod train. All the river's speed wasn't enough to suit him, though, and he stroked powerfully, doubling his speed until he heard the metallic protestations of the rearmost pod getting close. He grabbed it and held on as the pod tossed wildly in a sudden twist in the tunnel. The fingers of the metal frame screeched when they slammed into the rock, but they distorted and bounced back into shape afterward.

Remo could hear Chiun approaching, but his body also felt the vibrations of the agitated water coming from ahead of them. The ride was going to get a lot worse very soon. The first of the pods let out a loud screech of impact and then was muted abruptly, and Remo knew the watercraft was completely submerged. He held on with one hand and reached out with the other, snatched Chiun's wrist in his grip and held on as the pod train lurched ahead.

The albino's pod shuddered, crunched into the wall of rock in its turn and was dragged down underwater. The train was in a black passage where there was no air, only chaos.

39

Remo could feel people dying. He could hear their terror in the churning water. He watched their last precious bubbles of air seep away from the pod train.

He and Chiun clung to the back of the last pod, each with an arm looped in the steel braces of the frames. They had instinctively filled their lungs, and now they allowed the carbon dioxide to leak from their lips in tiny blips. They could survive underwater for some time—but the captives on the other pods, even the albinos in the last pod, would be clawing at their throats by now.

Remo couldn't just let them die.

He looked around the back end of the pod and drew his head back in again as a rock wall slammed into the steel framework. Nobody was steering the pods. The river drove the pod train along and pushed it where it wanted. The water was made into a maelstrom by rock falls too numerous to count. When the pod train wasn't being hurled into boulders it was floating to the top and being dragged, scraping and squealing, along the rocky roof, where shimmering pockets of air slipped by just out of reach.

Remo heaved himself around the end of the pod, only to be manhandled into place again by an insistent, unbreakable clamp on his ankle. Chiun's quick grab kept Remo from putting himself in the way of the dislodged stalactite that loomed up, as big as a redwood trunk. It crunched into the pod with such force the springy metal couldn't bounce back.

Remo turned on Chiun, ferociously pushing the old man's hand away from him.

"They're all dying!" Remo shouted, loud enough for Chiun to understand him under the water.

"What would you do?" Chiun barked.

Remo felt the truth wilt him—there was *nothing* he could do, even if he did manage to climb into the pods without being torn off. He allowed himself to dangle from the rear of the pod as the subterranean voyage continued endlessly.

Another impact spun the pod train to the side, and Remo found their pod rolling along the ceiling for seconds before the train came to a teeth-jarring halt. The pod train had become draped around a rock column.

The glow stick, hung on his neck, was bright enough to watch the cataclysm that followed. The pod strained on its lead, and out of the chaos of black water another pod swung into them, fast, heavy and unstoppable. Remo felt the weight of the disaster even before it struck him physically—the pods had to get free now or there would be no hope of any survivors.

Remo turned, his eyes meeting Chiun's in the near blackness, and they pushed away just before the stunning collision fused the two pods into a single ruined mass.

"Help them!" he shouted underwater. Chiun nodded in understanding. The old man found a new handhold on the tangled metal.

Remo's internal clock told him that the pods had been underwater for only minutes, but it felt like an eternity. It felt like the endlessness of existence beyond the Void.

He was angry at Jacob Fastbinder III, and he was angry at Jack Fast. This was one of the most inhumane things he had ever witnessed, and somebody was gonna pay for it. Remo's fingernails penetrated the steel framework of the pod. His swift crawling made a mockery of the gigantic impetus of the river's flow. When he reached the front of the pod he made out the barrel-thick rock column formed by the fusion of a stalactite and a stalagmite. What was it doing here in the river flow?

He slashed the braided steel cable with his fingernails, and the pod chain leaped ahead. Remo was snapped like a whip. His hand didn't release its grip on the rear of the pod, but the rear of the pod couldn't stand the opposing forces. It separated with a series of overlapping metal snaps, and Remo found himself floating along with a section of the jagged cage. The foam interior of the pod disintegrated and scattered its cargo of albinos.

Remo swam hard, trying to outrace the current again, heartened by the changing vibration of the water that told him the current was slowing and widening ahead of him. He shot to the surface in a wide cavern and slipped toward the gleam of green. Chiun had activated his own glow stick and was dragging the pod chain to an eroded rock landing.

Somebody was coughing. At least one of the captives had survived the ordeal.

40

Whiteslaw had been waiting for days in a sleazy Oklahoma hotel, doing nothing. It was driving him batty. No phone calls. He couldn't even go to the bar for fear of being recognized. He had nothing to do but watch television, where the best thing on was a T & A soap opera from south of the border called *¡Excito Totalamente!* Whiteslaw didn't understand a word of it, but he enjoyed watching the big-busted Latino women bickering and embracing in their skimpy halter tops.

And he brooded. Here he was, on the verge of scamming himself into the presidency of the United States of America, and he was too afraid to leave his hotel room. Those assassins were his ticket to glory and the bane of his existence. Why couldn't Fastbinder and his idiot-genius kid kill them already!

Fastbinder finally called. "I gotta get out of here, Jacob," Whiteslaw barked.

"There is a problem."

Whiteslaw didn't like the sound of that. "Don't tell me you missed them again."

"You have lied to us from zee very beginning about these assassins and what they can do."

"We've been through this and through this, Jacob."

"You never told us they could walk up zee walls, Senator."

"What?"

"You never explained that zees men punch through brick walls with bare hanz." Fastbinder's accent always became more pronounced when he became excited. "Also, Senator, zee assassins are adapting to zee weapons we used on them."

"So you missed," Whiteslaw accused.

"If a Tomcat fighter plane fails to shoot down zee B-2 stealth bomber, would you say zee Tomcat missed? No. It was eluded by a great unt zophisticated foe. Just so, we were outmaneuvered by superior cababiliteez. What else did you not tell us, Senator?"

"I told you all I knew from the start. Remember my telling you how the young one ripped the door off a limo and threw guys around like softballs. I never said I knew their limits. How would I know they could walk up walls, huh? The point is, your brat's traps didn't work—am I right?"

"Wrong. Jack's traps did work, but zee assassins got around them. They destroyed zee last of zee large proton-discharge devices, but zee devices had negligible effect because zee assassins shielded themselves some way. We are back at square one."

Whiteslaw should have been afraid, but he was just angry. "That idiot kid had the one weapon that would work and instead of killing those assholes at the very start he gave 'em just enough of it to teach them how to adapt."

"Do you know what Jack thinks?" Fastbinder asked sardonically. "Zat these assassins are using something other than technology. He says they use some sort of highly enhanced human skills."

"Like superpowers?"

"Yes."

"Like Batman?"

"Exactly, like Batman."

"Fastbinder, your kid's an idiot. I don't know why you let him call the shots."

Coldly, Fastbinder replied, "It is I who call zee shotz."

"Who you trying to kid? That brat's working you like a puppet. Lord knows why you let him do it. Take a look around you, Jacob. Who's the real worm king, huh? Who're the cavemen really afraid of? It ain't you."

"Senator—"

"Hey, Fastbinder, I'm giving you twenty-four hours to make those assassins dead. If you fail again, our co-operative relationship is dissolved."

Whiteslaw felt good about the threat, and about the cold silence that followed. He had what he needed to spin the political parties into decades of chaos if they didn't give him what he wanted. And once he was President, Fastbinder needed him as an ally. They both knew it.

"They will be dead in twenty-four hours," Fastbinder stated.

"I have your word?" Whiteslaw demanded.

"You haff my word. I will see to it perzonally."

41

"Why the long face, Pops?" Jack asked.

"Whiteslaw is showing his fangs," Fastbinder said acidly. "He called you stupid for believing our assassins have supertalents, and he called me stupid for putting my trust in you. I am beginning to think he is right. You are only a boy. I've given you entirely too much leeway."

"A boy? Gee, Pop, you could at least call me a young man, or even a teenager."

"Sometimes you act like a young man, and sometimes you act like a little boy. You are a brilliant boy, but I have seen enough of your mistakes and missteps to know that you lack the wisdom that comes with age, Jack. Zee assassins are *not* Batmans."

Jack laughed, short and haughty. "Batman didn't have superpowers, Pop."

"I don't care. It is make-believe."

"Maybe there are people out there with abilities that are different from ours, Pops, ever think of that?" Jack demanded.

"Hogwash."

"Hey, Pops, look at something for me." Jack snatched at the curtain on the chiseled window and stabbed a finger at the toiling albinos in the central court of the emerging city. "Those cave people were just like us until a few generations ago, and look how much they devolved. They think you and me have superpowers, right? So how can you say there's not another bunch of people who are further evolved than us?"

Fastbinder shook his head tightly. "The Albinoids are not devolved, Jack, just degraded. They're genetically zee same as us."

"Okay, fine, so they were normal humans and then they degraded. So maybe somebody else was a normal human and then they advanced—and maybe they had something that helped them advance."

"Jack, you are in a fantasy. Zee assassins do not have superpowers. We are all just people, zee Albinoids, us and zee assassins. Some of us simply have better brains." Fastbinder stalked to the door, waving down Jack before the teenager could speak again. "It is time for you to grow up, Jack."

42

"We should never have breathed life back into them," Chiun said.

"No kidding." Remo caught a female captive under one arm and reached for the scummy-looking man whose pores oozed nicotine. The scummy guy was making a high-pitched siren sound, but it stopped when Remo paralyzed them both.

"This is for your own good," Remo told the middle-aged woman who was trying to scramble up the walls.

"You can't make me go back in there!"

"You stay here and you'll starve to death," Remo pointed out. "There's no other way out."

"I'd rather die!"

"That's just the terror talking," Remo said reasonably. He stepped up onto her rock—the rock she had climbed for two minutes to reach. She goggled at him. "How'd you—"

"There, there." He paralyzed her and leaped down to the landing with her slumped on one shoulder, then inserted her into one of the sockets in the watercraft pod. It was the least damaged of the three salvaged pods.

They wouldn't use the other pods. After all, there were only eight survivors. The neat row of nonsurvivors stretched across the back wall of the cavern where they had landed.

"If you intend to send the other floating prisons into the river as a decoy, then these bodies should be placed into them," Chiun pointed out.

"Keep your voice down, will ya?" Remo said. "You know what Fastbinder will do with the ones that arrive dead?"

"Feed them to his subjects," Chiun said with a shrug.

"Shh!" Remo hissed, but it was too late. The paralyzed captives were practically having seizures with their eyeballs. "Nice goin', Chiun."

"Fastbinder will be suspicious of the disappearance of the captives when the decoy pods arrive empty. But it is you who is Reigning Master. Naturally, I accede to your authority, " Chiun sniffed.

"Which is your way of saying this is gonna be a real disaster and you want me to look like the moron instead of you. What's so hilarious?"

"Remo," Chiun said, wearing a smirk, "I could never look like a moron, and you never couldn't."

Remo rolled his eyes and stepped into Pod Two, weaving his arms and finally bellowing, "Hey!" This failed to get the attention of the struggling captives, until Remo lifted the glow stick and began waving it slowly back and forth. The captives found blessed distraction from panic in the swaying point of green light.

"My name is Remo and I'll be your tour guide today. Not sure where we're going or what we're going to do when we get there, but I know one thing—it's going to be the ride of a lifetime. In fact, it's gonna be the last ride of your lifetime unless you do what I say, okay?"

He briefly explained that he would have gladly made them all unconscious, but they needed to stay awake to keep their lungs saturated with oxygen. "Every breath could be your last one for minutes at a time, so make them last, people! Thanks for joining us today. I'd like to remind you that gratuities are not included in your tour price and are graciously accepted."

All he got in response were rolling eyeballs.

"It's like we're going into Splash Mountain with a bunch of Cookie Monsters," Remo said.

Chiun offhandedly tossed Pods One and Three into the river current and gave them a few minutes' start before stepping onto the last pod and nudging away from the shore with one sandaled toe. He crouched alongside Remo at the rear of the pod.

"We're gonna kill them all, Little Father," Remo said morosely as the pod picked up speed.

"Abandoning them would be worse." Chiun shrugged. "They would starve until their hunger compelled them to feed on their dead companions. Giving them a slim chance of escape is better than condemning them to a few extra days of life as cave people."

"You know, that actually made me feel better," Remo said.

THE HOOTING OF THE ALBINOS called Jack's attention to the window. A band of men was wading into the rocky shallows that served as the city docks.

More raiding parties were returning with their booty. Jack only hoped there was more to salvage than last time. The pod train from the Oklahoma raids was not in the best shape. In fact, half the raiding party was DOA.

He jogged downstairs and across the city, heading for the Fastbinder Docks, which were nothing more than a dam in the river created by blasting out the walls, widening it by a hundred feet and filling the riverbed until it was only as deep and strong as a woodland creek—even if it was a mile wide. It caught anything bigger than a cave minnow.

As he reached the docks his spirits sank. The latest arrivals were nothing but dead albinos, some still in pod chains. One wrecked pod rocked gently nearby, empty except for some tattered polystyrene foam.

"Anything to recover, Jack?" It was his father. The old man had to have been waiting nearby for the Wichita raiding party. He knew it was overdue. He couldn't pass up a chance to rub failure in Jack's face, could he? It was the old man's new hobby.

Jack squinted into the darkness of the cave mouth. "More pods," he announced.

These two were in better shape, although they had also become separated from each other. Fastbinder, standing on the higher shore and watching them emerge from the tunnel, shook his head sadly. Jack hated him for it but refused to ask what the old man saw.

Jack saw it himself soon enough. The pods were empty. No captives, no cargo. The rears of the frames swung open on their hinges.

"There's one more still coming," Jack reminded Fastbinder sullenly.

They waited in silence for ten minutes. Fastbinder was ready to leave when Jack said, "I see it."

The remains of the last pod were only floating because the foam interior had broken up and lodged in the pointed nose of the frame. When the jabbering albinos dragged it onto the rocky shallows, the foam fell to the bottom. There was nothing else inside.

"Now do you see that this was a mistake?" Fastbinder demanded.

"We should have gone with the onion-layers design like I wanted," Jack said, examining the last pod. "My fiberglass impact-mitigation panels would have worked. It *will* work."

"It's wasteful, and the fiberglass panels are too expensive!" Fastbinder snapped.

"Foot transport would take days," Jack called back, examining the wreckage.

"But it would actually get the goods and the prisoners to us. Do you realize that the only successful raid was the one you made in JED?"

Jack didn't answer, but then he stood up quick. "Pops, these pods didn't break down at all. Somebody broke them. See the cable ends? That cut is so straight it looks like a laser did it. Same in the front."

"The assassins," Fastbinder said. "They are coming!" He turned and strode off.

"'Bout time," Jack Fast said.

43

Paul Pirie tried begging.

"Please don't leave us!"

"No," said the man with the eyes of death.

Paul Pirie tried bribery. "I've got lots of money. I'll make it worth your while."

"No." They couldn't see much of the man. The only light was the dim plastic stick he had on a cord around his neck. The glow was enough to cast his features into deep shadow, but you could swear something malevolent glimmered in his black eye sockets.

Finally, Paul Pirie pulled out the big guns. "You get me out of here, or I swear I will file a grievance with my local union representative."

The cruel-looking younger man didn't even dignify that with an answer. What kind of a man disrespected the unions so much that he could casually ignore such a threat? Even the company, the great enemy of all good, honest, God-fearing people, trod softly when it came to the union. There was only one possible explanation.

"You're from Mexico!"

The man with dead eyes and unusually thick wrists said, "Yeah, whatever."

Paul Pirie's mind spun out of control, remembering all the wild talk he'd heard about the Mexicans conspiring to steal American jobs. Everybody knew the Mexicans stole American technology, they bribed the evil managers of American companies and, the sleaziest trick of all, those lousy Mexicans worked for a lower wage. But in the secure haven of the union hall, Pirie had heard people whispering about Mexicans who sabotaged American factories and the products they made.

"The Mexico guvmunt sends them Mexicans to take our best people down there. Like Phil Leary. Best foreman we ever had, and the Mexicans stole him away in the night!" The old man who explained this hadn't missed a meeting of the union local in forty-three years, so he had some credibility—but it was widely known he hadn't been sober in forty-three years, either, and was now senile to boot. So you took what he said with a grain of salt. But now Paul Pirie knew the truth. The old man was right.

"The old man was right," Pirie declared forcefully.

"Who gives a hoot about the old man?" said Alma. "It's the young stud muffin I want to get my hands on."

She was chained up next to Paul Pirie in the battered pod. They had all managed to survive the grueling, endless second phase of their trip down the subterranean river, thanks to the two strangers, but the two strangers refused to let them out of the pod now that they had beached it.

"He's a Mexican," Paul accused.

"Doesn't have a Mexican accent."

"Alma, I know you've lost your marbles but you gotta listen. We've been captured by the secret Mexican technology railroad! We've discovered how they're stealing America's factories and stuff and taking it to their own places south of the border. It explains everything!"

"And you're calling me crazy?" Alma scoffed. She said to Remo, "Where ya off to, big boy?"

Remo Williams tipped his imaginary hat. "You folks sit tight while we scout on ahead."

"Why can't we go with you?" demanded one of the other captives.

"This is the safest place for you. Trust me."

"I'll never trust a Mexican secret agent!" Paul Pirie shouted defiantly. "Don't try to deny it!"

"Stupid gringo, we're not Mexicans, are we, Little Father?"

"Certainly not," squeaked a voice out of the darkness where the old one had been standing idly as the young one pulled the pod above the waterline. "The Mexicans could never stand against us."

"Besides, this place has belonged to us way longer than the Mexicans."

Pirie thought hard. The Mexicans' ancestors were the Spanish who first claimed the Americas for the civilized world. The only quote-humans-unquote who were here before that were the—

"You're redskin Indians!"

"Exactly," Remo agreed.

"I am not!" protested the old man.

"You're trying to take it all back for the Cherokee nation!"

"Cherokees are kitty cats compared to us. Now we go kick-um some heap big paleface butt. Don't wander off."

The malnourished-looking man with the long face was shouting accusations, the scraggly woman was proclaiming her willingness to perform various services and the other captives were simply trying to scream their fool heads off. The sound followed them for a mile.

"Guess they didn't want to be left behind," Remo said. "Can't say I blame them."

"It would have been deadly for them to accompany us, for I would have annihilated them myself."

They had beached the pod when they felt eddies of air swirling back in their faces, potent with albino smell. Knowing Jack Fast and Jacob Fastbinder, there would be nasty surprises awaiting them. It was better to leave the captives behind and retrieve them later. Hopefully. Now they walked along the river's edge.

Thousands of years ago a massive river carved a wide tunnel, then the water flow dwindled. The reduced river created a much smaller channel on the floor of the old tunnel during the next age of erosion, leaving walkable banks on both sides. The signs of albino foot traffic showed that they used it regularly.

"Chiun," Remo said, and lifted the glow stick. Above their heads, where most eyes would have seen only pitch-blackness, they could make out a man-size access tunnel and a bundle of explosives affixed to the ceiling. More bundles stretched across the roof in an arch.

"I don't get why they'd close up the river tunnel," Remo said. "Unless they thought they could bring it down on top of us."

"If so, they missed," Chiun observed. "That is not a mistake I would expect of this young madman."

"Yeah. So what's he planning?"

"I know not, but he will have a plan," Chiun said confidently.

As they followed the river, walking shoulder to shoulder, Remo conjured the image of a beautiful garden grove on the Mediterranean shore of Spain.

"What troubles you?" Chiun asked.

"I was thinking of Barcelona. We knew there was something out of the ordinary waiting for us inside that mansion. That was the first time we had a run-in with the Fastbinder arsenal of doodads and gizmos, and we got our asses kicked."

"It was the proton-emitter device that weakened us. Without it, all the silly army toys would have been ineffectual," Chiun said.

"Doesn't matter. The emitter was there and we almost got whacked."

"This, perhaps, is not the best time to discuss the results of the emitter."

Remo smiled. "When we went into the hotel room in D.C. those emitters were just as strong, but they didn't give me the same sort of a mind-suck. I've grown calluses in my head."

"You don't know this."

"Yeah, I feel it."

"You cannot trust this intuition," Chiun said. "You must not take foolish risks. What if you are wrong?"

"I went beyond the Void," Remo declared flatly.

"Talk not of this now," Chiun said quietly.

"There was nothing, Chiun. All my senses were stripped away from me. It was an absence of everything. It was the greatest agony I could imagine."

"Remo, what is the purpose of this? Let us discuss it another time."

"I'm not gonna live my life dodging it."

"But why now?" Chiun demanded.

But he could see that Remo had closed his eyes.

"Stop, young fool!"

Remo was conjuring the darkness of the Void in his memory, and then he beckoned to the absence of darkness that was beyond it. He felt the darkness drift away, replaced by nothing.

"Stop, imbecile! You would obligate me to drag your comatose white body back to the world above?"

Chiun's discordant singsong faded away, and was replaced with the rush of blood in Remo's own skull, and then that too went away, until there was nothing.

The rhythm of the river flow, the cool, aged scent of the rock and the water, these dimmed and were gone, and Remo was once again in nothingness. In this place he had spent days that felt like years. He remembered it now. It was endless. He had been unthinking but miserable. There was nothing for him to sense and even his memories were wiped away and inaccessible. He had nothing to cling to.

Then a voice came through the nothingness beyond the Void. The voice was not real sound, nor real words, but was a glimmer of something. He clung to the sweetly spoken words, and centered his entire being on them until, by the force of his will, he clarified the words.

It was a gentle, exquisite voice, a young woman, and the memory she spoke of was—just the same. The floodgates opened and Remo was filled with memories of Freya, his daughter.

Vividly he saw beautiful Freya, the brilliant summer sun, the landscape of Arizona. He smelled the desert perfume, he heard the breeze and the voice of Freya as she spoke to the coyote she held in one hand....

That was how the emptiness beyond the Void was driven away, and now, as Remo Williams allowed himself to descend into the emptiness yet again, he conjured his memory of a memory.

He opened his eyes, surprising Chiun.

"I beat it, Little Father. It took me once, but I escaped it, and now I will always know how to escape it."

"Cretin. You aged me ten years."

"Don't you see, Little Father? Going beyond the Void wasn't all bad. It sucked at the time, but it made me strong in a new way. The nothingness won't get me again."

"Going into the nothingness cannot be a good thing," Chiun declared.

"But it wasn't fatal."

Chiun looked away from his protégé. "You mean to comfort me, but you do not know how close it came to being fatal. For I did not know how to summon you home."

But someone did, Remo Williams thought, and he heard again, like a waking dream, the sweet voice of Sarah Slate.

REMO CRUSHED the glow stick and stepped off the trail into the water when they saw the first twinge of light filtering upriver, then they drifted with the current until they saw the sallow moon where the river emerged. They were at Fastbinder's underground city.

"Chiun, remember how we thought this proton gizmo was some new kind of weapon that would neutralize us? A weapon custom-made for fighting Sinanju?"

"You were quite wrong. I said so when you first postulated this ridiculous notion and I say so now."

"But for a while there you believed it, too," Remo maintained.

"You are mistaken."

"Whatever. What I'm trying to say is, if Fastbinder starts microwaving us with proton beams, let me handle it."

"Glory hound," Chiun sniffed.

The earth suffered a spasm at that moment, then behind them they heard the crash of a massive explosion, followed by the collapse of a thousand tons of solid rock.

44

"What have you done?" Fastbinder demanded, storming into the command center looking over the city.

Jack didn't turn away from his panoramic view. "Blew the roof out of the Stinx River," Jack answered vacantly. "I'm gonna stop those guys."

"You can't know if you got them—they could be anywhere in zee tunnel."

"I'm not trying to bury them in the rock. I'm going to flood them out and slice them up. See?"

Fastbinder didn't want to see, but he was drawn to the window, where the city lay before them, raw and exposed, more stark than he remembered ever seeing it before.

"Why is it so bright?" he demanded.

"The illumination grid is more complete than I let on," Jack said without emotion. "We've got 687 functional lights."

The extra three hundred lights showed Fastbinder the activity at the mouth of the river entrance that his son called Stinx. A ceiling-mounted boom was lowering a welded metal rectangle over the entrance as a knot of albinos and slave topsiders steered it into place. The lower half of the frame disappeared into the water. Brackets, bolted into the stone, accepted the frame readily and it was obvious that it covered the entire opening. Topsiders balanced precariously on both banks to spin giant nuts into place to secure the frame.

"What is it?" he demanded.

"It will assassinate the assassins."

"How? What will it do?"

There was a shout of alarm at that moment from a topsider on a ladder. While he was turning one of the top bolts, the rock crumbled under one foot of the ladder. He fell toward the water as it flowed out of the opening. Part of his body was inside the frame, and his flesh vanished, When he bobbed to the surface, Fastbinder briefly saw two-thirds of a man with his head and shoulder sliced cleanly off.

"Wire," Jack droned. "Really, really small gauge. High tensile."

"I see."

"I diverted the Flix River into the Stinx. I'm gonna wash those jerks right through the wire, Pops. They'll be shaved thinner than roast beef from the deli."

Fastbinder got it now. Yes—the force of the combined water flow would be inescapable. The assassins would be hurtled through the mouth of the tunnel. If the wires held long enough...

"It just might work."

Jack turned on him, eyes blazing. "It will work, old man."

At that moment Jacob Fastbinder III, the king of the

Underworld, became afraid of what he saw in the eyes of his own beloved son.

"WATER," REMO SAID as the boom of the explosion died into a new rush of distant sound.

Chiun raised one hand from the river and waved his soaked kimono sleeve magnanimously. "I am humbled by your powers of observation."

"Come on, Chiun, that brat's sicced the Mississippi River overflow on us. We gotta get out of here."

They both saw something pass over the entrance then, and as it settled into position the lights behind it brought into contrast the skeins strung tightly across it.

"The fool would attempt to net us or electrocute us?" Chiun said. But the glittering fineness of the strands revealed its purpose.

"I don't want to be grated," Remo griped. "Let's find somewhere to ride it out." He searched quickly but saw only walls worn smooth by aeons of water flow. The approaching tidal wave made a discordant moan, and the pressure of the air being shoved ahead of it was getting powerful itself.

Remo sprang from the water and chopped into the stone wall with a flat hand, then used the gash as a handhold as he reached to the ceiling of the cavern and tapped the rock with his knuckle. The rock felt solid. He was looking for a weakness in the strata. There was always a weakness. The gale-force wind couldn't mask the thunder of the water wall that was chugging. Chiun raised his eyebrows in impatience.

Remo found the sweet spot he was looking for and gave it the perfect one-hand bash. It would have cold-cocked a large sea mammal, and it caused an almost perfect disruption in the structure of the stone ceiling. A chunk of rock separated and thudded into the river, just as wall of water swept through the tunnel with the force of an avalanche.

45

The albinos were fleeing. The topsider slaves were wrestling with their manacles as the wind blast grew. Some of them toppled into the water, others flattened on the banks, and then the surge came. A shaft of foamy water blasted out the mouth of the tunnel, sprayed the interior and washed out a hundred human beings.

The pressure equalized and a minute later the surge became only a strong flow of water. The scattered slaves and albinos began collecting themselves and collecting the dead, which included most of the slaves.

"See? It's still there, Pops," Jack Fast announced disdainfully.

"But what of zee assassins? How will we know if they went through it and were sliced to little bits?"

Jack nodded to the rear of the city, where a fresh crew of topside slaves appeared with dozens of skim nets. They trooped to the banks and began scooping detritus from the deep pool at the base of the river mouth, while others waded over the rocky dam to search for remains caught in the shallows.

"The wire mesh is spaced with six-inch gaps. If they went through, there will be pieces big enough to find."

Fastbinder touched his son on the shoulder. "Time for us to leave here, Jack."

Jack Fast turned on his father abruptly, saw the man's look of fear and spun back to the city view. Something was moving in the tunnel, behind the wire mesh. There was a man waving his hands.

No, two men, and where the men waved their hands the wire mesh parted like a stick going through spider webs.

"Jack, we will go now." Fastbinder squeezed his son's shoulder insistently.

"Fuck off!" Jack swung his fist behind his back, connecting hard with Fastbinder's head. The old man slumped against the cold stone, more stunned by his son's harsh words than by the blow.

"Attack and kill those men," Jack shouted, and the city-wide public-address system blasted his orders throughout the cavern.

The assassins allowed themselves to drift out of the river mouth with the water flow, then stroked with uncanny speed into the shallows and erupted onto the shore, befuddling the blind albinos who attempted to track them by smell.

"They're on the bank," Jack bellowed throughout the cavern.

The younger one looked right at him, from a quarter mile away, and gave him a deadly smile.

"Hiya, Jack!" the man shouted, as loud as Jack's amplifiers.

The albinos moved in for the kill. Jack suddenly felt a profound lack of confidence in his Albinoids. But there were a hundred of them—the assassins didn't stand a chance!

The assassins solved the problem of the Albinoids easily. They stepped up on top of them and stepped lightly from head to head, leaving the attackers behind in a state of confusion.

Jack swallowed his chagrin and turned to go, only to find he was alone. No Pops. Pops's personal computer workstation, the one he never used but insisted on installing, was now moved aside to reveal a tunnel no bigger than a sewer hole.

Pops had to have had it carved out when Jack was on his mission to Texas. But why? Pops would never double-cross his own son, would he?

Jack knew the answer. He rushed to the secret tunnel and was about to crawl in when he saw the brilliant sparkle of lightning from far below. Pops's secret tunnel went right to Jack's Earth Drill—and Pops was escaping in JED without Jack!

"You don't leave *me* behind, you jerk! I'm the one who leaves you!"

The sparkle of the earth drill was already getting faint. Pops was on his way topside, and Jack had no way to follow him.

Jack ran back to his window and caught a glimpse of the assassins, who had somehow scurried atop a rock protrusion that was being carved with sleeping niches. They leaped off the boulder, surely to fall to their deaths—only to land ten feet away on a partially completed defensive wall of stone rubble.

They were coming fast.

"Hey, sonny, is your dad at home?" the younger one called.

Jack Fast stumbled through the door and dropped through the small shaft into the emergency escape pod.

"Just in case the cave dudes go ballistic, Pops," Jack had explained weeks ago when he unveiled it.

"You'll never catch me resorting to that contraption, Jack," Fastbinder had said at the time.

"Rot in hell, Pops," Jack grunted now as he slid into the safety harness, slammed the support cage shut and slapped the glowing emergency escape button.

The escape charges fired. The force of the ejection blast turned everything black for teenage genius Jack Fast.

REMO FELT THE PRESSURE WAVES and slipped over the wall just as the base of the cliff building shattered. An orange burst of fire split part of the wall and revealed something metal behind it.

"What now?" he demanded of Chiun as they waited out the explosion, then he scrambled atop the wall in time to see the EEP reach the river. It was a metal cage that rocketed over the stony surface with a spray of sparks and slammed into the river beyond the dam.

"Mother of Murgatroyd!" Remo flew from the wall and sped after the pod. "I am so damn sick of your gizmos and gadgets and robots and supersecret pen decoders and whatever the hell this thing is."

Whatever it was, it was a better machine than the river pods the albinos had used, constructed of a dully gleaming alloy. It compressed and sprang back when it glanced hard off a sharp rock ridge. It swayed in the current, creaked in protest against the shrunken orifice at the far end of the cavern, then deformed itself to slither inside the narrow slot that channeled away the combined water flow from all three rivers.

Remo came to a halt at the bank, too late. "He got away."

Chiun came up behind him. "That river continues its descent. It will carry him deep into the earth."

Remo stared at the opening, thinking dark thoughts, fighting the urge to pursue Jack Fast. "Who knows what sort of gadgets he equipped himself with?"

"He had no earth drill, and this tunnel is unlike the others, Remo. It is a steep shaft. I think he'll not walk out this way."

Remo nodded tightly. "Not this way. But some way."

Chiun was standing calmly in the blazing overhead floodlights as his kimono emitted slivers of steam. His eyebrows moved together.

"What?" Remo asked.

Chiun was looking at the jumble of boulders that formed a narrow, long drainage gap for the heavy river flow. They were, the old Master noticed, of a nearly uniform size and shape. Could they possibly have been carved and placed by human hands?

He touched one of the corners. If man worked the block into this shape, then he did so long centuries ago, for the corner was smoothed by time.

He did not withdraw his hand, but touched the surface of the stone, smearing the coating of fungal slime. He found the tracing on the rock that the slime disguised, and he ran his ancient fingers over the hidden etchings until their shape became clear to him.

Chiun lifted his hand away quickly.

"I think there's air space down there," Remo said, squinting into the drainage gash. "Think I should go down after him?"

"No."

Remo raised his head. "Something wrong, Little Father?"

Chiun cursed himself that he had let the quaver come into his voice. "I saw just one occupant of the pod," Chiun pointed out. "It was only the mad brat, not the mad scientist himself. The brat is not coming back."

"You're sure of that, huh?"

"I am sure."

"How come you're sure?"

"Remo, should we not leave? You appear to have earned the enmity of an entire geographic race." Chiun nodded to the albinos that were marching upriver. There were hundreds of them—more men, women and children were skittering out of openings in the rock like cockroaches swarming.

"Okay, let's scram."

They moved swiftly into the room with the overlook, where Jack Fast had been watching the city, and they found the escape tunnel. Slithering inside, they found it led to an empty crystal tunnel, whose walls gleamed magnificently, even under the light of a single glow stick. Nearby it intersected a natural entrance to the city cavern.

"Same crystals we found in New Mexico," Remo said. "Let's go."

The tunnel followed a broad curve, then straightened into an upward slope. Something white and brilliant shimmered far ahead.

"That's what you call an earth drill?" Remo asked. "Where's the big screw on the front? Where's the big engine? This thing's—I don't know what."

"Pretty," Chiun suggested.

"Yeah! This is a girlie earth drill, not a real man's earth drill. ERB's gotta be spinning in his grave."

As they closed in on the thing, they could feel the sizzling heat and electricity of the lightning and Chiun suggested, "A girlie earth drill will be no challenge for a real man such as yourself."

Remo watched the patterns of the static electricity and couldn't find a gap big enough to get through, although he could make out an oblong space against the rear hatch where the lightning didn't touch. He just had to reach that place.

"This is gonna hurt," he announced.

"Probably," Chiun agreed.

Remo sprinted headlong into the flickering bolts of electricity, felt his body dancing with the fire and sizzle, and then he was flat against the rear of the earth drill.

"Did it?" Chiun called. "Hurt?"

Remo scowled, extinguished his T-shirt here and there, then went inside the earth drill without answering.

46

Jacob Fastbinder concentrated on what he was doing. He had never spent more than a few minutes behind JED's controls, and it wasn't as easy as it looked. Where was Jack's main tunnel? It should be right here!

Then the wall opened up in front of the drill, and Fastbinder found himself inside an identical, well-used crystal tunnel. Now he could turn off the nerve-racking electric drilling mechanism and simply drive to the surface. He flipped off the charger and raised the dark glass from the windshield.

"You have got to be kidding me," Remo Williams said, startling Fastbinder almost out of his skin.

"Who are you?" Fastbinder cried. "Oh, it's you."

"Yeah, it's me, and I just fried my follicles getting inside of this glorified minivan, and now you turn the bug zappers off."

"I—I don't need it anymore," Fastbinder said lamely, gesturing to the long tunnel that stretched out for miles in front of them.

"I see that," Remo declared angrily.

"What will you do with me?" Fastbinder asked.

"Take you up with us," Remo said.

"Why?" asked Chiun. Fastbinder was startled again by the silent appearance of the old man. "Let's just kill him here and be done with it."

"Nope. We're taking him up with us."

"Are all sons imbeciles?" Chiun asked of Fastbinder.

"What—what became of my son, by zee way?" Fastbinder asked, thinking he might actually have a chance of not dying today.

"He took some rocket-assisted carnival ride into the main drain," Remo said. "Where's that go, by the way?"

Fastbinder looked stricken. "I don't know," he said in a shallow voice. "We tried to probe it with tethered robots, but they kept getting ruined."

"Here's what I'm getting at—think the little brat's gonna find a way out of there?" Remo asked. "And FYI, I'll know if you fib."

Fastbinder's eyes grew shiny. "Not even Jack," he said hoarsely, "could come up from there." Fastbinder sniffed and said, "I so wish I could have just died under zee deserts of New Mexico."

Remo sighed loudly. "You and me both, Pops."

SENATOR HERBERT Whiteslaw never wanted to go be-lowground again, but now was not the time to allow his personal preferences to get in the way of his maniacal obsessions.

"Why do I have to meet you in a fucking cave, Jacob?" Whiteslaw said.

"It is just a small cave," Jacob Fastbinder said with a sniffle.

"Something the matter, Jacob?"

For a moment Fastbinder said nothing, then he spoke tenuously. "My son is dead. He was killed when zee assassins came into my city."

"Holy mother of crap! How'd they find it?"

"They followed in one of Jack's transport pods. Jack destroyed them, but he was destroyed himself in zee cataclysm."

"Yeah, well, that's really awful and all—but you did it, just like you said you would. You killed them within twenty-four hours."

"Before he died, one of the assassins gave me much intelligence."

Herbert Whiteslaw gripped the phone hard. "How much?"

"The conspiracy is vaster than we expected. You will wield great mastery over zee political parties."

"That's wonderful!"

"I wish I could share in your delight."

Herbert Whiteslaw took a shower. The shower hadn't been hot once during his extended stay at the Comforts of Home Motel in Wheeless, Oklahoma, but this time the chill was invigorating. He checked out and drove happily into New Mexico for the rendezvous with Fastbinder.

"Gimme a *P*!" he sang. "Gimme an *R*! Gimme an *E, S, I, D, E N, T*! What does it spell?"

THE GOOSE CREEK CAVE was on private property, outside the boundaries of the Kiowa National Grassland, unmarked and forgotten by almost everybody. While most cavern entrances across the nation were being watched by tanks and soldiers, the Goose Creek Cave sat alone in a small copse of trees a few miles off a country road.

The interior was no bigger than a living room in a trailer home, but Whiteslaw found the fresh opening in the rocks near the back. He crawled inside, stood up and flipped on the flashlight.

Somebody took the flashlight away from him.

"Jacob, is that you?"

"Yes, it is me, Senator."

"What'd you take the flashlight for?"

"That was me." The flashlight came on in the hands of a dark-haired man.

"I know you!"

"And I know you."

"You're one of the assassins!"

"And you're—wait, don't tell me."

The second assassin, the freaky little old Chinaman in the party dress, materialized out of the glimmering darkness of the crystal tunnel. "I believe you referred to him as a loser."

Remo Williams snapped his fingers. "That's right, yeah, loser. That's you."

"Jacob?" Whiteslaw called out. "You said they were killed."

"I told him to say that, Senator Coleslaw. Had to get our hands on you. You're as slippery as rotten cabbage. But, now, well, here we all are at last!"

"Let go of me!" Whiteslaw pounded the hand that

was holding his shoulder, but the hand felt like tempered steel.

"My God, are you one of Jacob's robots?"

"No way." Remo said. "I'm sick to death of robots and mechanized marvels and whatnot. Guess what else I'm sick to death of?"

"Jacob, we can make a deal!" Whiteslaw cried.

"The mad German scientist is not in the position to negotiate," explained Chiun in a merry, singsong voice. "Observe."

Whiteslaw found the great German industrialist Jacob Fastbinder III lying on his back with his limp wrists held up over him, like a dog lounging on its back, but his wide, rolling eyes spoiled the similarity.

"Fastbinder, what's the matter with you?"

"Coleslaw, what's the matter with you?" Remo asked as he paralyzed the senator with a quick love squeeze, tipped him over on his back and chained one ankle to the rear end of the earth drill alongside Fastbinder.

"Everybody ready to go?"

"Not I," Chiun said. "I don't understand this pointless and messy display."

"Easy dyin' is way too good for this pair," Remo insisted. "Coleslaw's been a prickle in my posterior for months, and Fastbinder put me in the freaking hospital. Besides, this is kind of poetic justice, don't you think?"

Chiun sniffed. "What you know of poetry would fill the back of a postcard. Get this outrageous display over with so we may leave."

"One outrageous display coming up!" Remo gave the thumbs-up to the paralyzed pair and stepped into the open hatch at the rear of the earth drill. It started up. He stepped out again as the drill began to crawl away. There were no lightning displays—it was returning into the crystal cavern it had created already. It left a glistening red trail in its wake.

"Ouch. The floor must be really sharp, huh, Little Father?" Remo said. "I bet that hurts something awful."

Chiun rolled his eyes. "Amid your immature antics you forgot something important."

"What did I forget? Oh, shit." Remo bounded down the tunnel and soon found himself stepping through a grisly obstacle course before catching up to the creeping earth drill.

"Hey, Mr. Loser, you're not gonna be needing that rental car anymore, are you? Mind if I take it?"

The flopping torso of Herbert Whiteslaw didn't answer.

"I'll take that as a yes." Remo gingerly fished the keys out of the pants pocket and jogged back to Chiun.

"Shredded like coleslaw," he announced cheerfully.

Chiun could not have been more disgusted.

47

Smith could not have been angrier.

"We did *not* want Whiteslaw assassinated."

"Smitty, no way in hell was I letting Whiteslaw be not dead. He should have been taken out of the picture months ago, along with Orville Flicker. Instead we ignored him and look what trouble he caused."

"The President, in particular, requested that he be captured alive," Smith said sourly.

"Why take the chance? That slippery little weasel would come back to haunt us, guaranteed. Now he never will. Fastbinder, same solution. Even his freaka-zoid kid couldn't put him back together again."

"There is also the matter of the earth drill. The DOD could have put it to good use."

Remo looked over both shoulders. "Smitty, where's the dingbat you're talking to? Because nobody in this room is stupid enough to believe the DOD would do good with any Jack Fast invention."

"Remo, hold your tongue!" Chiun ordered harshly. "Emperor, please forgive his impertinence. He is still recovering from his period of extended unconsciousness. It causes him to experience seizures of irritability and idiocy."

"What's the status of the survivors, Junior?" Remo asked. "How many made it out?"

Mark Howard felt as if he were getting quite skilled at operating in this environment of flaring anger. These days it was the normal state of things when Remo was around. "They rendezvoused with the rescue teams this morning at a subsurface depth of 10,031 feet. They rescued the bunch you tied up in the transport pod. They claimed that there were no surviving topsiders in Fastbinder's city, which was reverting to the anarchy of albino control. Apparently, the albinos were so busy gorging in the Fastbinder food stores they didn't lift a finger to stop the topsiders escaping."

"Remo—" Smith started.

"Smitty," Remo interjected, "tell me the U.S. of A. has enough sense to leave well enough alone in Fastbinder's city."

"Don't interrupt!" Chiun snapped.

Smith looked uncomfortable.

"That's what I thought," Remo muttered. "They're sending in the Army to find out all about it, right? Tell me when you find out they're all dead."

"They already are all dead," Mark Howard reported, then wished he hadn't and shrank into his chair. "Their last reports said they were outnumbered and taking catastrophic casualties," he added lamely.

"The logical thing to do now is to send down even more military," Remo said snidely. "Is that what the President is doing?"

Mark kept his mouth shut. Smith glowered.

"I thought so." Remo breathed out, long and slow. It was a cleansing breath, but he didn't feel especially clean when it was all done.

"Are we done? 'Cause I think I'm going to throw up."

"He is jesting, Emperor. He is trained too well to allow any malady to cause involuntary purging."

"We are not done," Harold Smith said sternly, feeling as if he were rejoining a lost conversation. "Remo, you and I must set some matters straight once and for all. We cannot go on like this."

"You got that right."

Smith had the sinking feeling that this was not going to go well. "We've been exposed, dangerously, and there is a grave risk to the security of CURE unless this exposure is neutralized. Specifically, I speak of the Sun On Jos. Of your son, Winston, your daughter, Freya, and your biological father, Sunny Joe Roam."

Harold Smith could feel Chiun's tension level, especially.

"Smitty, let me ask you this," Remo said, confused. "How could you not know about the family in Yuma? I haven't exactly tried to hide their existence, right? In fact, I think I told you I was going visiting kinfolk."

"I assumed you were joking. Of course we had some idea that you spent time with the Sun On Jo tribe, but you had met Sunny Joe Roam on the set of the movie fiasco in Yuma, years ago. We thought you were simply friends with the man."

"Didn't you have the local buzzard population reporting on my activities?" Remo demanded.

"We were giving you your privacy," Mark Howard said.

"Thanks so much. So it was okay for me to go visit my buddy Sunny Joe, but not my natural father Sunny Joe?"

Chiun scowled. "Why must you be deliberately obstinate?"

"I'm trying to figure out what I did wrong here, because dammit, I don't know."

Smith sighed. "The problem arises when the Sun On Jos become knowledgeable of CURE."

"The knowledge you gave them," Remo added insistently and began ticking off facts. "Winston knew who you were. Freya overheard you on the phone to me. You were the one who called, and you were the one who sent Junior driving around the reservation like an idiot in the middle of the night. You screwed up, Smitty."

"The fact remains, Remo, that the situation is dangerous and cannot be allowed to continue."

"Emperor—" Chiun began.

"Allow me to continue, Master Chiun," Smith said, nodding respectfully to the ancient Korean. "I merely suggest that you make them forget."

"No way," Remo declared. "Too risky. This is my family we're talking about."

"The risk is marginal."

"No."

"The only alternative—"

Remo was there, inches away from the nose of Harold W. Smith, and he had a fire in his eyes that was like the rage of an old and powerful Korean, but there was a smoldering glow of fire red that lingered behind the veil of humanity. "Old man, you don't want to know the alternative."

Harold Smith felt as if the blood were boiling in his brain, furious and afraid. He had been plenty angry with Remo, more times than he could count, but he had never been quite so afraid.

"Besides, what they know isn't enough to do anybody any good," Remo was saying when Smith focused again on his office and found everything back to a state of uncomfortable normalcy. "You're looking for a problem where there isn't one."

Smith considered this long and hard, and filed the subject away for further consideration. "Then shall we return to a more insistent problem?"

"I think we've done enough for one day, don't you?"

"The problem of a lack of a chain of command in the CURE hierarchy," Smith continued, not flustered.

"Right. The problem is, I'm not part of the chain of command," Remo said. "More like the bucket at the end of the chain. You say, 'Remo, go kill this guy,' and I'm supposed to just do it. Like I'm nothing more than hired muscle."

"You are a hired assassin," Chiun clarified.

"I'm a grunt. I'm a doer, not a thinker, right?"

"It is a role in which you excel, my son," Chiun assured him.

"Okay, maybe, but I'm not quite as yak-stupid as you think I am, Little Father."

Chiun considered how to respond, but Remo didn't give him time. "Sometimes, I know what to do when other people don't know what to do. Maybe, every once in a while, I have good judgment. Amazing, but true!"

Smith considered this carefully. Mark Howard looked like a kid at a dogfight, waiting to see who ripped whose ear off first.

"You think I'm full of beans?" Remo demanded of Smith. "I was right about Whiteslaw, wasn't I? We should have nailed his sleazy ass to the wall when we had the chance. Think of all the crap that wouldn't have happened."

"The responsibility rests with me," Smith said.

"The fact is, we should have done what I thought we should have done."

"The fact is, you do whatever you please anyway," Smith said. "You need to fall in line. That means, follow directions, maintain contact with myself and Mark. You need to carry a phone."

"You need to get real."

"You are failing to fulfill your contract, Master of Sinanju."

"Yeah, okay, let's talk about that," Remo said, and then he reached for his back pocket and pulled out a thick, folded wad of parchment. He flicked open the contract and said, "I've been reading this over—"

"Remo! What are you doing with that?" Chiun demanded.

"It's my contract."

"It is my contract, ignoramus! You had nothing to do with it!"

"Well, maybe I had nothing to do with figuring it out, but it's all about me, isn't it? Don't you think it is fair that I get to see it?"

"You have no understanding of such things," Chiun spluttered. "I doubt you can make any sense of it whatsoever."

Remo shrugged. "Won't argue with you there. I can't make heads or tails of it."

"So what is your point?" Smith said.

"Somebody needs to explain it to me. You know I actually found an 'ipso facto' in here? I thought 'ipso facto' was a made-up word, like 'McNuggetts.' I don't know what ipso facto means. Chiun does. Problem is, he doesn't have the patience to explain it to me."

"Because you have not the wits to comprehend it!" Chiun said, stamping his foot and growing red-faced.

"And if he stamps his foot about explaining one little word, imagine how mad he'd get if I ask him to explain all the words." Remo was ignoring Chiun for the moment. He had already earned months of penance for this little scene, but he was committed to going whole hog. "Now, I could ask you or Junior to explain it, but I can't trust you guys to give me the straight dope. You're the party of the other side. So what I need is a lawyer."

"You will stop these childish games!" Chiun squeaked.

"This is perfectly legitimate. See, in this country

you're allowed to have a lawyer to help you understand any contract you're a part of. So, I'll get a lawyer and have him sort out this gobbledygook."

"That would clearly violate CURE security," Smith said in exasperation.

"Lawyers don't violate their customers' privilege," Remo insisted. "CURE secrets would be safe."

Smith fumed. "For the sake of argument, what then? You would condemn this lawyer to death once his work was finished. CURE could not allow yet another security breach—"

"I'd keep him under retainer indefinitely," Remo said.

"And that would be intolerable," Smith responded quietly.

"Oh." Remo said, nodded and stood up. "Then I quit."

"Remo Williams, you will not break the sanctity of a contract signed by a Sinanju Master," Chiun declared.

"Hey, if they deny me legal representation in regards to the contract, then they can't enforce it. The contract is void. They can't even sue me because then they'd have to let me get a lawyer."

"This is ridiculous!" Smith was on his feet, as excited as he had been in years.

Remo stood at the door. "Ridiculous is putting your head in the sand while Whiteslaw murders a hundred more innocent people. This is just crafty, if I do say so myself."

"Do not do this impetuous thing," Chiun warned.

"Chiun," Remo said, "it's done."

Then he was gone.

Epilogue

The nightmare ended with a crash, then oblivion.

Then consciousness, followed by confusion. How could he tell if he was conscious or unconscious when both were simply utter darkness?

He walked this way, then that, trying to shake off the thousand points of pain, and after several days only the worst bruises still bothered him. By then it was the hunger that mattered more.

He went back to the sound of the water and found the crushed and mangled metal scraps. There had been food. Where was the food now? Washed away?

Food materialized, eventually. It fell from above and made a horrible noise when it hit bottom.

He felt its face. The eyes were grown over with flesh. He felt the limbs. An adult, recently deceased, nicely chilled by the river.

So what if it was human? He was starving. He hadn't had anything for days, and he was hungry enough to eat a horse.

He chewed thoughtfully, felt his strength coming back, and began planning his future. Step one: find a way up through four miles of solid rock.

Step two...

Stony Man is deployed against an armed
invasion on American soil...

THE
CHAMELEON
FACTOR

A brilliant new development in portable stealth technology,
Chameleon is a state-of-the-art jamming device that blocks
all kinds of magnetic frequencies, making it the ultimate death
shield in the right hands. But in the wrong hands, it would
mean the obliteration of America's defense and communications
systems—and open season on its citizens. When Chameleon
is stolen by a traitor who provides a fiery demonstration of its
doomsday power, Stony Man must retrieve it at any cost.

If Chameleon is deployed...shutting it down is not an option.

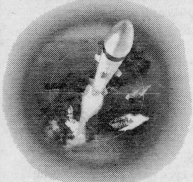

STONY
MAN ®

*Available
December 2004
at your favorite
retail outlet.*

James Axler
Outlanders®

ULURU DESTINY

Ominous rumblings in the South Pacific lead Kane and his compatriots into the heart of a secret barony ruled by a ruthless god-king planning an invasion of the sacred territory at Uluru and its aboriginals who are seemingly possessed of a power beyond all earthly origin. With total victory of hybrid over human hanging in the balance, slim hope lies with the people known as the Crew, preparing to reclaim a power so vast that in the wrong hands it could plunge humanity into an abyss of evil with no hope of redemption.

Available November 2004 at your favorite retail outlet.

Or order your copy now by sending your name, address, zip or postal code, along with a check or money order (please do not send cash) for $6.50 for each book ordered ($7.99 in Canada), plus 75¢ postage and handling ($1.00 in Canada), payable to Gold Eagle Books, to:

In the U.S.	In Canada
Gold Eagle Books	Gold Eagle Books
3010 Walden Avenue	P.O. Box 636
P.O. Box 9077	Fort Erie, Ontario
Buffalo, NY 14269-9077	L2A 5X3

Please specify book title with your order.
Canadian residents add applicable federal and provincial taxes.

GOLD EAGLE®

GOUT31

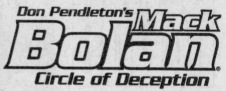